Praise for
*Prophet So*

## Winner of the Booker Prize 2023

"A beautifully written, slow descent into the maelstrom . . . This horrifying yet lovely novel would be a masterpiece even in a time of halcyon equality and justice for all. But that time is not this time."
—**Maureen Corrigan, NPR**

"As illuminating and haunting as any real-life history of descent into authoritarianism."        —*The Week*

"A triumph of emotional storytelling, bracing and brave. With great vividness, *Prophet Song* captures the social and political anxieties of our current moment. Readers will find it soul-shattering and true, and will not soon forget its warnings."
—**Esi Edugyan, Chair of the Booker Prize 2023 Judges**

"Gripping . . . As Eilish's circumstances deteriorate, Lynch's dense, lyrical prose barrels down on you relentlessly. As you read, you feel precious time slipping away, the inexorable future rushing toward you. He eschews quotation marks and paragraph breaks, and the result is a chaotic, disorienting whirlwind that amplifies the furious action of the narrative and plants you firmly in Eilish's weary, fractured mind."        —*Boston Globe*

"Stunning in every sense of the word . . . In masterfully controlled and powerful prose, [Lynch] yanks the reader headlong into the experience of living in a country that is taken over by an authoritarian government—slowly, slowly, and then suddenly and completely . . . *Prophet*

*Song* is a brilliant, disturbing reality check. Lynch insists that we understand 'the end of the world is always a local event.'" —*Tampa Bay Times*

"[A] beautifully written, ingenious, holy terror of a novel." —*Minneapolis Star Tribune*

"Harrowing . . . The lesson for readers is not necessarily to wake up to signs of totalitarianism knocking at our doors, but to empathize with those for whom it has already called." —**Kristen Martin, NPR**

"A horror story, with the new political order serving as the monster now inside the house . . . This is not a book that presents political oppression as an intellectual problem to be anticipated or solved. It aims for the limbic system, and it does not miss." —*Los Angeles Times*

"Unsettling." —*The New Yorker*

"Many, many lines and passages of great beauty and power." —*New York Times*

"A story mirroring today's headlines." —**PBS NewsHour**

"If there was ever a crucial book for our current times, it's Paul Lynch's *Prophet Song* . . . A brilliant, haunting novel." —*The Guardian*

"Thunderously powerful." —*Times Literary Supplement*

"Deeply harrowing . . . An extraordinary achievement." —*Highbrow Magazine*

"A speedboat of a novel that hurtles the reader through ever-heightening waves toward a dark shore, a stark vision of total societal breakdown . . . Lynch understands that totalitarianism doesn't simply storm into power; all too often it creeps in."    —*BookBrowse*

"A disquieting novel from an exceptional writer."
—*Crossville Chronicle*

"Lynch's novel is full of dread, but it's neither hopeless nor nihilistic. For in focusing the novel on the commitment of a dedicated mother, he invites the reader to dwell in the path of the propulsive wonder of love, an experience that is, in its finest moments, downright awe-inspiring."    —*World*

"In this chilling, Booker Prize–winning novel, author Paul Lynch takes us inside the slowly-unfolding nightmare that is his protagonist Eilish's mind . . . The personal and public atrocities mount up and we readers see them happen as Eilish does and we cannot look away or un-see them . . . A great novel, well deserving of the praise and awards."    —*Enchanted Circle*

"A superb novel."    —*Deadly Pleasures*

"A novel that allows darkness a corporeal form—something that breaches thresholds and follows."
—*The Wire*

"An exceptionally gifted writer, Lynch brings a compelling lyricism to [Eilish's] fears and despair while he marshals the details marking the collapse of democracy and the norms of daily life. His tonal control, psychological acuity, empathy, and bleakness recall Cormac McCarthy's *The*

*Road* (2006) . . . Captivating, frightening, and a singular achievement." —*Kirkus Reviews* (starred review)

"A disquieting novel from an exceptional writer." —*Shelf Awareness* (starred review)

"Irish writer Lynch (*Beyond the Sea*, 2020) conveys the creeping horror of a fascist catastrophe in a gorgeous and relentless stream of consciousness illuminating the terrible vulnerability of our loved ones, our daily lives, and social coherence. Eilish muses over the fragility of the body, its rhythms and flows, diseases and defenses. The body politic is just as assailable. A Booker Prize finalist, Lynch's hypnotic and crushing novel tracks the malignant decimation of an open society, a bleak and tragic process we enact and suffer from over and over again." —*Booklist* (starred review)

"I haven't read a book that has shaken me so intensely in many years . . . *Prophet Song* becomes a testament to a world unraveling. The comparisons are inevitable— Saramago, Orwell, McCarthy—but this novel will stand entirely on its own." —**Colum McCann, author of *Apeirogon***

"Surely one of the most important novels of this decade." —**Ron Rash, author of *Serena***

"Monumental . . . You remember why fiction matters. It's hard to recall a more powerful novel in recent years." —**Samantha Harvey, author of *The Western Wind***

"The work of a master novelist, *Prophet Song* is a stunning, midnight vision whose themes are at once ancient

and all too timely: fear, complicity, resistance, and what becomes of us when hell rises to our homeland."
—**Rob Doyle, author of** *Threshold*

"It was gripping and chilling, and terribly prescient—a novel with a darkly important message about this particular moment in time."
—**Sara Baume, author of** *Spill Simmer Falter Wither*

"Part cautionary-tale; part dystopian-nightmare; part fever dream. Whichever way you skin it, there is no denying the gathering power of Paul Lynch's writing. This is at once fearless and affecting prose with a ticking clock inevitability and a clanging bell payoff. Both urgent jolt and slow furnace, *Prophet Song* takes you to the edge of the chasm and insists that you look down. A masterclass in terror and dread."
—**Alan McMonagle, author of** *Ithaca*

# Prophet
# Song

# Prophet Song

## Paul Lynch

Grove Press

*New York*

First published in 2023 in the United Kingdom, Republic of Ireland, and
Australia by Oneworld Publications.

*Published simultaneously in Canada*
*Printed in the United States of America*

First Grove Atlantic hardcover edition: December 2023
First Grove Atlantic paperback edition: October 2024

ISBN 978-0-8021-6352-3
eISBN 978-0-8021-6302-8

Typeset by Tetragon, London

Library of Congress Cataloging-in-Publication data is available for this title.

Grove Press
an imprint of Grove Atlantic
154 West 14th Street
New York, NY 10011

Distributed by Publishers Group West

groveatlantic.com

24 25 26 27   10 9 8 7 6 5 4 3 2

*For Anna, Amelie and Elliot*

*The thing that hath been, it is that which shall be;*
*and that which is done is that which shall be done;*
*and there is no new thing under the sun.*

*In the dark times*
*will there also be singing?*
*Yes, there will also be singing.*
*About the dark times.*

BERTOLT BRECHT

# 1

The night has come and she has not heard the knocking, standing at the window looking out onto the garden. How the dark gathers without sound the cherry trees. It gathers the last of the leaves and the leaves do not resist the dark but accept the dark in whisper. Tired now, the day almost behind her, all that still has to be done before bed and the children settled in the living room, this feeling of rest for a moment by the glass. Watching the darkening garden and the wish to be at one with this darkness, to step outside and lie down with it, to lie with the fallen leaves and let the night pass over, to wake then with the dawn and rise renewed with the morning come. But the knocking. She hears it pass into thought, the sharp, insistent rapping, each knock possessed so fully of the knocker she begins to frown. Then Bailey too is knocking on the glass door to the kitchen, he calls out to her, Mam, pointing to the hallway without lifting his eyes from the screen. Eilish finds her body moving towards the hall with the baby in her arms, she opens the front door and two men are standing before the porch glass almost faceless in the dark. She turns on the porch light and the men are known in an instant from how they are stood, the night-cold air suspiring it seems as she slides open the patio door, the suburban quiet, the rain falling almost unspoken onto St Laurence Street, upon the black car parked in front of the house. How the men seem to carry the feeling of the night. She watches them from within her own protective feeling, the young man on the left is asking if her husband is home and there is something in the way he looks at her, the remote yet scrutinising eyes that make it seem as though he is trying to seize hold of something within her. In a blink she has sought up and down the street, seeing a lone walker with a dog under an umbrella, the willows nodding to the rain, the strobings of a large TV screen in the Zajacs' house across the street. She checks herself then, almost laughing, this universal reflex of guilt when the police call to your door. Ben begins to squirm in her arms and the older plainclothesman to her right is watching the child, his face seems to soften and so she addresses herself to him. She knows he too is a father, such things are always known, that other fellow is much too young, too neat and hard-boned, she begins to speak aware of a sudden falter in her voice. He will be home soon, in an hour or so, would you like me to give him a ring? No, that will not be necessary, Mrs Stack, when he comes home could you tell him to call us at his earliest convenience, this is my card. Please call me Eilish, is it something I can help you with? No, I'm afraid not, Mrs Stack, this is a matter for your husband. The older plainclothesman is smiling fully at the child and she watches for a moment the wrinkles about the mouth, it is a face put out by solemnity, the wrong face for the job. It is nothing to worry about, Mrs Stack. Why should I be worried, Garda? Yes, indeed, Mrs Stack, we don't want to be taking up any more of your time and aren't we damp enough this evening making calls, it will be hard work getting ourselves dry by the heater in the car. She slides the patio door closed holding the card in her hand, watching the two men return to the car, watching the car move up the street, it brakes for the junction and its tail-lights intensify taking the look of two eyes agleam. She looks once more onto the street returned to an evening's quiet, the heat from the hall as she steps inside and shuts the front door and then she stands a moment examining the card and finds she has been holding her breath. This feeling now that something has come into the house, she wants to put the baby down, she wants to stand and think, seeing how it stood with the two men and came into the hallway of its own accord, something formless yet felt. She can sense it skulking alongside her as she steps through the living room past the children, Molly is holding the remote control over Bailey's head, his hands flapping in the air, he turns towards her with a pleading look. Mam, tell her to put my show back on. Eilish closes the kitchen door and places the child in the rocker, begins to clear from the table her laptop and diary but stops and closes her eyes. This feeling that came into the house has followed. She looks to her phone and picks it up, her hand hesitating, she sends Larry a message, finds herself again by the window watching outside. The darkening garden not to be wished upon now, for something of that darkness has come into the house.

Larry Stack moves about the living room with the card in his hand. He stares at it frowning then places the card on the coffee table and shakes his head, falls back into the armchair, his hand taking grip of his beard while she watches him silently, judging him in that familiar way, after a certain age a man grows a beard not to enter manhood but to put a barrier to his youth, she can hardly recall him clean-shaven. Watching his feet seek about for his slippers, his face falling smooth as he rests in the chair, he is thinking about something else it seems until his brow grows taut and a frown creeps down his face. He leans forward and picks the card up again. It's probably nothing, he says. She bounces the child on her lap watching him closely. Tell me, Larry, how is it nothing? He sighs and drags the back of his hand across his mouth, moving out of the chair, he begins to search about the table. Where did you put the newspaper? He steps about the room looking though not seeing, the newspaper might be already forgotten, he is seeking something within the shade of his own thinking and cannot alight upon it. He turns then and studies his wife as she feeds the child on her breast and the sight of this comforts him, a sense of life contracted to an image so at odds with malice his mind begins to cool. He moves towards her and reaches out a hand but draws it back when her eyes sharpen towards him. The Garda National Services Bureau, she says, the GNSB, they are not the usual crowd, a detective inspector at our door, what do they want with you? He points to the ceiling, would you ever keep your voice down? He steps into the kitchen chewing on his teeth, turns a glass upright from the draining board and lets the tap run, seeing out past his reflection to the dark, the cherry trees are old and will soon go to rot, they might have to come down in the spring. He takes a long drink then steps into the living room. Listen, he says, almost watching his voice as it falls to a whisper. It will turn out to be nothing, I'm pretty sure. As he speaks he finds his belief fall away as though he had poured the drink of water into his hands. She is watching how he gives himself again to the armchair, the body pliant, the automated hand flicking through the channels on the TV. He turns to find himself imprisoned with a look and then he leans forward and sighs, pulls on his beard as though seeking to lift it from his face. Look, Eilish, you know how they work, what it is they are after, they gather information, they do so discreetly and I suppose you have to give it to them one way or another, no doubt they are building a case against a teacher so it would make sense they would want to talk to me, give us a heads-up, perhaps before an arrest, look, I will ring them tomorrow or the day after and see what they want. She is watching his face aware of some nullity in the centre of her being, mind and body seek the supremacy of sleep, in a moment she will go upstairs and slip into her nightwear, counting the hours until the baby wakes for his feed. Larry, she says, watching him recoil as though she has passed electricity into his hand. They said to call at your earliest convenience, call them now on the phone, the number is on the card, show them you have nothing to hide. He is frowning and then he inhales slowly as though taking measure of something looming before him, he turns and looks her full in the face, his eyes narrowed with anger. What do you mean, show them I have nothing to hide? You know what I mean. No, I don't know what you mean. Look, it's just a figure of speech, Larry, please go and ring them now. Why are you always so bloody difficult, he says, look, I'm not going to ring them at this hour. Larry, do it now, please, I do not want the GNSB to darken our door again, you hear the talk, the kind of things that are said to be going on these past few months. Larry leans forward in the armchair without it seems the ability to stand up, he frowns and then he is moving towards her, takes the baby from her arms. Eilish, please, just listen a moment, respect is something that runs both ways, they know I'm a busy man, I am the deputy general secretary of the Teachers' Union of Ireland, I do not hop, skip and jump to their every command. That is all well and good, Larry, but why did they call to the house at this hour and not to your office during the day, tell me that. Look, love, I'll ring them tomorrow or the day after tomorrow, now, can we let this rest for the night? His body remains standing before her though his eyes have turned to the TV. It's nine o'clock, he says, I want to hear what's on the news, why isn't Mark home by now? She is looking towards the door, the hand of sleep reaching around her waist, she steps towards Larry and slides the baby out of his arms. I don't know, she says, I've given up chasing after him, he had football practice this evening and probably had dinner at a friend's house, or maybe he's gone to Samantha's, they've become inseparable this last while, I just don't know what he sees in her.

Driving through the city he has grown vexed with himself, how the mind roams this way and that, pressing against something he seeks yet feels the need to draw back from. The voice on the phone was so matter of fact, polite almost, I apologise for the lateness of the hour, Mr Stack, we won't take up too much of your time. He parks on a lane around the corner from Kevin Street Garda Station, thinking how the main road used to be most nights, it was busier for sure, this city over the past while has grown much too quiet. He finds himself biting down on his teeth as he steps towards the reception and releases his mouth to smile, thinking of the children, Bailey no doubt will know he went out, that child is all ears. He watches the pale, freckled hand of a duty officer who speaks inaudibly into a phone. He is met by a young detective bony and brisk in shirt and tie, the face waxen and correct, matching the voice to the speaker from earlier on. Thank you for coming, Mr Stack, if you will follow me, we will do our best not to take up too much of your time. He follows up a metal stairwell and then along a corridor of shut doors before he is shown into an interview room with grey chairs and grey panelled walls and everything looks new, the door is closed and he is left alone. He sits down and stares at his hands. He reads his phone and then he stands and walks about the room, thinking how he has been placed on the back foot, shown a lack of respect, it is well past 10pm. When they enter the room he unfolds his arms and slowly pulls a chair and sits down, watching the same narrow officer and another his own age growing stout, a mug in the man's hand filmed with coffee spatter. The man eyes Larry Stack with the trace of a smile or perhaps it is just geniality resting in the wrinkles of his mouth. Good evening, Mr Stack, I am Detective Inspector Stamp and this is Detective Burke, can I offer you some tea or a coffee perhaps? Larry looks to the soiled cup and signals a no with his hand, finds himself studying the speaker's face, searching for an image he feels is known. I have met you before, he says, Dublin football wasn't it, you played midfield for UCD, you would have met me up against the Gaels, we were a powerhouse then, that was the year we put you into the ground. The detective inspector stares at his face, the wrinkles have collapsed around the mouth, the gaze grown opaque, an inscrutable silence fills the room. He speaks without shaking his head. I do not know what you are talking about. Larry is sensitive now to his own voice, he can hear it when he speaks as though he too were in the room watching the interview, can see himself from across the table, can see himself watching through the peephole in the door, there is no other way of looking in, not even the one-way mirror you would see on TV. He hears his voice grown false, a little too chatty, perhaps. It was you for sure, you played midfield for UCD, I never forget an opponent. The officer takes a drink from his mug and swills the coffee against his teeth, he stares at Larry until Larry finds himself looking down at the table, he runs a finger across the nicked varnish then lifts his eyes again to the detective inspector. The bones in the face have thickened, for sure, the frame grown stout, but what is told by the eyes never changes. Look, he says, I want to get this over with, I should be home with my family getting ready for bed, tell me, how can I help you? Detective Burke motions with an open hand. Mr Stack, we know you are a busy man so we are pleased to have an opportunity to speak with you, an allegation has been received that is of the utmost importance, it is an allegation that concerns you directly. Larry Stack watches the gaze of the two men and feels his mouth go dry. Something is moving in the room, he can sense this now, for a moment he remains frozen and then he looks up and sees the domed ceiling light where a moth is trapped and beats berserkly against the glass, the amber cupola soiled and filled with the bodies of moths past. Detective Burke has opened a folder and Larry Stack sees before him the bloodless hands of a priest, sees placed onto the table between them a sheet of printed paper. Larry begins to read the sheet, he blinks slowly then bites down on his teeth. Footsteps pass down the long corridor and are absolved by a closing door. He hears the muffled beatings of the moth, grows aware for an instant of something inside him beginning to wither. He looks up and sees Detective Burke watching him from across the table, the eyes regarding him as though they have the power to roam freely inside his thoughts, seeking to free something within him that isn't there. Larry looks towards the detective inspector who reads him now with an open face and he clears his throat and tries to smile at the two men. Officers, surely you're having me on? He watches them feeling the smile slide from his mouth, finds himself lifting the sheet and waving it. But this is nothing but madness, he says, wait until the general secretary hears about this, she will be on to the minister directly, I can assure you of that. The young detective coughs smartly into his fist then looks to the detective inspector who smiles and begins to speak. As you will be aware, Mr Stack, this is a difficult time for the state, we are under instruction to take seriously all allegations that are put before us—— What the hell are you talking about? Larry says, this is not an allegation, it makes no sense, you're twisting something, taking one thing and turning it into something else, it looks like you typed this up yourselves. Mr Stack, you will be aware no doubt of the Emergency Powers Act that came into effect this September in response to the ongoing crisis facing the state, an act that gives supplemental provision and power to the GNSB for the maintenance of public order, so you must understand how this appears to us, your behaviour looks like the conduct of someone inciting hatred against the state, someone sowing discord and unrest – when the consequences of an action affect stability at the level of the state there are two possibilities before us, one is that the actor is an agent working against the interests of the state, the other is that he is ignorant of his actions and acting without the intention of doing so, but either way, Mr Stack, the result in both cases is the same, the person will be serving enemies of the state, and so, Mr Stack, we exhort you to examine your conscience and make sure this is not the case. Larry Stack is silent a long time, he is watching the sheet without seeing it and then he clears his throat and squeezes his hands. Let me understand you correctly, he says, you're asking me to prove that my behaviour is not seditious? Yes, that is correct, Mr Stack. But how can I prove what I am doing is not seditious when I'm merely just doing my job as a trade unionist, exercising my right under the constitution? That is up to you, Mr Stack, unless we decide this warrants further investigation, in which case it will no longer be up to you and we will decide. Larry finds himself standing out of the chair with his knuckles pressing against the table. What he sees in the face is will and he can see how he was brought here to be broken against this will, this will but a sanction of some absolute that has the power to make a yes into a no and a no into a yes. I want to be very clear about this, he says, the minister is going to hear about this and there's going to be trouble, you cannot threaten a senior trade unionist out of doing his job, the teachers in this country have a right to negotiate for better conditions and to engage in peaceful industrial action which has nothing to do with this so-called crisis facing the state, now if you don't mind I'm going home. The second detective slowly opens his mouth and Larry is almost sure he sees it, he thinks about this as he walks back to the car and sits inside for a long time watching his hands quake on his lap. How the moth seemed to fly free of the officer's mouth.

First Ben to crèche and then the children to school, Molly stepping from the passenger door of the Touran with headphones on while Bailey slams the back door, Eilish watching over her shoulder as he stands pointillist by the glass pulling at his Parka hood. She is moving out onto the road when a hand bangs on the window, Molly is shouting for her to stop, the door pulls open and Molly grabs her gym bag from the floor and is gone. This winter light, a cold November smear, she is moving through traffic sensing her own exhausted emotion, her motions automatic, resting at the red light she sees not the day ahead but how the day will pass without impression, another day forgotten and absorbed into the silent reckoning of days, seeing herself at work and how she no longer thinks of her work as a career – the real work of a microbiologist is standing at the bench for long hours seeking evidence, testing hypothesis against reality, against whatever an individual might seek to believe, the answer true or false is found in the result. Now she spends her days on email and phone, specialist become generalist without a white coat, managing personnel, adrift during meetings, asking the wrong questions. She sits to her desk and looks at her email and reschedules a call for 5.30pm. She picks up her phone and rings Larry. Did you fill out the passport forms like I asked? she says. Listen, love, I'm still a bit rattled, I cannot get it out of my head. He speaks as though the air had been released from him while he slept, waking to find himself deflated, how he sat on the side of the bed staring at the floor. Did you tell them at work? she says. She hears him speak to a colleague for a moment with his hand covering the phone. I left them on the desk upstairs. Left what on the desk upstairs? The passport forms. Larry, you should ring Sean Wallace and talk to him, emergency powers or not, there are still constitutional rights in this country. I want to take this directly to the general secretary but she is out today with a virus. Tell me, is Sean still parading about with that young one? Sean Wallace is buried up to his balls in that Fitzgerald trial right now, I don't want to trouble him, tell me, who is cooking dinner tonight? I still think you should ring him, it's your turn to cook. Grand so, I have a meeting scheduled for 6.30pm but I'm going to cancel, I'm not in the mood. Larry. What love? Oh, nothing, I picked up some mince yesterday, you can make burgers, look I have to go. She ends the call but sits for a moment with the phone in her hand aware of some ill feeling. She looks at the phone and reaches back into the call, following her voice into Larry's phone, the signal has to be relayed to reach Larry's mobile, it is picked up and relayed through a network transmitter. Of a sudden she hears her own voice as though she were listening to herself in another room. Talk to him, emergency powers or not, there are still constitutional rights in this country. She is suddenly cold, stands abruptly out of her chair and moves towards the office kitchen, thinking, in other countries, yes, but we don't have that kind of carry-on here, the gardaí, the state, they are not allowed to listen in on calls, there would be outrage. She thinks about the car last night parked outside the house, she thinks about the GNSB and the whispers she has heard about what is said to be going on, stepping now towards the kitchen she feels for a moment as though she does not know the room. Paul Felsner, the new global account executive, is standing at the coffee machine pulling at the cuff of his shirt. The machine stops whirring with a soft smack and he turns around and smiles without the smile reaching his eyes. Oh, Eilish, I was hoping to see you, you didn't respond to my voice message, they had to reschedule that video call with Asakuki to 6pm. There is something false about his face, she thinks, his eyes should be dark but instead they are green and she finds her sight drawn to the hooped party pin of the National Alliance on his lapel, the NAP, this new emblem of state. She looks down again at his hands and sees they are a little too small. Oh, I didn't see, she says, I'm afraid I won't be able to make that call, but thanks for letting me know.

There is a blue horse on the shore and it comes to her, riding now beside the water and she is ageless, riding in light, the phone ringing downstairs in the hall, she rides up out of the dream into the room. Larry is sitting on the edge of the bed rubbing his eyes. For goodness' sake, she whispers, it is quarter past one, who is ringing at this hour? It better not be your sister, he says. He leans forward then steps towards the door reaching for a shadow that wings open into dressing gown. The padding of slippered feet down the stairs while she lies listening to Ben's breathing in the cot, a smothered cough from the boys' room next door. Larry's muffled words reach upstairs and come shape-less into the room and she wonders who the call might be from, thinking of her sister Áine in Toronto, it hap-pened once years ago, oh my God, I'm so sorry, sis, I got the time zones in reverse, I've just had a few drinks. She closes her eyes and seeks the blue horse on the strand, seeking it in memory, what age were you? It is winter, the sky low over the sea, touching the flanks with her heels, the shuddering vitality beneath, Larry's weight pressing down on the mattress beside her. I was just falling back asleep, she says. He does not speak but stares at the wall and seems leaden, belaboured of breath, she reaches out and squeezes his arm. What is it, Larry? She turns on the lamp and sits up, seeing him by the light's caress made into a child, a frowning, quizzical look as he turns and clears his throat. That was Carole Sexton, Jim's wife, she was near hysterical on the phone, Jim left the office yesterday and didn't return home. Is that all, Larry, I was afraid for a moment you were going to say somebody is dead. Listen, Eilish, she said they took him in. Who took him in? Who do you think, the GNSB. The GNSB? Yes, that is what she said. But that doesn't make any sense, Larry, what does she mean, took him in? Arrested, I suppose, detained, turns out somebody saw him being put into the back of a car but didn't think to let anybody know, she found out later after she rang around. Jim Sexton, that big mouthpiece, what has he ever done? The thing is, Eilish, nobody has heard a word from him since. But did he call the union solicitor, whatshisname? Michael Given, no, nothing, he didn't even call his wife. But you can't just arrest somebody like that without giving them legal recourse, there are rules about these things. Carole says Michael is over there now at Kevin Street but they are giving him the runaround and he is going home for the night, you can't even get through to the GNSB it seems, they don't have a direct number, I don't understand why I didn't get a phone call from anybody at the union, this sounds like a right mess. That is not true. What is not true? There is a number on the card for that detective inspector who called here the other night, a mobile number, you rang it yourself, tell me, Larry, what is going on? I don't know, love, he is furious apparently. Who is furious? Michael Given. Make sure that you give it to him, the card. Yes, I hadn't thought of that, I will find it now, where did you leave it? I put it down on the mantlepiece in the living room, then I slid it under the clock. Listen, Eilish, Carole said they took him in last week, that they told him that an allegation had been made against him and she said he just laughed at them, you know Jim, apparently when he asked if he was under arrest and they told him no, he recited in full Article 40.6.1, section three, right there in front of them, the right of citizens to form associations and unions, you know the drill, and he having half the secondary teachers of Leinster busing into the city if the strike goes ahead. Her hand is searching the bedside locker, she takes hold of a glass of water without looking and takes a drink. Larry, how much of our constitutional rights can they suspend under these emergency powers? I don't know, not this much, not like this, any powers of detention are still subject to the law but what is the law if this kind of thing is going on, look, keep this quiet for the moment and don't tell the kids. Larry, there is nothing you can do at this hour, please come back to bed.

She stands looking out onto her father's garden. Old memories stamp on wet leaves, swing on rope, huddle in the bushes, voices calling out from the past, ready or not, here I come. Watching the ash tree that he planted for her tenth birthday towering over the narrow plot. Bailey swishing through the long grass and kicking at leaves while Molly takes pictures of the wintered plants. Eilish turns from the table where her father sits with his nose in a newspaper, Ben asleep in the car seat by her feet. She lifts two mugs and peers inside them, squeaks her finger around the rim. Dad, look at these mugs, why won't you use the dishwasher, you really need to wear your glasses when washing up. Simon does not lift his eyes from the newspaper. I'm wearing my glasses right now, he says. Yes, but you need to wear them while washing up, these mugs are ringed with tea. You can blame that useless cleaning woman who comes around here, there was never a dirty cup in this house when your mother was alive. Watching him now she enters into the feeling of her childhood, seeing her father as he used to be, the hawk-like nose and quick, scrutinising eyes, the figure that now shrinks in the chair, the back rounding in the wool cardigan, the fine bones of the fingers voicing through the papery skin. He folds the newspaper and pours tea and begins to drum his fingers on the table. I don't know why I still read this thing, he says, there is nothing in it but the big lie. She takes up the paper and begins to nick at the crossword with a pen. His fingers have ceased their drumming, without looking she can sense him examining her but when she lifts her eyes he is frowning. Who is that in the garden with Eilish?

he says. For an instant she looks outside then turns to
her father, taking his hand. Dad, that is Bailey outside
with Molly, I am sitting right here. A bewildered look
passes across his face and then he blinks and dismisses
her with a wave of his hand, pushes back his chair. Yes,
of course, he says, but she sulks about the place just
like you, never sunny like your sister. She regards him
now with a pained smile. So the both of us are just like
you then, she says. She is watching outside to Molly,
seeing herself in the same body, the clock winding to
chime in the hall bells three times from her childhood.
There is nothing wrong with that girl, she says, she is
fourteen, that is all, it is a difficult age, I remember it
all too well. Her gaze returns to the crossword. Badges
of office, she says, eight letters down, fifth letter is a G.
Simon lets slip the word insignia as though it has been
waiting in his mouth all along. She looks into his face
pleased for him, seeing the wattles cording about the
neck, the eyes withdrawing behind the hooded skin,
and yet the mind wings down. She pours tea, thinking,
do not tell him anything just yet, watching Bailey so
very fine in his bones whereas Mark is all brawn like
his father. She looks up and says, Larry is having some
trouble in the union, the government doesn't want the
TUI to go on strike, they took him in, Dad, and more
or less threatened him, can you believe that? Who took
him in? The GNSB. Simon turns and regards her without speaking then shakes his head and looks down at
his fingers. Larry should be careful with that crowd,
the GNSB, the National Alliance brought them in to

replace the Special Detective Unit soon after they came
to power, there was some noise about it for a week and
then it died away, suppressed no doubt, we never had
secret police in the state until now. Dad, they lifted the
area organiser for Leinster, no phone call, no solicitor,
he is being detained, the union is making a big bally-
hoo but the GNSB are silent. When did this happen?
Tuesday night—— Molly screams outside and they
turn to see her squirming and flapping her arms while
Bailey hangs from old rope pincering her with his legs.
A sudden, swooping look from her father. Tell me, he
says, do you believe in reality? Dad, what is that supposed to mean? It is a simple question, you took the
degree, you understand what it means. When you put
it like that, yes, I know what you mean, but spare me
the lecture. He looks away momentarily towards the
sideboard stacked high with yellowing newspapers,
dog-eared current affairs magazines, the old smile pulling to reveal his teeth. We are both scientists, Eilish,
we belong to a tradition but tradition is nothing more
than what everyone can agree on – the scientists, the
teachers, the institutions, if you change ownership of
the institutions then you can change ownership of the
facts, you can alter the structure of belief, what is agreed
upon, that is what they are doing, Eilish, it is really
quite simple, the NAP is trying to change what you and
I call reality, they want to muddy it like water, if you
say one thing is another thing and you say it enough
times, then it must be so, and if you keep saying it over
and over people accept it as true – this is an old idea,

of course, it really is nothing new, but you're watching
it happen in your own time and not in a book. She
watches his eyes travel down some distant thought,
trying to see into his mind, the mottled hand that pulls
a wrinkled handkerchief from the trouser pocket, he
blows his nose then puts the handkerchief back. Sooner
or later, of course, reality reveals itself, he says, you can
borrow for a time against reality but reality is always
waiting, patiently, silently, to exact a price and level
the scales—— Ben sputters awake and casts his eyes
about. He begins to bawl and Eilish pushes back her
chair and shushes at him, picks him up and puts him
to her breast under a scarf. She wants the old comforts,
she wants to call the children in and gather them round
but instead she meets a feeling of darkness, a zone of
shadow seeking increase. She draws in a breath and
sighs and tries to smile. We just booked our holidays
for Easter, we are going to stay with Áine and her gang
then tour around for another week, Niagara Falls if we
can get to it, a few other places around Toronto, the kids
will have a ball. Simon's eyes are adrift before her and
she is not sure if he has heard or not. He lifts his hands
from the table and stares at them then puts them down
again and looks up. Perhaps, he says, you should give
some thought to staying in Canada. She finds herself
unlatching the child, she is standing out of the chair
looking down at him. Dad, what is that supposed to
mean? It means I'm too old to do anything now, but the
kids are still young, they can easily adapt, there is still
time to make a fresh start, they'll pick up the accents

in no time. For goodness' sake, Dad, would you listen to yourself, don't you think you are over-reacting, and what about my career and Larry's job and the kids with school, and then there is Molly's hockey, they're going to win the Leinster schoolgirls' junior league this year, they're nine points ahead already, and Mark has just entered the senior cycle at school, who is going to keep an eye on you when you can't even clean the cups, Mrs Taft comes in just once a week, what if you fall and break a hip, tell me, what then?

The winter rain falls lush and cold, the passing days held numb within the rain so that it seems to mask time's passing, each day giving to faceless day until the winter is at full bloom. A strange, unsettled air has filled the house. It came with the two men who called to the door and has worked its way throughout their home, this feeling now as though some unity within the family has begun to unravel. Larry working late into the night and in the mornings he is irritable and withdrawn, moving it seems within some quiet savagery, his hands tense, his body seeming to tighten as though under the influence of some great screwing pressure. For too many evenings now he has come home late, Eilish watching through the blinds then releasing them so as not to be seen, like some old spinster, she thinks, a curtain twitcher, waiting for him in the hall as he comes through the door. You were supposed to bring

Molly to practice, Larry, I had to cancel another call with our partners, I have only just returned back to work after maternity leave, how do you think this looks? He stands by the door with a foot half-pulled from his boot and then he lowers his eyes like some abject and beaten dog, he shakes his head and looks her full in the eye and she sees a change come over him, his voice an angry whisper. They are trying to disrupt us, Eilish, they are spreading lies within the union, you will not believe what I heard today—— His voice falters before her narrowed gaze and then his eyes seek the floor again. Look, he says, I hear what you're saying and I'm sorry. He shows her a small pay-as-you-go phone, a burner phone he calls it. Even if they wanted to listen in, they could not know the number. She watches him thinking of the children listening to them whispering in the hall. You are behaving like some criminal, Larry, listen, it looks like Bailey is coming down with a virus, he's gone upstairs—— Larry brings his hand into the air and cuts her off. I am hardly a criminal when they are trying to break the union, arresting members of our organisation without sanction, they are not going to stop this march. He steps past her into the living room and goes into the kitchen closing the door. She watches him through the glass as he rests his satchel on a chair and goes to the sink and washes his hands, leans against the sink looking out. She wants to go to him, seeking for the mind within the body, the good, proud man within the mind, urgent and moral and committed, the war within him growing against this something they cannot measure. Thinking how of late he wants to be alone, in the end, all men seek the same isolation, she saw this once graffitied on a wall. She opens the door and leans her head into the kitchen. Do you want dinner? she says. No, I'm fine, I had a late lunch, I might eat something later. Molly steps into the room wearing a respirator. She has been disinfecting door handles, taps and toilet flushers, erects a cordon outside the boys' room using Sellotape and refuses to eat at the table. She will not listen to Eilish who explains that the virus can hardly be stopped, seeing in her mind how the virus invades the host cell and replicates, a silent factory within the body, the virus riding unseen on the breath. The next day Molly and Mark take sick to their beds and then Larry too, she is glad to have them all home, even Larry seems to be his old self again, laughing at how she and the baby are immune, ribbing Mark as he comes through the door with his hair over his eyes snuffling into a tissue. The head on you, Larry says, I could pass you on the street and hardly know you. Anybody else but Dad want coffee? Mark says. They gather round to watch a film and Mark returns with drinks, she is watching the long, solid body, he is almost seventeen and as tall as his father. Scooch over, Mark says, sitting down beside her, he rests his arm over her shoulder and she cannot recall the last time everybody was home like this, Molly curled up by her side, Bailey on a bean bag spooning ice cream, Larry before the TV, Ben asleep on her lap. Ah, come off it, Mark says, how many times before have we watched

this sentimental shite? I like it, Bailey says. Yeah, me
too, says Molly, it's very sweet, remind me, Mam, how
you two first met? Larry laughs and Mark groans and
says, how many times have we heard that before, don't
you know that Dad is the great romantic and had to
chase after Mam for months with a net. That's not true,
Eilish says, smiling at Larry. Well, part of it is true,
Larry says, I am of course a great romantic and as for
the rest of it, it was a potato sack I used. When Ben
wakes in her lap she looks into his face trying to see
the man he will become, both Mark and Bailey have
proven this kind of thinking wrong, an orange can fall
from an apple tree and Ben will become his own man
for sure. And yet she seeks within the child for some
semblance of Larry, hoping he will measure up to his
father, knowing how it is so that all boys grow up and
pull away from home to unmake the world in the guise
of making it, nature decrees it is so.

The child startles awake with a cry as though astonished at waking and she finds herself rising upward
through sleep until her sleep lies broken in the dark
room. She slides a foot towards Larry but his side of the
bed is cold. She lifts the child from the cot and puts him
to her breast, the small mouth gasping and devouring,
the little hand clawing at her flesh. She gives him her
finger and he grips it with such tiny might she knows
his innate terror, the child clinging as though for dear

life, as though there is nothing else to bind him to life but his mother. The dawn birds are sounding the quiet when she robes and carries Ben downstairs. There is Larry seated at the table in darkness, his face illumined by the laptop. He has not heard her come and so she watches him freely, the sad and burdened face, the unblinking preoccupation. She reaches to the wall and turns on the lights and he looks up and sighs then smiles, motions for the child, stands him on his lap, letting the boy take his own weight. Did he sleep through the night? he says, I didn't hear him wake, how come you're up so early? I could ask the same of you, Larry, you look as though you didn't even go to bed. Larry lifts the child nose-to-nose. Look at you, little man, first you take us by surprise and now you'll soon be weaned. She stands at the coffee machine with her arms folded then turns and watches Larry with such intensity his face grows estranged, the eyes to blood from lack of sleep and the hair askew, the beaten herringbone jacket over the merino sweater, comparing herself to him for a moment, he has begun to age more quickly it is true, the beard half-run with grey. It is then she is met with the realisation she cannot remember how he used to look, cell renewal is both fast and slow, you start out with one body and over time it becomes another, he is the same and yet he is different, only the eyes remain unchanged. She takes Ben from his arms and stares at him. It is not too late, she says. He is watching her and begins to frown. What is not too late? This game you're playing with the government, there is still time to stop.

He is silent a moment and then he sighs and folds the laptop, feeds it into a leather case and stands up. For goodness' sake, Eilish, the wheels are in motion, you cannot just pull out from something like this, it would be a huge embarrassment to the organisation, the teachers would abandon us in droves, the march has to go ahead. Yes, Larry, but Alison O'Reilly hasn't returned to work yet, why do you think that is? Her husband says she has the flu. That flu is going on three weeks. Yes, I know, it does seem a little strange, look, I have to be in early, there is a media briefing before—— She has turned her back, watching outside to the garden wet and dark, everything hung in damp suspension, the trees bowing to the cold. Without turning she can measure the strength of his will set against her will, both wills locked in silent adversary, circling each other and then grappling before withdrawing bruised and sore. Larry is moving towards the living room when he stops and says, Mary O'Connor's mother died last night, I got a message just before midnight, she was ninety-four, the last of the titans if ever there was one. Eilish shakes her head and places Ben into the rocker. She was fierce in her day that woman, when is the funeral? Saturday morning at the Church of the Three Patrons. She is stepping towards Larry wishing it were some other morning, she places her hand on his wrist and squeezes. Larry, Alison O'Reilly isn't sick and you know it. Eilish, you can't prove that. The GNSB are not to be messed with, if you open this door, Larry, you cannot know what is on the other side. Eilish, listen, you need to relax, the GNSB are not the Stasi, they are just applying a little pressure, that is all, some disruption and harassment to get us to back off, we are fifteen thousand strong and the government is nervous but they cannot stop a democratic march, just you wait and see. She is close enough now to see the stippling in his eye, the muted shades of red and amber, no eye has unison colour. Tell me, Larry, where is Jim Sexton now? He blinks, frowning, and turns away. Really, Eilish—— He shakes his head and lifts his briefcase, steps into the living room but does not go to the door. She can hear him standing motionless and then with a long sigh he sits down. For an instant she feels overcome, looking again out the window she sees the trees glistening in the leaden day, thinking, how quickly the dawn passes, grey light fresh upon the leaves, the shadow shapes in the trees of rattling magpies. This urgent feeling in her hands as she enters the living room, seeing Larry very still in the armchair as though watching some thought made manifest before him. He looks up and shakes his head and says, maybe you're right, Eilish, this is not the time, it is madness to go ahead, I'll give them a call, tell them I'm out sick. She steps towards him sensing victory, looking down upon him. She goes to speak but something comes free inside her, a trickster magpie taking flight, and she stands before him shaking her head. No, she says, this has to be done, it is not about you or me anymore, the NAP seem to think they are above the law, everybody knows this emergency legislation is just a grab for power, who else will stand up for our constitutional rights if the teachers don't stick it to them? She watches the way he is seated heavy about the bones, a boy holding the grown mind in his hands and then in an instant he is standing up and has assumed the old unswerving aspect. Right so, love, it is a dirty day for a march, I'll follow them for a pint afterwards but I won't take a drink, I can still collect Molly from practice. She leans against the door watching as he puts on his green hiking boots in the hall. He reaches for his raincoat and tries to sleeve it over his jacket, the arm of the raincoat is inside out and for a moment he is stuck on the threshold of the door doing battle with the sleeve, she thinks he is still unsure, he looks up and meets her eyes. Go, she says with a smile, go and be done with you.

She steps into the office after lunch nursing an oblique thought. Something is hidden yet asking, the searching mind alighting upon other things, Ben's change of clothes she forgot to pack for crèche, the passport renewal forms she was supposed to post. It is then she thinks of the mobile phone left behind on her desk. She picks it up expecting some missed calls but there are none, it is unlike Larry not to call from a march. She moves towards the kitchen and Rohit Singh's eyes intercept her over the top of his screen, he is speaking into the phone yet telling her something with his eyes, it is a look she cannot read and so she shrugs and curls her lower mouth into an expression of mock universal grief. It is then she hears her name being called and she turns to see Alice Dealy stepping out of her office with a look of hesitation. Eilish, are you not watching the news? No, I'm just back from lunch. As soon as she has spoken she knows what is told in Alice's face, moving now towards the office and for an instant she has been slowed into an upright swim, she is wading forward, taking a mouthful of air as she steps inside, seeing them gathered around Alice's large screen. What she sees on the news is the piercing image of sudden horses charging through a street become some dim and smoking inferno. She sees police with batons, they are beating the marchers into grovelling shapes, they are beating them into the corners of the street, tear gas skulking within some slow time occurrence while without the marchers flee in repeat clips. They cringe in the doorways with the necks of their clothing pulled over their noses while an image repeats of a teacher being dragged by plainclothesmen towards an unmarked car. She is met with a feeling of helplessness, finds herself at her desk with the phone to her ear, it is ringing, ringing out, Paul Felsner is watching through the office blinds. She sits down behind her screen trying to see him in her mind, Larry, but instead she sees Felsner's slow and examining look, sees herself thirty minutes before eating a sandwich while time was already on the march, time had already marched past her. She must go to him, feeling him now, feeling some obscure sense of guilt. She sweeps her security pass and her belongings

into her bag, steps through the office sleeved in one half
of her coat, the stairwell reverberant with the smack of
her shoes and then she is standing on the street with
her phone to her ear, Larry's phone does not answer
and when she rings it again his phone is turned off. It
is then she looks up and it seems as though the day has
come to be under some foreign sky, feeling some sense
of disintegration, the rain falling slow on her face.

# 2

Towards the car with the baby in her arms, Eilish
urging the children onwards, urging herself on in silent
wish. She turns to see Molly stropping silently with two
shopping bags, Bailey playing with the trolley as she
calls him back. She clicks Ben's baby seat into place
and he meets her eye with a sleepy smile while Molly
drops the bags into the boot then slides into the front
seat placing headphones over her ears. Eilish wants to
reach out, to touch and speak, Bailey with flung arms
running towards the car. He climbs in the back and
slams the door then leans between the two seats and
studies his mother in the rear-view mirror. Mam, he
says, when is Dad coming home? The long drop of her
heart through her body and still its falling. She searches
for the words that will not come, finds herself looking
away from her son, sensing that Molly is watching her
also. For a moment she looks onto the darkening street,
a group of teenagers passing by, knowing them in their
heedless bones as they harass and sport each other,
seeing the Molly to come and losing her, perhaps she is
already gone. She turns to Bailey inhaling slowly, seeks

his gaze in the mirror and holds it. I've told you, love, he had to go away for work, he'll be back as soon as he's able to. She watches the lie growing out her mouth, the lie unseen doing its work, Bailey falling back onto the seat with a humph, seeing how he takes whatever she says as fact. Bailey reaches forward and pulls at Molly's seatbelt imprisoning her until she turns and tries to slap at his hand. She gives her mother a sharp look and Eilish looks away, thinking how Molly must have known something was wrong when nobody came to collect her from hockey, she could not get through to her parents on the phone, standing outside the clubhouse watching her teammates go one by one in the dusk until Miss Dunne saw her home. Her face as she came in the door puce with rage and later how she fell silent, what had to be told to Mark and Molly that night, that there has been a round-up of key personnel from the union, that we are living in difficult times, they will have to let him go soon, you must remember your father hasn't done anything wrong, he is being sub- jected to intimidation by the government but both of you need to be careful now, you cannot speak about this outside the house and cannot say a word to anybody at school. Seeing the terror in Molly's face, pleading with them to keep it a secret from Bailey, he is too young to understand. The girl's anger abating into silence, the bedroom door locked, Eilish standing outside afraid to be the knocker. Mark taking the news with some strange quality of reserve, a single question was all he asked, why aren't they allowing him access to a solicitor? She keys the ignition afraid now for what lies must follow, the lies growing further out her mouth, seeing how a single lie told to a child is an outrage, that there can be no untelling it and once the lie is known it will remain outgrown from the mouth like some dead-tonguing poisonous flower. She drives through labouring traffic, the children silent in the car, they are almost home when the phone rings in her bag by Molly's feet. She asks for the phone and then she asks again, of a sudden she screams at Molly and sheers the car to the roadside, she reaches for her bag and pulls the headphones from Molly's ears, the girl staring aghast at her mother. The missed call is from an unknown number, she stares at it and decides to ring back. Hello, yes, this is Eilish Stack, I have a missed call from this number. It is Carole Sexton who wants to talk. Look, Carole, I cannot speak right now, I'm in the car, can I give you a call tonight? Bailey watching sullen in the mirror. Why can't I call him on the phone, Mam, are you getting a divorce, is that what's going on? When she parks in the driveway she opens the door and goes to step outside but hesitates as though a chasm has opened before her on the gravel. The sensing step after each sensing step, sensing the long night to come.

Michael Given makes his calls house-to-house, it is not safe to discuss things over the phone, one must always suspect they are listening. She watches him stoop into the kitchen almost sorry in his manner, the knitting of his yellowed fingers as he sits down, watching how he opens his phone and removes the battery and places it on the table. She slides Ben into the rocker and continues to study Michael Given, seeing how he is smoking himself past cough into hurt. You look tired, Michael, can I make you something to eat? He bats away the request with a long hand but she places biscuits before him on a plate and he picks one up and turns it in his hand without eating. Listen, Eilish, there is talk they are going to move them. She has been absent from herself watching the water jet into the kettle's mouth, she is holding her breath, she turns off the tap and places the kettle down. Move them where? The talk is of internment camps in the Curragh, it is only a rumour but still, one must imagine they cannot hold all of them in the city when so many have been arrested, they had them there during the war, in the Curragh, those at the time who were considered a security risk by the state. What are you saying, Michael, that Larry is now a security risk? She watches Michael Given surrender his hands into the air. God no, Eilish, it's just a figure of speech, that's the term they are using. Larry is being held for political reasons, Michael, I do not want to hear that kind of talk in this house. Michael Given seals his lips inward, his eyes widening like a surprised child, he nods towards the sink. You don't want to leave that thing resting in there, he says. She turns and sees the electric kettle in the sink. Aren't I some eejit? she says, shaking her head. She wipes the kettle dry and places it on the stand, looks again at Michael Given seeking the source of her anger, seeing him as prey, yellow and insect before the table. They are lifting people from everywhere now, he says, did you hear the journalist Philip Brophy was taken, a fucking journalist, the NAP have some nerve, it has been all over the foreign news but not a word said about it here, they are controlling the newsrooms now though social media is alive with it. She is watching Michael Given as he speaks, thinking how he seems to sway softly in the seat, a willowy tiredness passing through his body as though he were underwater. Husbands and wives, mothers and fathers sinking under the water. Sons and daughters, sisters and brothers disappearing down, down into the down. She finds herself breathless seeking upward for air, moving into the living room, seeking something within her thinking as she picks up the remote and finds a news channel and puts it on mute. This sense now she is living in another country, this sense of some chaos opening, calling them into its mouth. She steps into the kitchen feeling her wrath then squeezes the air with her hands as though she has reached around the throat of the problem. Michael, she says, the fact that you are not allowed to see him, that is what I cannot understand, I've looked up the law myself, the treaties, it is a flagrant breech of international law, so tell me, why are they being allowed to do what they like, why has nobody shouted stop? Her words beat upon Michael Given's silence and she searches the face that seems both sad and perplexed, a baffled dog met with some alien injunction, he puts his hands up and goes to speak but she is upon him again. The state is supposed to leave you alone, Michael, not enter your house like an ogre, take a father into its fist and gobble him, how can I even begin to explain this to the kids, that the state they live in has become a monster? All this will blow over, Eilish, the NAP will have to back down sooner or later, there is outrage all over Europe—— Then why is the GNSB arresting more and more people each day, Michael, calling this a time of national emergency, the plain-clothesmen who came into our office on Tuesday and took a young fellow from his desk, Eamon Doyle, a statistical scientist, the last fellow on earth to be causing trouble, and do you know what he said when he fetched his coat, he asked that somebody call his mother, and this two weeks before Christmas. She sits down and pours coffee with an aggressive swing of the French press. She is out of her body and the body must follow, standing again before the TV pretending to watch the news, she tries to stifle a sob. Michael Given is talking about rumours of protests in Cork and Galway that were shut down on sight but she isn't listening, she is thinking of the children upstairs in bed, she is thinking of Mark who any moment will put his key in the door and wheel his bike through the house to the patio out back, there is nothing she can say to him. Michael Given leans his voice into the living room so she can hear. They've gone too far now, Eilish, the mood of civil unrest is growing though you'll not hear that on the news, the NAP want to turn this country into a security state and have said they'll start drafting for the Defence Forces, can you imagine that in this country, the streets are full of talk, people want to put a stop to it now, that is what I'm hearing—— She finds herself standing before him with a snapping mouth. If the country is full of talk, then who is passing among that talk listening? She watches him until he makes a rueful shape with his mouth and turns away. Look at you lot, she says, the unions bowed and silent, and at least half the country in support of this carry-on and casting the teachers as villains—— Something inchoate within her knowledge has spoken and she feels afraid, she can hear it now and speaks it silently to herself. All your life you've been asleep, all of us sleeping and now the great waking begins. This night-haunted feeling that won't let her go, thinking of Larry hesitating at the door, Larry sliding his feet into his green boots and then fighting to get into his raincoat. He knew what they were up against and he gave you the power to say no, he sat down on that chair and gave himself utterly to you. The nights now are the longest, this is what she would like to say, looking at the sallow hands resting on the table. Sleeping in the cold bed with Larry's odour in his pyjamas beside her on the pillow. She turns again to Michael Given and sighs and sits down and doesn't know what to do with her hands. I'm going to lose my job if this carries on, she says. Have you told them? he says. Look, you know how it is, there are party types in the company working their way into senior positions, you have to be careful now, one fellow inside seems to

be able to do what he likes. You can request annual
leave, Eilish, there's always that. I cannot go on leave
after being on maternity leave for six months. Yes, but
these are extraordinary circumstances, in any case,
there are union funds available if you run into trouble,
all you need do is ask. Yes, Michael, but who will be left
in the union to disburse them? He is silent awhile
watching the long, yellowed fingers asking the mouth
for a smoke. She finds her hands restless on her legs,
stands again out of her chair and looks down feeling
her might upon him. Michael, I want my husband back.
Look, Eilish, we are doing what we can—— You're not
listening, I want you to get him before a judge, a judge
will return him to his children. Eilish, if this were any
other time we would have filed a complaint to the High
Court for unlawful detention, we would have him out
but habeas corpus has been suspended under the
national emergency legislation, in effect, the state has
special powers and has silenced the judiciary. You're
not listening, Michael, I want you to listen, I want you
to make something happen, I want my husband back.
Look, Eilish, you're not being reasonable, this is
unprecedented, there is an air of hysteria in the country, you cannot just click your fingers and expect the
state to do your bidding—— In her mind she is moving
towards his throat with both hands, she has grabbed
him by the larynx and wrenches the mouth open,
reaches in and yanks the craven tongue, holds it a
moment by the stalk then roots it out. Watching the
way he opens his hands upon the table, the smokeless

hands meek and half-expressed as though they speak the true waiving of his power. He lifts his face and she sees the eyes of a man who has not slept and is met with pity for him, for what is known by the telling of the hands, how the man has been trained for the rules of the game but the game has been changed so what now is the man? A seam of anger opens inside her. I want you to go and bring him back, she says, and if you won't go, I will go myself and bring him back, that is what I will do, I would rather die than see his absence parading all day in front of the children. Michael Given stands up and levels his eyes at her and looks at her a long time as though making up his mind. Eilish, you need to listen to what I'm about to say, I did not want to tell you this but I'm afraid I must do so now, we have been told directly by the GNSB that if we continue to press on this, if we continue to petition for a writ for habeas corpus, we too will be arrested and detained. Her mouth opens but no sound comes out, she has been thrown free of the body to become a single black thought, the thought intensifying, expanding darkly until it has swallowed all matter. When she finds herself again in her body a whisper leaves her mouth. Michael Given is moving from the table, he goes to the sink and washes his hands. They are saying we are in for some stormy weather, he says, Storm Bella she's called, hold onto your hat the next couple of days. She turns upon him sensing the wish to let fly into madness but instead she begins to the window looking out. The cherry trees held the sleet this morning when she

awoke but now the trees in their witless conspiracy
are nodding to the dark.

She wakes on Larry's side of the bed into night.
Somewhere in the dark of her body a candle is burn-
ing for him but when she seeks the candle to light out
past her body she meets only darkness. She has heard
in sleep the wind calling and now it sounds about the
house as though the front door had been left open. She
steps to the window looking out, swept and running
orange are the clouds, looking upon the city and long-
ing for it. She walks about the unlit house feeling her
feet grow cold, feeling she has become a ghost to her
past. Standing outside the children's rooms listening
to them sleep while the wind blows without. What can
be more innocent than a child at sleep, let the children sleep and when he has returned we shall go on
again. She slips into bed and rubs her feet and wakes
into wild light, hearing a hoarse shout of wind, the
window slapped with wet gravel. She steps drowsy to
the window feeling as though the house were in flight,
the house turning in the wind. Across the street the
Zajacs' green bin is lying on its side, paper and tins and
pizza boxes strewing the driveway, a handful of rain is
snatched by the wind and flung to the bare willows.
Then she sees it, a lone magpie tricked to a tree, watching for a time how the bird flicks its wings yet remains
fixed to the branch as it bends with the wind, seeing

now that it is not she who must hold on but Larry, he must hold on and meet whatever he is being met with, sensing his strength now and knowing it, stepping inside his strength and clasping it to her body.

Come the morning she stands by the front door calling Bailey down. It is almost twenty past eight, she says, Molly will be late for school and so will you—— Mark wheels his bike towards the street then stops and looks to the sky. She follows his glance sensing calm in the muddled air, watching him swing his leg over the seat as he propels the bike in fluid motion without saying goodbye. Hold on a minute, she says. She studies his face as he turns to look at her, a lone eyebrow raised beneath the curling chestnut hair. She does not know what she wants to say, she does not want to say anything at all, she just wants to look at him. Your hair is very long, she says, I want you home for dinner, you are hardly home as it is. Mark rolls his eyes then smiles and says, I love you too, Mam, he turns and pedals up the street. She finds herself crossing the road where she rights the Zajacs' green bin then studies the house, the lights should be on, the front door open, Anna Zajac should be harrying the kids into the Nissan but instead the blinds are drawn and the house looks empty though the car is parked out front. She meets Molly stepping out the door. Where is your brother? she says, we are going to be late for school, tell me, have the Zajacs gone

back home for Christmas already? Molly shrugs, how
am I supposed to know, I don't think Bailey has left his
room, he did not come down for breakfast. Eilish clicks
the child seat into the car and asks Molly to wait with
Ben. She steps inside and stands in the hall calling for
Bailey, turns and sees herself true in the mirror, the
pale and raddled face giving to the sunken eyes, the
eyes asking the question and almost laughing at it,
mirror, mirror on the wall. For an instant she sees the
past held in the open gaze of the mirror as though the
mirror contains all it has seen, seeing herself sleep-
walking before the glass, the mindless comings and
goings throughout the years, watching herself usher
the children out to the car and they are all ages before
her and Mark has lost another shoe and Molly is refusing to wear a coat and Larry is asking if they have their
schoolbags and she sees how happiness hides in the
humdrum, how it abides in the everyday toing and
froing as though happiness were a thing that should
not be seen, as though it were a note that cannot be
heard until it sounds from the past, seeing her own
countless reflections vain and satisfied before the glass
while Larry waits impatiently in the car, he is standing
in the hall taking off his raincoat, he is shouting for his
slippers as he slides out of his green boots. She calls
for Bailey and goes upstairs and finds he has locked
the door. She shakes the handle and bangs the door
with her fist. Since when do you have a key to this
room, open this door right now, you're going to be late
for school. When the key turns in the lock she pushes

the door open and sees her son in the curtained gloom climbing into bed. She pulls the key from the lock and drops it into her pocket, goes to the bed and pulls back the duvet, stands over him with her hands on her hips. Right, mister, you have two minutes to get dressed and into the car. It is then she meets the smell from the bed, Bailey tucking his legs towards his belly and she can see the pyjama bottoms are sodden. She falls silent, goes to the window and snatches at the curtains, dirty light unmasking the room. She bends to pick up the clothes from the floor and speaks without looking at him. Go undress and wash quickly, you are holding everybody up. Bailey moves towards the door and she begins to strip the sheet from the bed, asking herself how many times this has happened since Larry has gone, he had never wet the bed before. She turns to see Bailey standing by the door with a look of whetted malevolence, he cries out at her, you sent him away, didn't you, that's what you did, you're nothing but an old bitch. She finds herself stopped with stuttering hands, her mouth quivering, she bundles the wet sheet and sees herself in flight down the stairs. She will lance the evil in his eye like the pricking of a boil, she will lock the front door and climb into the car and let him stew alone in his room. She has not moved, her eyes have dropped to watch her feet when she hears it fall from her mouth, the truth about his father, she is explaining the illegal arrest and detention, the efforts being made to get him before a judge, the fact that nothing will happen before Christmas. Her heart grows pained as she watches the boy's frowning disbelief, the sliding look in his eye, how his mouth slopes and then he buckles silently to the floor ringing his arms about his knees. What she sees before her is an idea of order coming undone, the world slewing into a dark and foreign sea. She holds him in her arms, seeking in her whispers to rebuild for her son the old world of laws that lies broken at his feet, for what is the world to a child when a father without word can be made to disappear? The world gives to chaos, the ground you walk on flies into the air and the sun shines dark on your head. Molly is leaning in the door. What's going on? she says, we're waiting outside in the car, we have to go to school. Bailey straightening himself up, he pushes past her into the bathroom.


It is past nine o'clock when she hears faint knocking on the door. She looks out past the blinds and sees a small car parked in front of the house, Christmas lights twinkling from under the eaves and electric candles flickering in the windows though the Zajacs' house is dark. Mark and Samantha are flopped on the couch holding hands, their minds entwined with the screen, they barely look up when Carole Sexton droops past them with a faltering smile, looking too tall in her flat shoes as she follows Eilish into the kitchen. Eilish sneaks another look at the clock, Bailey and Molly have just gone upstairs to bed, soon as Carole is gone out the door she will give Samantha the nod to go home. Carole fetches a hand into a tote bag and removes three biscuit tins. The long hours of the night in her eyes and when she speaks her voice is burdened. I'm sorry to impose on you like this, Eilish, but I needed to see you. She is searching about the room with her eyes, examining the counters, she has never been here before, Eilish seeing her own kitchen as though for the first time, the disorder of cups and plates by the sink, the dishwasher half-full with the door open, the basket of soiled clothes waiting to be washed, if Carole had called in advance she would have had time to tidy up. You have a lovely tree, Eilish, I wish I had a Christmas tree like that, I didn't put one up this year, it seemed, I don't know, it just seemed—— She goes to speak again but waves her hand. So, anyway, let me tell you, I had a taste for soda bread last night, I'm not even sure I like soda bread, you know, the traditional kind, but I suddenly developed the taste, the first loaf came out alright, the second was much better, and I had bought so many eggs you see, once you get in the mindset for baking it is hard to stop even if you don't really know much about it, I haven't done any baking since home economics in school, but I had such an urge last night I thought I'd make some oat cakes as well, the smell of them fresh from the oven, my goodness, and some fruit scones too, and I went from there to a fruit cake, an old recipe I dug out of my mother's cookbook, and it was then it occurred to me that last year for Christmas, Eilish, I didn't bother to get a Christmas cake, I was just so busy, you know, and he made a comment, Jim, he said he would have liked to

have had some Christmas cake, so I made one of those
as well last night, but anyhow, when I was done I had a
good laugh at the idea of myself baking all these things
when I only wanted some bread, and I have no appetite
at all whereas you have several mouths to feed, so look,
I brought some over for you and I have one here for you
as well, a Christmas cake, there are some scones also
and some crumble cake—— The smell of baking has
brought Mark to the glass door, he is watching with his
nose, his eyes asking if he can come in. Eilish shakes
her head but Carole waves him in, studying him as he
takes a plate and begins to fill it with cake. Take some
for your girlfriend as well, you've grown so tall, she
says, big at the shoulders just like your father—— A
sudden shadow seems to crawl down her face as Mark
mutters thanks and steps out the door fisting cake into
his mouth. Carole turns to Eilish opening her hands.
I'm so sorry, she says, I wasn't thinking. Eilish watches
the woman's discomfort and for a moment she is glad,
seeing the hair uncombed, the roots pulling on an inch
of grey, she remembers her at a gathering some years
ago heeled taller than the men, the sensuous mouth
given to taunting and laughter, the way her hand would
creep onto Larry's wrist and remain there while talking
with him, she was always so difficult to like. In short
time she will climb into her car and set out for home
to a childless, silent house. Eilish reaches out and takes
Carole's hand. Never mind, she says, he's not angry
with you at all, he's angry at me, at the world, my other
son won't even look at me, I've tried to speak with Mark

about what's going on but all I get is this unnerving silence, he knows, you see, he understands only too well what is happening to the country, he wants to go on and study medicine, you know, I think he will make a good doctor. She pours Carole tea and lets her talk without watching the clock, sensing how the woman's words have been housed too long in silence, seeing how she makes sense of herself through speech, the words leave the mouth and the mind follows after the words and some sense of understanding is made. She listens thinking about what she would like to say but cannot, how she too has sought to hide from relatives and friends, telling herself she must give herself to working, seeking the hours that are given to fill the hollow body, seeking to lose herself in the children though it is the children that take her back to their father. Carole takes a long drink of tea then stares into space. I cannot tell you how many people have fallen silent since Jim has been arrested, it is as though I am guilty somehow, why are we being made to feel guilty when it is an evil that has been done to us? Eilish finds herself watching the clock, she stands up, shaking her head. This is not a time to speak, she says, but a time to keep silent, everybody has grown afraid, our husbands have been taken from us and placed into this silence, there are times at night when I hear this silence as loud as death but it is not death just arbitrary arrest and detention, you must keep telling this to yourself over and over. She finds herself standing with nothing to do, she goes to the sink and begins to tidy up. Our family holiday has been booked for Easter, she says, I still believe we will be going. When she turns she sees Carole leaning forward in the chair watching past her reflection in the glass, seeing out to the garden, her eyes fierce as though seeking to perceive some augury in the darkness. What's that outside, Eilish, the white on that tree? Ribbons, Carole, white ribbons, every week since her father is gone, Molly takes a chair outside and ties a piece of ribbon to the tree. They are silent for a time watching the ribbons swaying in the lower branches. I have this feeling, Eilish, that sooner or later, I will take matters into my own hands. Eilish turns from the window and studies the face that rests as still as a mask. Whatever do you mean? Carole remains silent and then she shakes her head as though breaking free of some reverie, she sweeps the crumbs on the table into her hand and stands up, delivers them into the bin. The doctor has given me sleeping tablets, Eilish, but how can you sleep, I haven't slept a full night since he's gone, the other night I found my wedding dress in a box in the attic and took it down, would you believe I still fit into it after all this time.

She has left the office forty minutes before lunch wrapped against the cutting breeze, her walk brisk, the winter light uncertain, a sense of snow in the air. A bicycle courier slows to a red light between traffic and balances to a standstill without resting his feet and she watches for an instant met with the feeling that the city has stopped and time has ceased but for a shadow that glooms across the street and then the cyclist awakens and bends to the green light. She rounds onto Nassau Street thinking of her shoes which are starting to bite, looks up and sees Rory O'Connor holding the hand of a child. She makes to cross the street but he calls her name and she turns feigning surprise. You've let your hair grow again, Eilish, I almost wouldn't know you. Rory, she says, looking at the Christmas shopping in one hand and the young boy in the other. Is this your son? she says, I didn't know you had a child. She smiles down at the boy seeing the father in the plump fresh face, the skull wired with the same reddish hair she remembers Rory having years ago, seeing now the thinning strands of copper and grey, he could be any middle-aged man. A rare day off for the both of us, isn't that right, Fintan, you're looking well, Eilish, how long has it been? Fintan, she says slowly, wondering if the name suits the face. How long has it been, Rory, it must be ten years or more? He is quick to speak about old times and she watches his face hurrying him along with her eyes, a bus pulls away expelling hot diesel smoke and Rory steps back, his scarf stirring to reveal the party pin on the lapel of his jacket. She has taken a step backwards, swallows and closes her eyes, Rory smiling with his teeth. So how is Larry, the same old, same old, I suppose? She cannot lift her eyes from the party pin, she looks across the street then steals a glance at her watch. Oh, Larry is just fine, she says, he's up to his eyes, never a moment's peace, he is no longer teaching at Mount Temple you know, he is working full-time now for the— look, it was lovely to meet you but I must run, and you too little Fintan, I'm in a mad hurry, I have to get to the passport office, we're off to Canada with the kids at Easter—— She has stepped out in front of a transit van and makes a dash for the far pavement feeling the pinch in her shoes, watching herself with Rory's eyes as she continues at a clumsy jog as though to prove her hurry. This hollow feeling as she turns onto Kildare Street, seeing before her the Rory O'Connor she knew from before, the blushing, amateurish young man who palled around with Larry, this creeping sense of double time as though her life were unfolding twice along parallel paths.

Warm air blasts the doorway as she enters the passport office on Molesworth Street and takes a numbered ticket, stands by a Christmas tree untying her scarf, watching for a seat to come free. She has so much to do, she makes a list in a notebook and watches an obese man with an egg-shaped head shuffle towards hatch thirteen, she takes his seat and watches him return blinking with small eyes at a form. She will store all this for later, seeing Larry's face across the table, his disgust when she tells him about Rory O'Connor, he was always a feckless eejit Larry will say. She must call the office to tell them she will be late. It is four minutes past three when her number appears on the ticker and she is met by a woman with hardly a face. I received this yesterday, Eilish says, there must be some mistake. A hand motions to see the letter, then fingers begin to type. Can you pass me your ID? Eilish slides her driving licence under the screen and the woman takes it then wheels back her chair and steps away. Eilish chews the inside of her lip, she is speaking to herself the words she will say when the woman returns, she looks up and sees a man approaching. He slips neatly into the chair and meets her with a colourless look. Well, he says, Mrs Eilish Stack, you can have this back now. He slides her ID under the glass and continues to watch her openly so that she is forced to look away. So, Mrs Stack, you are planning on leaving the country, is that right? Yes, we're going on our holidays. Your holidays. Yes, to visit my sister in Canada for Easter, the flights are booked. The flights are booked. Yes, that is what I said, I'm sorry but I don't understand what difference this makes to you, I am just applying for a renewal for my eldest son and to get a passport for my infant. Faintly she can smell menthol cigarettes from the other side of the hatch. The procedure has been changed, Mrs Stack, you must now go through a security and background check before you can apply. She finds herself watching the face so intensely she is met with the feeling of an existence unalterably separate from hers, can feel her smile uncoupling from her face, the smile sliding past her jaw onto the floor. She stutters for a moment then clears her throat. I'm sorry, she says, I don't understand what you're talking about, I've never heard of such a thing, I'm just applying for a passport like I've done before. Yes, but you did not take the preliminary step, Mrs Stack, you must now go through a full security and background check with the Department of Justice before you can apply, all this is provided for in the Emergency Powers Act introduced this year. She watches the man reach for something as she leans towards the glass. So what you're saying is I need to do a security and background check to get a passport for my infant and teenage son? The official allows a narrow smile. That is correct. I follow the news, she says, there was nothing said about this anywhere, I want to speak with your supervisor. The man slides a form under the window. Mrs Stack, I am the supervisor here, my name is Dermot Connolly and I'm on secondment from the Department of Justice, this is the form you need, F107, you just need to fill it out and apply for an interview, it will take a few weeks at best, is there anything else I can help you with? She finds herself staring into a face that does not alter from its single expression, the colourless eyes, the mouth and what it says although the mouth does not speak – your husband is in detention, Mrs Stack, you have been deemed a security risk. It is then she is struck with the sense that some wild animal has entered behind her and is pacing the room, she takes the form and slowly folds it, places it into her bag, watching the supervisor leave the chair, hearing the silent steps of the animal, sensing its rank breath on her neck, she is afraid to turn around. The silent, seated faces gaping into phones.

On Christmas day she walks with the children by the sea, mortar the sky and the water, this easterly breeze blowing cold hell upon Bull Island yet cooling the mind to think. Ben strapped to her chest while the children fan outward, sensing the anger in their hearts, knowing them by the shape of their walk, Molly alone and careful with her feet as though sounding for something within her body, Mark with his hands in his coat pockets watchful and removed until he grabs at a ribbon of seaweed and swishes it after Bailey, slaps him on the ass. Watching the other families on the beach, her footprints lone upon the sand, searching in the faces of those that pass by for what she feels herself. Watching the light upon the beach, thinking, this time of light, how the days pass by gathering the light and releasing, light into night, and we reach but cannot touch nor take what passes, what seems to pass, time's dream. And yet these days have given the snowdrops to bloom. She saw one wild and solitary in the car park printing the air with white and bent to examine it, met in that instant an image of all that Larry has missed. Telling him how it was as she turned to see Ben sitting up unassisted, and on another day, his hands plump with strength as he hoisted himself to standing. The darkening brow and bolting height of Bailey who stands almost as tall as his sister. What time has passed without Larry and she sees herself doing nothing, capable of nothing, but there is nothing you can do, a small voice says, hating that voice, what is it you think you can change? Michael Given has stopped returning her calls. She has written to the ministry, to the head of the GNSB, to human rights agencies knowing her voice remains silent. Soon the snowdrops will be gone into the earth and there will be other flowers. She drives back into the city where the houses look onto the sea, watching each passing car, seeking past the liquid-seeming glass for the faces within. These are the nameless who have brought the present into being, yet what she sees are faces the same as her own, faces that pass by as ever in this city as it breathes the ceaseless exhalations of night into day.

She steps towards her father's front porch with the keys in her hand and is met at the door by a growl. She stops and stands uncertain as the growl unrolls from behind the door and snaps into high barking. She looks back towards the car as though asking for help and sees Molly staring into her phone. Something comes forward into thought asking to be remembered, she doesn't know what it is, it is something to do with Mark, she approaches the door and rings the bell, knocks loudly on the window while the woofing continues, Simon's voice calling out, hold on, hold on, he shouts the dog quiet. When he opens the door he is holding a dark and meaty dog by the collar, she thinks it is a brindled boxer, Simon's hands in gardening gloves, his hair damp from the earlier rain. Yes? he says, frowning, what do you want? Yes? she says, pushing past him into the hall, staring at the dog. So now I'm going to be attacked when I call to see my own father, what are you doing with this dog? She bends and picks up the mail from the floor, wet dog smell in the hall and when she turns she sees in her father's eyes a look of glassy bewilderment. Dad, I said I was coming around, we were to take you shopping, we arranged this last week. In an instant he has taken the post out of her hand and seems to be himself. Why aren't you at work? he says. Dad, today is Saturday, who owns the dog? Simon sends the boxer into the kitchen with a tap of his foot and the dog turns and licks its black lips, stands by the door measuring her with a hungry look. I thought you were somebody else, he says, the other day I had some trouble at the door. Trouble, she says, what kind of trouble? It's hard to know exactly, three men called to the door and I did not like the look of them, they said they were from the party, they looked like thugs, they said I wasn't on the local register and wanted to know if I would put my name down—— What party, Dad, do you mean the NAP, who are these people? I told them not to call here again but they knocked on the door a few days later and banged on the window, I could hear one of them laughing before they went away. She is looking towards the dog's dark snout, something muttered blackly as he watches her. Why didn't you tell me,

Dad? I told Spencer here, he says, nodding to the dog as he sneezes twice and lowers onto his paws. Spencer, she says, shaking her head, this dog's fully grown, who did you get him from, tell me, how are you going to be able to mind him on your own? Simon lifts his jacket from the coat stand. In no time at all they have taken over the garden, he says. She turns to look at him from the door. What has? The climbing roses, I'm cutting them back on my own as nobody has bothered to offer any help. Come on, she says, we haven't got all day, it's going to rain soon, why don't you ask Mark to help, he came over last summer and did loads for you then. I won't bother, he says, I'll do it on my own.

The tarmac darkens before the downpour as she advances through the car park, the bodies fleet and hunching in the rain while those with umbrellas take their leisure. She slows up and indicates for a space, watching a balding woman standing crooked to the rain as she fills her boot then gets into her car clutching the lapels of her coat. Eilish sends Molly to fetch a trolley and Bailey is gone out the door without a word pulling on his parka hood. He runs after his sister with flinging heels while Molly jogs with tucked elbows. I hired that new solicitor, Eilish says, Sean Wallace put me on to her, Anne Devlin, she seems to be specialising in cases like this, we're not the only ones you know, she really has her hands full. Simon's fingers begin to drum on the dashboard. Has she filed a petition yet? he says. She takes her meetings outside, Eilish says, I had to leave my phone in the car, she is very brisk, a petition will be the next step. She will be lining her coat with your money but the outcome will be just the same as that shill from the union. Dad, she is working pro bono, she says the government has taken control of the judiciary by putting their own people in, that's the nub of the problem, once you get your own people in you can do whatever you like. The rain grows thunderous in volume and they both look out as the water comes to boil on the tarmac. She can see Molly fighting Bailey for control of the trolley, then Molly pushes her brother away and he throws his arms up in despair, directs a look of fury towards the Touran. She says, I had trouble getting Molly out of bed this morning, this is the second Saturday in a row she won't go to practice, she is one of their best players but not for long if she continues like this. She is watching the sky certain the rain will ease and then it falls quiet in an instant. She reaches for the door but Simon takes hold of her wrist, a rheum of panic in his eyes. They are going to vote them in, Eilish, it is unthinkable for a country like ours—— She watches him without emotion, telling herself it is not true, how the face has ceded yet more to gravity, the levator muscles losing grip as the eyes continue to sink, the skin riding down the bones in sedate avalanche towards the end pulling on the muddled mind within. She sighs and shakes her head. Dad, they came into power two years ago. Simon is frowning, he turns to look outside then shakes his head. Yes, yes, of course, I know, what I meant was—— She watches his hand go to the door. Dad, hold on a moment, I have a brolly in the boot. Simon is gone out the door and passes before the Touran in tweed and odd socks, his feet in gardening clogs, his body moving through the rain with swinging fists and he does not look cold or wet or even old anymore, seeing in him again the look that once ruled them all.

She roams the aisles of the supermarket watching her father's clogs, muck and dried grass clung to the heels as he moves ahead of her gripping a tin of peaches, Ben in the trolley seat gnawing on a ring. She is standing at the fish counter when Molly steps towards her urgent and flushed, alerting her mother with a warning look. Mam, she whispers, you need to come. What is it? I said come here will you. She steps after Molly thinking of Bailey, whatever has he done now, yesterday he squirted ketchup into Molly's hair then stormed out of the room. Molly pulls her mother by the sleeve then stops and nods down the aisle. Don't let him see you're looking. Don't let who see, do you mean Bailey? No, him, that's him, isn't it? She follows the pointed finger past an elderly woman whispering to a list, past detergents and toilet rolls, alighting upon a woman plump in jeans and a man alongside her idling over a trolley. She knows who Molly thinks this is, but it is not him, the build is too small, he is wearing the wrong clothes, a Dublin football jersey underneath a hiking rain jacket, she looks down at his feet and sees cheap running shoes. He is just some other man with nothing to do, following mindlessly after his wife, she wants to ask Molly how she saw the man who is not this man, she must have seen him from the front window that night when they stood at the door. It is then the man turns and she knows it is him, the detective inspector, she looks away feeling her mouth go dry, she looks again to the face thinking of his other face, the face of the official who stood at the door, he seems another man entirely. She finds herself walking towards him without knowing what she is going to do, she is going to speak with him, yes, what is there to lose, what is he but an ordinary man, she will ask for a quiet word in front of his wife. The detective inspector looks across and finds her gaze and there is a moment between them where he puzzles at her and then he smiles and it is the smile of somebody you know to say hello to on the street, a husband, a father, a volunteer in the community, and yet behind that smile lies the shadow of the state. She turns abruptly and seizes hold of bottled bleach, stands a moment pretending to read the label, returns through the aisle scouring herself.

She has fallen behind at work and is distracted before the children. She tells her boss she has an appointment and drives across the city, seeking Bird Road, parking two houses down from the detective inspector's house, it was easy to find where he lives. She looks to the dashboard clock and sees she has been here almost ten minutes, she must return to work soon. She squeezes her hands checking again the driveway is empty, this feeling of looking out upon a dream, this feeling as though she were riding the edge of some chasm afraid to be the looker down. She paints her face in the mirror and combs her hair. Watching the light now as it broods upon the street, a slow pulsation that gives to sudden clarity then dims, thinking about what lies hidden, seeing that what is revealed in the soft blooming light is the everyday occurring, the centre of the middle charged with the ordinary, the evergreens and the rhododendron, the paths designed for wheeling buggies, the cement stamped by growing feet, the troopings to school, the endless orbiting of SUVs, the elderly stooping after dogs and stopping to speak, the crows watching down from the utility wire, the grand parade of the year marching them all towards some glorious summer under the bannered leaves. When she crosses the street she does not move within her body but is watching herself as though from the window of the house, thinking herself onward, she begins to feel her way into her body, the measure of the body in the air, the hand knocking on the door. The woman's face that greets her is not the face she recalls from the supermarket but is older now, plain and unpainted. I wonder if I might have a word, Mrs Stamp, it is a private matter, I won't take up too much of your time. Lime walls and the open face before her folding into a crease. Is this about Sean? she says, what's that boy done now? Standing in the kitchen she sees it is a room made cosy for wet days, background chat on the radio, a shuttle near the stove amidst a corona of coal dust. She pulls a chair and sits to the table and does not want to breathe until she has spoken, looking out for a moment onto the rear plot, bird feeders on maturing apple trees, a goldfinch blazons for a moment and is gone. She watches her own hands as she speaks about her husband, the fingers weaving and interlocking, the hands as though wringing pain, placing the pain on the table as an offering. She watches Mrs Stamp's countenance drift before her as though the features were a puzzle of light, the eyes she thought were bright have become dark, the woman's hands increasing in size. She sees the listening face grow sullen, the sudden tightening of lips. Mrs Stamp stands from the chair and goes to the counter and pulls at a box of cigarettes. You don't mind, do you? she says. Eilish shaking her head as the woman lights up and steps to the back door and takes a long drag, she exhales outside then turns and looks Eilish up and down in the chair. What did you say your name was again? she says. Eilish watches the broad shoulders but does not speak her name. Please, she says, I'm just asking that you put a word in, surely you'd do the same in my position. The woman is frowning now, she begins to shake her head, sucks hard on the cigarette. Really, she says, this is quite absurd, you speak to me

as though my husband has done something wrong, a
Garda detective inspector, during a time like this. I just
wanted to speak to you as a wife, a mother—— It would
have been better if you had not spoken at all. Their
eyes have met and rancour passes in open exchange
and Eilish hears herself speak, the words falling out
her mouth so that she looks down at them aghast after
she has spoken them. So I'm to remain silent, bowed
and broken like every other fool in this country? A bin
lorry whines along the street and Eilish looks away,
then nods towards the garden. They look like fine apple
trees, do you get much yield from them? Mrs Stamp
turns, the spell of her thinking broken, she stares at
the trees without seeing them then waves her hand in
the air. They've come into their own this past few years,
Kerry Pippin, John brought them back from the family
farm. Mrs Stamp, my husband is just an ordinary man,
a father, a teacher, a trade unionist, he should be home
with his children. She is being measured with narrowed eyes, then Mrs Stamp wets her lips and mutters
something to the window. I'm sorry, Eilish says, what
did you say? Mrs Stamp turns around with a sneer.
Scum, she says, that is what you are, you and your trade
unionist, coming to my house and insulting my husband, a decorated man who has given twenty-five years
of his life to this state, let me tell you, whatever-you-
call-yourself, your husband is where he is because he
is an inciter, an agitator against the state during a time
of great threat to this country, you people have no idea
what's happening outside in the world, what is coming

our way, you will see us all destroyed, this should be a time of unity for our nation but instead there's civil unrest up and down the country and we have to face down the likes of you, get out of my house this minute. Eilish sees in the woman's face the superior look of the party, finds herself on her feet wishing to give licence to her hands. She can see the woman speaking to her husband, the man doing a little detective work and making life worse for Larry. She moves towards the hall door feeling she has failed him, her fingers fumbling at the latch, seeing the Touran parked across the street as the woman comes behind her, she turns and walks the other way.

She wakes knowing that somebody has come into the room, she can hardly open her eyes, rising upon her hands, she can hear breathing from a figure seated in the wicker, it must be Mark, wondering what he wants at this time of night. The seat complains as the shadow leans forward and the light from the hall finds the face. It is the detective inspector, John Stamp, she cannot find her voice, she looks with fear to the baby in the cot and listens for his breathing. How did you get in? she whispers, the doors are all locked, you have no right to come into this house. The voice smiling in the dark. No right to come into this house. Yes. But that is only a belief you speak of. It is not a belief, it is a fact before the law. A fact. Yes, there is the rule of law, you cannot violate our rights like this. The rule of law. That is what I said. You speak about this word rights as though you understand the word rights, show me what rights were born with man, show me what tablet they are written on, where nature has decreed it is so. She goes to speak but he is moving out of the seat towards her and she is afraid to look into his eyes, is arrested by his stink, the admixture of food and cigarettes and something malodorous that comes from under the skin, she knows what it is, this stench that sets free her terror. You call yourself a scientist and yet you believe in rights that do not exist, the rights you speak of cannot be verified, they are a fiction decreed by the state, it is up to the state to decide what it believes or does not believe according to its needs, surely you understand this. His hand is sliding across the duvet, she is watching the hand afraid for what might happen should she stop him, the hand sliding towards her throat, she grabs hold of the wrist and tries to scream, yanks the hand free from her throat, is shouting now, I want to wake up, and he says, but you are awake—— She opens her eyes into the room, blue-cold light from the window and on the chair her folded clothes. She sits staring at the chair telling herself the room is real and not the dream, sensing her relief and yet there remains in her chest, in her throat, a small knot of fear, watching the door as though she does not fully believe. She lies for a moment drowsy, seeking the return of some blind and featureless sleep but the residue of the dream still infects her, that man and his stink, the words he has spoken have left her afraid, hearing the children downstairs, a burst of laughter and then Bailey squealing over the blare of Sunday morning television.

# 3

Molly stands by the sink in gym shorts and a coat running a glass under the tap when her hand jolts back, she makes a disgusted sound and drops the glass into the sink. Mam, she says, the water's brown. Eilish can feel the eyes of her daughter upon her back but chooses not to look. She leans forward spooning apple puree into Ben's mouth, thinking, it is her father she wants, the no that is a yes, the yes never a no. Last night in a dream they spoke about Molly, something he said that seemed hazed puzzled her as she awoke. She arrests a dribble of food using the spoon, seeing for an instant something far underground, a fragment of corroded piping coming loose into the mains, it is being whisked by the water, the water growing fouled by rust and lead contaminant, the water rushing onwards through the piping dark into the city's homes, its businesses and schools, passing out of the taps into kettles, glasses and cups, passing into their mouths, the lead being absorbed by the gastrointestinal tract, being stored by the tissues and bones, the aorta and liver, the adrenal and thyroid glands, the poison doing its work unseen until it makes itself known in the lab in the urine and blood. She turns and studies the water jetting out of the tap and says, just let it run out a while. The rattling of a key in the front door. Molly says, why don't we have bottled water in the house? She grabs an apple from the bowl and huffs into the living room while Eilish looks up listening, seeing inwardly the fall of light as the door opens, wishing upon her hearing for the familiar steps, the thwack of the umbrella into its stand, the sigh and then out-shucking of the coat, the call for missing slippers. Mark carries his bike through the hall and into the kitchen, passes without word through the French doors where he places his bike on the decking. She looks to Ben in the highchair and thinks about her eldest son, this silent process of growth, the cartilage extending and converting to bone, the bones solidifying, sustaining the child towards a future unknown and yet such a future must contain within it the sum total of all possibility. It was only a heartbeat ago when Mark was crawling on the floor and she turns to watch him as he steps into the living room, the future made instant. She hears hushed talk, Molly raising her voice, you have to tell her, she says. Eilish calls out, tell who, what's going on? Molly stands by the door and pushes Mark into the kitchen and he comes before her holding out a letter. She tells Molly to turn off the tap, takes the letter out of Mark's hand and reaches for her glasses. She does not notice that she has been brought to her feet, she reads the letter slowly again as though she cannot understand it, the meanings behind the words have become unfixed, the black text unintelligible. She looks up into her son's eyes and sees the child vanished. This cannot be, she whispers, searching with her hand for the chair but she is unable to sit. She closes her eyes and sees the glimmering dark of her eyelids. But you are only sixteen, she says, you'll have the Leaving Cert next year, they cannot do this now—— Mark hangs his jacket on the chair and stands for a moment sensitive and solemnly quiet. The date of registration is for the week after my birthday next month, he says. She does not see him as he goes to the sink, runs the tap and fills a glass and begins to drink. It is Molly who pulls the glass from his hand, don't drink that shite, she says, the water's brown, tell Mam to buy bottled water instead and tell her what they did, how they came into the school, Mark, tell her. Who came into the school? She is watching her son, seeing him distinctly by the sink, the frown weighing upon the brow, the brooding hair, the jaw forcing into expression the young man. I didn't think to tell you, he says, it was a doctor and some woman, an army official, they called all the boys in my year out of class and we had to go to the gym, they looked us over one by one without telling us what it was for, I had to stand in my boxers behind a screen while the doctor took my height and examined my feet and my teeth, asked if I had any allergies—— This sudden feeling of pressure within the body, it has begun within her heart as though something had climbed into it and begun to swell there, it is dilating outward, forcing upon the lungs the feeling of a scream. She finds herself sitting on the chair quick with fatigue, whispering now, it must be some mistake, you will only be seventeen. Her hands reaching out for her son, to nurse him now, to hold him to her cheek, to wash him in the balm of her fury. I want you to listen, she says, taking his hand, seeing that he is not listening at all but staring out onto the garden. You will not be leaving this house, do you hear, you will not be leaving school, they cannot call you up for national service like this. He turns away with a pained look. And how are you going to stop them, they can do whatever they like, what was it you could do to stop them taking Dad? It is Molly who turns upon her brother, shoves him backwards towards the sink. Don't speak to Mam like that. Shut up you, he says. Molly stays her brother with a venomous look, the dull pinging of a hammer from nearby and then Ben drops the spoon. Eilish bends to pick it up and carries it to the sink. At least the water from the hot tap is clean, she says. What's going on? Bailey says, stepping into the room. Mark takes the letter from the table and goes outside and closes the door taking a lighter from his pocket. She watches through the glass as he jets gas but cannot spark the flame, watches and has no urge to stop him, to ask him where he got the lighter from, the lighter clicks an amber flame that tastes the corner of the paper then forms a black mouth, watching the letter come to smoke in his hand and when he lets it drop he turns and looks through the glass with the blackest eyes of anger.

She is distracted at work, pacing within, seeing before her some shadowed obstacle and seeking a path around it, saying to herself over and over, they will not take my son. There are rumours in the company of a blood-letting, of a phased wind-down, none of it can be true. They are called into the meeting room where it is announced the managing director Stephen Stoker has been stood down, he did not come into work this morning, they are told that Paul Felsner will replace him. He comes before them pulling on the tips of his fingers with a small hand and cannot hide his delight. She watches about the room as he speaks selecting for his supporters by the clapping hands and smiles, seeing the wild animal among them, seeing how it has done away with concealment and pretence, how it prowls now in the open as Paul Felsner raises his hand in hieratic gestures speaking not the company speak but the cant of the party, about an age of change and reformation, an evolution of the national spirit, of dominion leading into expansion, a woman walks across the room and opens a window. Eilish finds herself stepping out of the lift onto the ground floor. She crosses the street and goes into the newsagent's, points to a pack of cigarettes. It has been a long time, she thinks, standing alone outside the office building, sliding a cigarette from the box, fondling the paper skin, running its odour under her nose. The cottony taste of cellulose acetate as she lights and pulls the hot smoke into her mouth, recalling the day she last quit, this feeling of some younger self, perhaps Larry was with her, she doesn't know. Memory lies, it plays its own games, layers one image upon another that might be true or not true, over time the layers dissolve and become like smoke, watching the smoke that blows out her mouth vanish into the day. Watching the street as though it belongs to some other city, thinking how it is so that life seems to exist outside events, life passing by without need of witness, the congested traffic fuming in the dismal air, the people passing by harried and preoccupied, imprisoned within the delusion of the individual, this wish now she has to escape, watching until she is brought clean outside herself, the light altering tone by tone until it becomes a lucent sheen on the street, the gulls nipping at food in a gutter are dark underwing as they whip up out of the path of a lorry. Well now. Colm Perry is standing beside her tapping a cigarette on its box. I didn't know you smoked, Eilish. She is squeezing her eyes as if to see an answer to a question she has not been asked and then she shakes her head. I can't say that I do. Colm Perry lights a cigarette and exhales slowly. Neither do I. She pulls the dark burn inside her and wants the burn some more, studying Colm Perry's wrinkled shirt, knowing the cerise face of a drinker, the look that rests sly in the eye of a man well in on the joke though he is laughing at them from the outside. He glances behind towards the automatic door. The gall of that man, he says, there will be a purge soon enough, they like their own kind so keep your head down, that's all I have to say. He looks again over his shoulder and pulls out his phone. Have you seen the latest? What she sees on the phone are images of graffiti on windows and walls denouncing the gardaí, the security forces and the state, triumphant scrawls in sprayed red paint. The writing looks like blood, the building looks like a school. St Joseph's in Fairview, he says, they are saying the principal called in the GNSB who came and arrested four boys, they haven't yet been released, it's gone on a few days but the story's only online now, there are parents and students gathering outside Store Street Garda Station waiting for the boys to be freed. My son has been called up for national service, she says, he is to hand himself over the week he turns seventeen, he is still just a kid in school, and this after they take his father. Colm Perry looks at her and then he shakes his head. Bastards, he says. He cups his hand to his mouth and thinks long upon a drag then extinguishes the cigarette on the smokers' box. You're going to have to get him out, he says. Get him out where? She watches him shrug and open his hands and then he puts them in the pockets of his jeans. He is looking across the street to a newsagent's. Right now, he says, I'd love an ice cream, an old-fashioned cone with a 99, I'd like to be on a beach freezing my butt off, I'd like for my parents to be still alive, look, Eilish, I don't know, England, Canada, the USA, it's only a suggestion, but you're going to have to get him out, look, I must go back inside.

She watches online the growth of the protest, parents and children dressed in white before the Garda station. They hold white candles and do not speak, waiting for the return of the boys. Their number is growing all day. By next morning it is past two hundred, it is said they are all from the school, a dark band of security forces standing in front of the station. She knows the square where they are gathered, a paved plaza with granite platforms to sit on, a stainless steel octagonal bi-pyramid in the centre that is a symbol for something or nothing perhaps. In a time not so long ago this square was designed for openness and light, for sitting down or taking one's time, this feeling now the protest has forced open a door, light reaching into a dark room. She can see Larry's face looking up as though in expectation, if the boys are soon to be released, she says, more will follow. On Saturday morning Molly comes into the kitchen dressed in white. Look, she says, have you seen this? Viral messages are being sent from phone to phone, one message says that a friend of a close friend says the boys are soon to be released, another message says the boys were released days ago and are with their family, the protest is a conspiracy, a plot to shame the state. Yes, she says, I've received them also, none of them are true, I forgot to remind you, Saoirse's wedding is next Saturday, I've told Mark he has to stay home till I get back. I don't need Mark to keep an eye on me. I know that, but it's better to have the both of you home to keep an eye on the two boys. Molly lifts a chair and brings it outside and places it on the grass under the tree. Eilish watching as Molly stands on the chair and pulls a branch towards her, she ties a white ribbon and watches it hang, the ribbons like long empty fingers playing the silent music of the tree, Eilish does not want to count them. Fourteen weeks, Molly says, stepping through the door with the chair, she puts it down and goes to the sink and runs the tap, leans down to examine the water with narrowed eyes, fills a glass and drinks. She puts the glass down half full and wipes her mouth with her sleeve. I'm going out, she says. Out where? I'm going into town. Eilish regards her for a moment, the white denim jacket, the white scarf coiled around her neck. If you're going into town, she says, you can take them off right now. Molly looks down at her body with mock surprise. Take what off right now? You know what I'm talking about. How do I know what you're talking about, how do I know what anybody is talking about or even thinking of for that matter if nobody says anything, if nothing is ever said in this house? Eilish turns to the table and lifts up a magazine and puts it down again. For goodness' sake, she says, where are my glasses? Your glasses are sitting on top of your head. Well, she says, aren't I a right eejit? When she turns around Molly is watching her strangely and then her mouth wrinkles as though she might cry. I want my daddy back, she says, I just want him back, why aren't you doing something? Eilish looks into her eyes seeking for something, she does not know what, something from the old Molly to hold onto, some sense of give, but Molly instead is pushing at her, pulling on some lever. And do you think going out like that is going to bring your dad back? Molly's face darkens, she turns and lifts the glass and slowly pours the water onto the floor. That's fine, Eilish says, do as you like, pour water onto the floor, go out onto the street dressed like that, maybe you'll get as far as the bus stop without somebody passing a remark at you or taking note of your behaviour to report it later on, maybe you'll get off the bus without being seen by the wrong person, or maybe you will, maybe there's two men in a car and one of them doesn't like how you look, maybe you're just wearing white because you like the look of it or maybe you're trying to say something else, something provocative, something the man doesn't like, maybe he stops and gets out and takes your name and address and creates a file with your name on it, maybe you'll be quiet or maybe you'll say the wrong thing and instead of taking your name and address he takes you, puts you in the car, and where's that car going to, Molly, have a think about that, maybe it's going to where all the other cars go, the unmarked cars that pull up silently and lift people off the street because of one thing or another, the people who do not return home again, you think because you're fourteen years old you can do what you like, that the state isn't interested in you, but they arrested those boys and those boys haven't yet been released and they're your age, you think I'm not doing anything, that I'm just standing about waiting for your father to return, but what I am doing is keeping this family together because right now that is the hardest thing to do in a world that seems designed on tearing us apart, sometimes not doing something is the best way to get what you want, sometimes you have to be quiet and keep your head down, sometimes when you get up in the morning you should spend more time choosing your colours.

Eilish moves about her father's bedroom searching for a tie. The green fleur-de-lis carpet stacked with yellowed newspapers and journals, clothes heaped on two chairs placed side-by-side to the wall, dirty cups and plates on the dresser. She rummages through a drawer meeting the odour of must, discoloured white shirts, a spider of old ties. She selects a pink tie and puts it to her nose sensing the past heavy within it yet grown obscure, she stands up and turns and meets her mother windblown in a photo, the young woman catching at her hair, the promise of her daughter's face secret in her own. Eilish moves the cups and plates onto the floor and arranges the photos in order. Jean leans into Simon and wipes water from her eyes on a cold beach. She is willow in a wedding dress gripping Simon's arm but does not see the photographer. Her gaze sharpens towards the camera as she sits on a chair with the two girls on her lap. Eilish closes her eyes seeking her mother as she was like this, stepping through their first house, she walks the shadowed rooms recalling, her fingers trailing the handrail of the staircase and upward past the window seat, towards her old room, each step sounding upon the boards, seeking the vast ceiling. She can hear her mother's voice now, recalling this not as a sound but as a feeling never decayed within the weakening of her memory. What she can see from the old bed, the window giving to sky, the open wardrobe mouthing the dark that invites the sleeping child to nightmare. Jean's mouth sours in a photo and her hair withdraws from her shoulders to her ears. She greys in a garden chair while the climbing roses bloom. She leans gaunt upon a stick by the waterfall at Powerscourt and seems caught by surprise, turning one last time away from the camera. Eilish carries the dirty cups and plates downstairs and stacks them in the dishwasher while Simon sits at the table forking bacon and eggs, his shirt open to the navel, his chest hairless and white. He seizes the salt cellar by the throat and shakes it over his eggs then gives her a rancorous look. I know what you were doing up there. She closes the dishwasher door with her hip. Dad, your room is a pigsty, the amount of plates and cups I had to bring down, button your shirt and put this tie on, I picked it to go with your shirt. Do you think I did not hear you up there, you can look all you like but you won't find anything. She finds herself galled before him, begins to fill the kettle though there is no time for tea. Dad, please, we are going to be late, the service starts in an hour. He straightens the knife and fork on the plate and pushes it away from him with the heel of his hand and turns to face her, the corner of his mouth yellowed with yolk. Do you think I keep it all stashed in my room,

none of you are going to get a penny. She looks into his
face aghast and then she grows afraid, seeking past the
face to what is changing inside him, seeing the self as
though it were a flame respiring in the dark, the flame
never still, the swollen flame tapering to its narrowest
self. He is but he is not, this is what she thinks, and yet
he seems to be himself again as he moves towards the
mirror and she stands behind him as he studies his face,
the skin pinkly shaven, a bleb of shaving foam behind
his ear, she smooths it away with her thumb. She turns
him around by the shoulders and buttons his shirt and
loops the tie around his neck. It's a lovely day for a wedding, don't you think, they got lucky with the weather. He
gives her a dismissive look and she knows he is himself
again. That cousin of yours, he says, I cannot see her
taking to the wedding bed. Dad, you cannot say things
like that, Saoirse is your niece. Saoirse is a middle-aged
woman approaching forty and her father is an ass, my
sister never had any taste. Yes, well, it's better late than
never, don't you think? She stands knotting the tie then
pats his shoulder and lifts her eyes and something in the
way he looks at her makes her think he is staring at his
wife. She looks away, seeing out to the garden to where
her mother stood, the climbing roses now ragged and
slashed to the wall.

From the university church the wedding party steps out
onto St Stephen's Green. She takes her father's arm as

they cross for the park, the women promenading in their clicking heels lit by plumed and coloured hats, the hushed sensation of trees. By the lake the bride and groom couple for photos while a groomsman loosens his tie. They exit the park towards a Georgian building strewn with ivy, the smell of freesias reaching to greet them as they are escorted inside to a reception room with tall windows overlooking the green. She looks across the room to her father who is speaking with her aunt Marie, sees the woman hide a yawn behind pink shellac nails, her eyes casting about until she snares Eilish with a summoning look. Oh, it's you, Simon says, I'm just telling Marie about this bill the NAP are putting through, they are looking to take control of the academy, they want to put their own people in, Marie, take charge of the board, it seems there is nothing anyone can do, it's simply grotesque, unbelievable——— Marie is squeezing her arm and turns away from her brother as though to keep Eilish to herself. Your father hasn't said a word about your little one, she says, I thought you might have brought him along, it must have been a lovely surprise at your age. Eilish smiles into the powdered face seeing the pink lips soft with spittle then feels her spirit fall, seeing now what has not been said, how their talk has been kept to questions about the children or how she is doing at work, nobody wants to talk about Larry. She looks into her aunt's face and sees the unspoken injunction that today shall pass under some absolute of happiness. She smiles and says, Larry would have loved to have come, can

you excuse me? She steps through the room looking
for somebody else to speak to, there are so few here
from her own generation, her father's cousins stooping into old age and yet the years between them are
not so very much, what is twenty-five years or thirty,
she orders a drink, thinking how this time of her life
will pass, it is passing already, it is past, the light as it
falls through the tall windows giving to them all this
moment, the world hushed to a murmur, the bride in
white beatitude. When the bell rings they take their
glasses into the dining room and find their places at the
round tables, the groom standing up as though to give
address but instead he raises his hand to his chest and
begins to sing the national anthem. Tattooed birds on
his hands, arcane symbols inked on his neck. Chairs
are pushed back and people stand and begin to sing
and someone is pulling at her sleeve, it is her father's
cousin, Niamh Lyons, whispering down at her with
crinkled lips, stand up, Eilish, for goodness' sake. She
looks across to where her father should be but his chair
is empty, he has gone to the bar for another drink, he
has got lost again on the way to the bathroom, she is
looking up into the mouthing faces and sees the eyes
watching down and feels her mouth go dry, Niamh
Lyons pulling again at her sleeve but she will not stand
and sing along with them, she will not sing the lie.
Without knowing it, she begins to arrange the white
napkin before her and when she looks up she sees the
groom's face and what is worn openly, what is worn in
the face of his groomsman and those standing around

them, the unmasked contempt of the party. The bride has closed her eyes and the groom is met by applause though not everyone in the room is clapping. A pale elderly woman with slender hands gives Eilish a quick benevolent smile that is gone the moment she looks for it. Eilish reaching into her bag, she pulls out a white chiffon scarf and ties it around her neck, stands up as the others sit down. Excuse me a moment while I go and look for my father, she says.

The oven alarm begins to bell and she turns calling for the children, spoons casserole onto rice-piled plates, would someone please set the table? Molly comes yawning into the room. The dusk has entered before her and enshrouded her mother. She turns on the lights and reaches into the drawer for knives and forks, stands a moment staring as though her thoughts had fallen into the drawer. Eilish calls out again, the dinner is ready. She can see Bailey stretched on the rug before the TV. She turns to Molly, tell Mark to come down. Down from where? Molly says, he's not upstairs. Where is he then? Molly shrugs and leans across the table setting down the knives and forks. How am I supposed to know, can you give me a lift later on? Eilish goes to the stairs and calls for Mark, she goes upstairs to his room then returns downstairs. He is not in the house, he is not in the garden, she rings his phone and it is ringing upstairs, she is scolding him as she ascends the stairs again knowing his response, how the mouth will grow tight and he will fix his eyes to the floor preparing some sly comment. She finds herself standing by the door to the boys' room, his phone is ringing on the bed, it is strange he does not have it on him. When she picks up the phone she looks at it as though it were some forbidden object, Bailey shouting from the kitchen that he is going to start eating, she hears two voices speaking, one that is a no, the other that is a yes, she listens for movement by the stairs. She reads her son's messages and clicks on the video he last watched, a prisoner in a red jumpsuit is on his knees wearing a hood, another man in black stands over him wearing glasses, a teacher or perhaps an intellectual ranting in Arabic, he tears off the prisoner's hood and brings up a large and sickled knife while the camera begins to zoom in slow motion as though seeking to perceive something in the eyes of the victim in the instant of his death. She throws the phone on the bed and when she picks it up again she scrolls through a search history of brutality and murder, videos of beheadings and summary executions. A feeling has entered her body that will not speak but sits black and knotted inside her, she can hardly talk during dinner. She is moving through the house picking up one thing after another, putting them back down again without thought, Bailey is tussling with Molly for the remote control who slaps him on the head and throws the remote across the room, Eilish shouts at them to be quiet. She is standing on the landing with the baby in her arms when it strikes her that what has entered her body is the feeling of death, that death has entered her son, seeing him now almost seventeen years old and the blood corrupt by rage and silent savagery. It is past eight o'clock when she hears the porch door slide back, the key going into the lock of the front door and she moves to cut him off, placing her hand on the bicycle to stay him, searching his eyes for some sight of the darkness growing within, seeking her old authority. His eyes slide past her while she speaks, her voice risen and sharp. You didn't tell me you wouldn't be here for dinner, where did you go? She has not seen Samantha coming behind him until she is stepping through the door, the girl stops as though afraid to enter and Mark turns towards her screwing his mouth in silent apology for his mother. It's alright, Mam, would you ever calm down, I had dinner at Sam's, I wanted to message you but I forgot my phone, I can never remember your number.

She drives through rain and hesitating light, her phone buzzing in her bag. She waits for the traffic ahead to stop then reaches for her bag and pulls out the phone. When she reads the message she looks up and sees the road before her vanished, her hand reaching to turn off the radio before she reads the message again. Two of the detained boys are dead, their bodies released to their families. Photos of the bodies with the markings of torture have been made public. The Touran is moving forward by itself, she can see the boys laid out before their parents, seeing the broken bodies and whispering to herself, it is one thing to take a father from a house but another to return the bodies of children. Feeling within her heart the coming tremor, knowing now it will come, the outrage and disgust that will rise up from the silent ground into their mouths. At home they gather around the table watching a live feed of the demonstration on the international news, the crowd has grown outside the Garda station, people are bringing their children, everybody is wearing white and holding lighted candles. The vigil spills around the bus station and onto the nearby streets and she goes to bed and cannot sleep, lies watching her fear parade before her like some wretched spectacle, a small voice that wants to speak is shouted down. By morning the crowd has outgrown the space and begins to march towards College Green. She stands to the window looking out, Mark and Molly watching her now, waiting for her to speak. The dormant trees are beginning to swell. Soon the trees will open their buds to see again the spring light, thinking upon this, the strength of a tree, how a tree abides the dark season, what a tree sees when it opens its eyes. It is then she sees that her fear is gone, this feeling of relief in her body that something now can be done. We shall wear white, she says, turning around, we shall go and join them. Watching the children go upstairs, this feeling of daring and excitement in the house.

Carole Sexton comes with an oaten loaf, some crumble cake and white candles. Mark has already gone ahead on his bike. When they drive into the city they meet traffic slowing to a checkpoint, Eilish turning to the children in the back. Zip up your coats, she says. The car ahead of them is directed into a search lane while a Garda steps towards the Touran, the face of an analytic youth in uniform leaning down to examine her licence, he seeks her gaze and holds it. Where are you going today? he says. What she sees of the face starburst with freckles is a youth a few years older than her son, the lie sliding out her mouth, it rides the air between them. The Garda leans down and studies Carole then visors his hand to examine the children in the back, Bailey snubbing his nose against the glass as he waves them on. The street along the quays is closed to traffic by motorcycled gardaí. She finds parking in a laneway beside a church and they set off on foot with Ben in the buggy, a pedestrian crossing clicking them passage across an empty street and it is strange to find the quays so quiet, sunlight surging along the water, this feeling of racing calm. Carole has not stopped talking since they left the car but Eilish is adrift, watching over her children as though from some great height, seeking to seize hold of her dread. She is speaking with Larry and watching his response though he remains within some shadowed interiority as if out of reach in a dark cell. There are others now walking among them dressed openly in white and they can hear the noise as they cross the river, walking the narrow streets of Temple Bar towards College Green, and then the crowd stands before them, a mass concentration of will, they say the protest has grown to fifty thousand to fill the plaza, her spirit rising so that she cannot breathe. She grips the hands of her children as they push their way in among the white-painted faces and white flags and banners, Carole following behind them, so many people are holding white candles and everyone seems to have brought their kids. A young woman offers to paint their faces, Molly tying up her hair. A stage has been erected before the old parliament and a young woman stands with a microphone calling out for an end to the Emergency Powers, for all political prisoners to be released. She receives enormous applause as another man takes to the stage, it is not even the words spoken, Eilish thinks, but the speaking of their bodies, for here before the world there is no place to hide. Bailey is watching the protest on a phone and she sees their image giant and alive and can sense her fear has gone, that her fear has become its opposite, wanting now to surrender to this, to become one with the larger body, the single breath, feeling her might grow in the triumph of the crowd. For an instant she is met with some inchoate feeling of death, of victory and slaughter in vast numbers, of history laid under the feet of the vanquisher and she stands as though with some great blade in her hand, she brings the blade down and shivers with exaltation then takes a sharp breath, two gardaí are walking among them with cameras recording faces despite booing and jeering from the crowd.

Looking up she sees the marksmen on the rooftops, men pointing long-range cameras, the sunless clouds signalling rain and she remembers she did not pack their raincoats or bring an umbrella. Carole hands out sandwiches and bottles of water while images appear on a large screen of the dead teenagers, photos taken when they were boys, one of them tow-headed and smiling, the other caught with a wide-eyed look. She does not know her hand has gripped Bailey's elbow until he has wriggled free, she is thinking about Mark, seeing him plucked out of school by the state and sent into the security forces, being deployed on the streets against his own kin, knowing the fury and resistance in his heart, she will not allow it to happen. She puts her arm around Molly and pulls her close, is struck by a memory of having belonged to another protest such as this, thinking now that the memory is false or exchanged somehow, the memory belongs to some other people in some other country, she has seen it countless times on TV. Ben wakes with a sharp cry and she gives him his bottle, he wants out of the buggy, he begins to scream until she places her coat on the ground and lets him sit on it, he is trying to crawl away. An elderly lady in jade on a portable chair asks to sit him on her knee. Bailey begins to flop his arms and then he slumps down on his bag giving out, he wants to go home, the smell of hotdogs wafting from nearby, he says he is starving, she sends him off with Carole to get some. Molly is texting on her phone. Mam, she says, Mark is trying to find us. She leaves for a moment and returns with Mark and some other friend they have not seen before. They are both wearing white T-shirts and white bandanas over their mouths and Eilish reaches out and pulls the mask down. What are you doing wearing that, you are not a yob, this is a peaceful protest. She is watching the smirking eyes of Mark's friend, there is something about him she does not like, she would like to know who he is. Carole proffers Mark a sandwich and in three quick bites it is gone. He asks for one for his friend. I want you home by eight o'clock, Eilish says, and Mark looks to Molly with a smirk and Molly wants to go with Mark but Eilish says no. There is the feeling of rain before rainfall and then the umbrellas open and the unity of the crowd becomes cellular. The children hive under the large brolly of a woman and Bailey asks for some tissues, he wipes his nose then begins to hang off her arm. People are passing through the crowd with their kids on the way home, there are dinners to be made and dogs to be walked, let the students and people without children remain throughout the night. As they turn to go she is watching down the length of the street towards the sky at Christ Church Cathedral, a slow furnace of light as though the world were on fire.

Carole Sexton will stay the night. It will be risky to cross the city, Eilish says, thinking of the crowds returning home buoyant over the bridges, the cars driving with white flags from the windows to be met by roadblocks, searches and arrests, the story is all over the international news. Carole is watching footage on her phone of military trucks and personnel carriers entering the suburbs, they are assembling in long rows along the canal. It looks as though they are preparing for an invasion, she says. There is talk online of cars being attacked with bats and bricks, people being dragged from their cars by men in balaclavas, cars being set alight. Eilish defrosts Bolognese and allows Bailey and Molly to eat before the TV while she puts Ben down to sleep, watching for a moment his tiny fists, she wants for him to remain like this and yet how long his childhood will be, he will know nothing of the first few years, it will all become lore, that time your father went away, that time he came back. She goes to the bathroom and wipes the make-up from her face, stares at the mirror and sees Mark, how fair he is, how young, she closes her eyes and can sense him being taken, his hand releasing, seeing them all as though they were on some dark sea, Larry the first to be pulled away, she is shouting for Mark to swim towards shore, she is shouting in the dark to be heard. She opens her eyes and leans towards the mirror and pulls with her finger at the claw reaching for her eyes. Carole is watching a live feed of the demonstration on a laptop. The protest has thinned to a few thousand people who sit in silence on the street with lighted candles in paper bags as though votaries before some religious event, the security forces standing by with water canons and batons. Eilish is watching the clock and listening for the door. It is a quarter past eight, it is ten to nine, soon it will be ten o'clock, Mark's phone continues to ring out. I cannot shake off the feeling that something terrible is going to happen, Eilish says. Carole is watching her carefully. They would have done it by now, don't you think? Done what by now? If they were going to attack. Eilish is watching the clock. I keep dialling Mark's number, listening to his voicemail, he sounds like he's in a rush. Bailey and Molly are fighting again, she had forgotten they are in the living room. She goes to the door and sends them upstairs, stands at the sink and empties her cup. Is it just me or does this tea taste funny? she says. She watches her phone again. Mark will be fine, Eilish, this is his fight now as much as yours, you have to let him do this. Yes, but I told him to be home by eight. Carole is looking down at the cup. I think you're right, Eilish, this tea does taste of must, it must be the water. Eilish is watching Carole's face thinking she does not know this woman who sits so upright in the chair, the face graven by sleepless nights, it is as though the very thing that had given her aspect has been slowly extracted, her grief feeding on the marrow in her bones. Eilish brings up a hand and touches her own face. Do I look tired? she says, I feel so exhausted, I cannot think anymore, I need to go to bed, Molly's bed is made up for you, she will sleep with me. When she turns for the door she is met with the feeling she has forgotten something and looks vacantly about the room. It's his birthday, Carole, in two weeks, Mark, she says, I'm talking about Mark, if these protests don't work, I just don't know what I'm going to do. There is talk, Carole says, of boys going across the border to avoid national service—— Eilish is watching the clock, she has forgotten to check if the back door is locked, there is a pile of laundry in a basket on the floor. But how am I supposed to get him out, she says, they won't issue him with a passport, a letter arrived from the Department of Justice, our application declined without explanation. Carole stands from her seat and takes hold of Eilish's hand and palms her other hand on top of hers. If they were to come looking for him, Eilish, if it were to come to that, he could live in my house for a while until the time came to— look, it might not come to that, but there is a granny flat at the back that gives onto an alley, nobody will look for him there. Eilish pulls herself free of Carole's hand but the touch remains on her skin. She rubs the feeling away from her hand, marches to the back door and tests the handle, stands to the glass looking out. The false colours of night, the world that remains despite the shadows that hide the harm being done. My son, she whispers, a fugitive, when he is supposed to be at school, palling about and playing football? Carole's reflection behind her in the glass is an apparition of grief. I can get him across the border to my brother's house in Portrush, let me speak to Eddie, he married a woman up there and will want to help. You don't understand, Carole, he's at school, he wants to go to university. When she goes upstairs Molly is already asleep in her bed. She can hear Carole cleaning up, wishes she could hear instead her husband and son goofing about in the kitchen, Larry taking

Mark in one of his strongman grips, soon it will be the other way round. She dials Mark's number again but his phone is turned off or the battery is dead. She has Larry's nightshirt balled in her hand and brings it to her nose, his odour is slowly fading. She falls into a sleep of shadowed faces, the babel of the crowd, wakes during the night into another dream where two become one, husband and son, she seeks the one that is them both but cannot find him there.

The window whispering the rain. She comes to be languid with the sense of being before memory, a hollow body filling with the sound of the rain until memory awakens and she is at spill, moving across the landing to see into the boys' room and Mark's empty bed. She returns to her room and puts on the bedside light, lowering the shade away from Molly, Ben lying in his cot as though flung into the depths of dream. What it is a child this age must fear from dreaming, the dread of falling from sudden height, the looming unintelligibility of faces, the terror of waking alone in a dark room. He awoke just once, she remembers now, her hands opening the laptop, she clicks onto the foreign news and a low sound issues from her throat as Molly stirs beside her. Mam, she says, what's going on? Eilish is scrolling, pulling at her hair, she looks at her daughter with a feeling of falling, she wants to shout everybody awake. They smashed the demonstration in the middle of the night, she says, thousands of people have been arrested, they put them all onto buses—— She tries to reach Mark but his phone remains off. They watch footage from the early dawn of the security forces moving in upon the demonstration with flash grenades, tear gas and batons, the protestors resisting in the rain and sodium light until live rounds are fired, the news shows thousands of people fleeing College Green, people being marched onto buses, a man lying prone on the street until he is dragged by the arms by two gardaí, she sees he is missing a shoe. She is barefoot on the stairs ringing the phone that does not answer, the house silent around her. She is standing by the kitchen table ringing again and then she puts the phone down and sits on a chair. The waters have swollen, she can see this now, the waters sweeping them along while she was asleep, taking her son, the tide broken against the shore wall. When Carole comes downstairs she is fully dressed and looks for something to do, Eilish folding her arms, she turns her back, wishing this woman out of the house. But how can you know? Carole says, you just can't know if it is true or not, at least give him a few hours to come home. Eilish turns sharply on the ball of her foot, watching the face that went to bed at what hour, this aroma of baking that does not belong to the house, the bread and brownies lying under teatowels, the floor smelling of pine antiseptic, the counters scrubbed down, you let her stay for one night and she treats the kitchen like it is her own. Look, she says, he would have rung somehow, he would have got his phone charged, he wouldn't have stayed out the night, I know my son. Carole begins scrolling through her phone, she pulls a chair and sits down. It says here they are using the National Indoor Arena as a detention centre, that must be where the buses are going. Molly drifts into the kitchen with a toothbrush in her hand. She sits down to the table and pours cornflakes into a bowl but does not reach for the milk, sticks the toothbrush into the bowl and stirs the dry flakes. Carole says, look, Eilish, if you want to go, I'll stay here and mind the children, I have nothing to do all day. Eilish is watching Molly carefully, she looks at Ben who is crawling on the mat, looks again to her daughter as though seeking permission for her to go. Do you want milk, love? she says, going to the fridge, she slides a carton of milk towards her. Let us wait a few more hours, she says, he's bound to return home. Ben has crawled into the living room and pulled himself to standing on the coffee table, he begins to bang on it with his fist. Soon he will walk and then he will run and the hand that pulls on the hand of the mother is the hand that will pull to let go.

She gets into the Touran and closes the door and keys the ignition then drops her hands. Soon it will be dinner time and yet she is afraid to go. She needs to speak to her father, she tries Mark's phone again then rings Simon, he doesn't answer, she tries again, watching out upon the street and for an instant she is met with a sense of stillness so absolute not even a bird breaks the Sunday quiet. This low and motionless sky, the windows with their blinds drawn, the street in silent witness as the people live out their lives, the cycles of births and deaths, the endless recurrence of human generation, a hundred years goes by. The phone clicks and Simon answers and she cannot tell him what she wants to say. That woman has taken my glasses again, he says. Did you look in all the usual places, Dad, did you look on the kitchen table or the bath-side chair? One of these days I'll catch her red-handed, she is trying to destroy my life, last week she stole your mother's crystal from the cabinet, I'll bet you didn't notice. She is watching her father's mind, seeing at work the neurological weather, a zone of low pressure giving to sudden inclemency, in five minutes' time there will be sunshine. Dad, I took the crystal last week to clean it, it was black with dust, you watched me wrap it up in newspaper, look, you need home help, you know you can't get by on your own anymore, Mrs Taft just moves things about when she's cleaning, I'll make sure to have a word with her, anyhow, did you see the news? I don't know what you're talking about, I never said I needed help, I never said she could come into this house. Her mind narrows down to driving, there is only this, the slur of motorway traffic, the wet road in ashes. She cannot get the interval right on the windscreen wiper, the wipers beating about her head, the GPS navigator tells her again to take the next exit.

By the toll booth she sees a man and woman arguing alongside two cars pulled into the lay-by, the woman pointing at the man and waving something orange as the car plunges ahead. She takes the exit and follows onto Snugborough Road watching for the right turn to the National Indoor Arena, there is nowhere to park, cars are lining the verge and blocking the bus lane while a crowd stands before the gates. When she gets out of the Touran she rings a scarf about her neck and zips her coat watching the sky. Something is being whispered into the afternoon, it rests between the rain as she walks and moves between the people standing before the gates, she doesn't know what it is. This feeling of winter enduring into spring, the cold rain seeping through her clothes, the cold seeking her heart as she stands watching the gates and the fencing crowned with barbed wire, the security cameras nosing down, armed soldiers standing guard in open-face balaclavas summoning people through the security gate one at a time to enquire at a window. She has forgotten to bring any food or drink. A trim, efficient woman in polar gear offers her some pick'n'mix in a freezer bag. I haven't heard from my daughter for two days, she says, and they won't give me any information, this morning I got a phone call, just a man's voice, telling me my daughter was in the city morgue but when I went there with my husband she wasn't there, my heart is going to cave in. A Garda prisoner van slows to the entrance but is given no room to pass, camera phones are pressed to the dark glass, a woman

in her sixties beats on a window with the base of her
fist as her handbag slides down her arm. A man in a
rumpled business suit shouts hoarsely at the soldiers,
take off your masks, what have you got to hide? The
gates open onto the sedate vista of a sports complex
as the van goes through. She turns watching the faces
that surround her, the faces pained with the vertigo of
staring into sudden abyss, all of these people the very
same, every one of them clothed yet naked, sullied
and pure, proud and shameful, disloyal and faithful,
all of them brought here by love. Sooner or later pain
becomes too great for fear and when the people's fear
has gone the regime will have to go. After an hour she
is searched and summoned through, steps towards the
glass watching a young woman in military uniform
glancing up from a screen. Identification, please. Eilish
touches her pockets with her hands. Oh, she says, I
didn't think to bring it, I might have left it in the car,
my son went to see his girlfriend last night and didn't
come home, I've been waiting here for hours. The
face that regards her is plain as milk, she drinks in
the face and smiles and something improves in the
young woman's stare, an empty seat beside her. Are
you sure you don't have it? she says, OK, I suppose it
doesn't matter, tell me, what is your son's name? Her
lips move to sound the name but a voice says no. She
looks down at her feet and cannot think, toes with her
shoe at the yellow line painted on the tarmac. The voice
that has spoken is Larry's. What if he's not inside? he
says, all they want are names, a name that goes into

the system cannot come back out, names are the source of their power. James Dunne, she says, 27 Northbrook Avenue, Ranelagh. She wants to go back to the car and buy more time, watching the woman key the name into the system, the slim engagement ring on her finger, seeing her attached to the arm of some young fella, a weekend footballer and drinker of stout, she does not look like a bad person, so few of them are, there is little to distinguish her from any other girl fresh out of college, a bargirl wiping down countertops, a trainee accountant counting the hours to lunch. A door opens inside and a uniformed man steps through, he pulls at the empty chair and places a sandwich packet on the desk and makes a low comment and the girl laughs without lifting her eyes from the screen. About that name, she says, I'm afraid I can't give you any information, can you take this form and fill it in?

The children won't go to bed until she shouts them into their rooms. She lies in the dark walking blind alleys of thought, she thinks she sleeps then wakes into a dark room watched by whispering faces finding herself judged. She sits up and checks on her son in the cot then goes downstairs, moves through the living room when she hears breathing from the couch. She is very still then turns on the lamp. There is Mark stretched out asleep in his jacket, an arm loose over the edge of the seat, a white bandanna around his neck, his clothes still damp from the rain. She fetches a blanket and kneels by the couch careful not to wake him, places his arm by his side. She is holding his hand, watching the face at rest, the features soft around the giving breath, he is at once a child. When he wakes she watches fiercely over him as he butters bread and takes a long drink of coffee, a shadow hiding under his expression, he will not meet her stare. I don't believe you, she says, the world around you is made up of lies, where will we be if you start lying to me also? I told you where I was, he says, there was no way I could get home until now. He slides back his chair and goes to his phone and sits down typing a message. Where did you leave your bag? she says. He looks away from his phone a moment then shrugs. They said we attacked them with metal clubs, he says, they shot a man in the chest and said he had a heart condition. Look, she says, you're lucky you weren't arrested, you need to keep your head down, you can stay home today and get some sleep but tomorrow you are going back to school. She stands by the table watching over him until he looks away. The hair unwashed for how many days, the damp, reeking clothes. You need to take a shower, she says, you need to go upstairs and sleep. He sighs and stands up taking his full height over her, his chin flecked with stubble and for a moment she does not know him. He opens his hands and looks away and when he speaks she senses his resolve, the stony calm in the voice. The world is watching us, Mam, he says, the world saw what happened, the security forces fired live rounds into a peaceful demonstration and then hunted us down, everything has changed now, don't you see, there can be no going back. She turns away searching for some might over him, the old supremacy of blood, she is watching outside to the garden, the wet light lustrous upon all things, the rain being pulled into the earth. You will have no part to play in what is to come, she says, they have taken your father, they are not going to take my son. She is squeezing her hands when she turns to face him and what she meets is the falsehood that has come out her mouth, one way or another, they will take her son, he stands before her taken. Bailey is pounding down the stairs and comes into the kitchen coughing with an open mouth. Cover your mouth, she says. Oh, he says, looking at his brother, when did you get home? He opens the fridge and pulls at the milk. Mam, the baby's crying, I have a cold, can I stay home from school?

She stands watching through the blinds onto the street thinking of the gardaí who walked the crowd recording their faces. In the towns and cities across the country the GNSB is knocking on doors and rounding them up, the subversives who occupied the streets, the terrorists hiding in the civilian population. Watching the cars that slow through the street or park nearby, the who of their occupants, this feeling as though a great sleep has been broken, that they are dreamers

awakened to the beginning of night. Hearing the sound
of the fist on the door in her dreams as though the
knocking has come. Protestors have set up roadblocks
and are setting fires in the streets, effigies have been
set alight in town squares, shop windows smashed
and graffiti-sprayed with slogans. There are women
in wedding dresses handing out pictures of husbands
who have disappeared. There are men wearing Garda
bracelets on their sleeves who are not gardaí but move
in packs upon protestors with bats and hurling sticks.
She watches news footage of a blockade in Cork, the
dark pouring of riot police, the rattling staccato of live
rounds fired above protestors' heads. A male student is
felled by a bullet and the video circulates on the international news, the slow-motion collapse of the body
torn into pixels as it is consumed by tear gas, the body
loaded into the back of a car and driven at speed down a
side street. She watches it again in disbelief, the known
contours of the street, the man in tan sandals with a
shopping bag in hand watching from a bus stop, the
historic arcade with cosmetics advertising in the windows, she shopped there only last year. Notice is given
that the schools are to be closed until law and order has
been restored. She is told to work from home. Molly
mopes about in her father's dressing gown refusing
to eat anything but breakfast cereal while Bailey complains his shoes are too small. Watching Mark caught it
seems within the same brooding savagery of his father.
Please, she says, I want you to stay in the house, but he
comes and goes as he pleases, he comes home late, she

does not know what to do. This unknown air, the soldiers placed at cash machines and banks, the soldiers
filing past in personnel carriers on their way into the
city. She watches an old man step onto the street and
spit at the wheels of an army truck. She adopts a neutral
business tone when she speaks to colleagues in New
York, speaks to her sister on the phone alert to her own
voice and the words she is choosing, the blurriness of
certain words, the precise ambiguity of one phrase over
another. I wish you would listen to me, Áine says, history is a silent record of people who did not know when
to leave. Eilish remains silent, watching the words form
around her until she takes her sister's bait, it is always
like so, the pair of you would tangle over a phone line,
her father always says, she does not care who is listening. That is easy for you to say having abandoned
our father to my care, tell me, where is your husband
now, he's at the institute teaching calculus, he'll drive
home in an hour or so and slide into his slippers and
put his feet up while you make him dinner, I'm not
going to move a bloody inch past my door until I see
my Larry home.


She drives to the supermarket and coins free a trolley,
slides her son into the facing seat and walks past two
soldiers standing guard by the doors while holding
her breath, the dark majesty of automatic weapons
in the arms of youths no older than her son, chins

that have no need of a blade, their faces aggressively expressionless. The shelves have not been restocked. There is no fresh milk or bread. She buys yeast and wholemeal flour, condensed milk, some tinned food and baby formula. She passes the soldiers on her way out the door and shields her son's head with her hand. She drives home along the canal and slows to a checkpoint, armed gardaí on the road, their faces grave, her throat clamping down on her voice. She is asked to open the boot while a Garda with a handgun at his hip leans down and takes a look at her son. She watches the precise movements around the car, drives away from the checkpoint with her gaze wild before her, thinking about Mark's birthday, watching the trees along the canal, the willows and poplars giving shade to the path while the swans glide the lengthening light, it has been like so all her life. She finds herself wishing for a stop to spring, for the day's decrease, for the trees to go blind again, for the flowers to be taken back into the earth, for the world to be glassed to winter. She arrives home and goes upstairs with Ben to put him down for his nap, hears the muffled click of the front door, the sliding of the front patio, quick steps on the gravel. She lifts the blinds and looks out. There is Mark getting into an old Toyota across the street, the car being driven by some youth, another youngster in the front seat, she has never seen either of them before, none of Mark's friends have a car. She rushes downstairs with the child in her arms and has reached the street when the car pulls away and she follows up the street waving at them to stop but the car slows to the corner and is gone. She stands very still sensing her feet grown cold, she looks down and sees she is wearing her slippers, Ben wriggling to be free of her arms.

# 4

They take a booth in a restaurant on a Saturday evening. There will be time to eat and relax and to bring Simon home before curfew. This feeling of pleasure seeing them seated before her, Molly and Bailey, Ben in a highchair, Simon in tweed by the booth's edge, Mark will be here any moment. In a booth nearby a man and woman eat in resigned silence but for the clinking of their cutlery, the woman with a remote and disappointed air watching her plate as she eats. Simon horns his nose into a handkerchief and Bailey turns towards Molly and pulls a disgusted face, Eilish reaching into her bag for her phone, her eyes falling upon the empty seat. She tells herself it is not true, Larry is here with us in some way, he will not forget Mark's birthday. For an instant she can see his hands resting on his knees, he is sitting on a bed in a prison cell, thinking his way into her thoughts, wishing for life to go on as it should, wishing for her to be strong. She straightens her back against the pleated leatherette and regards her children for a moment, telling Larry, it is Molly who needs our attention, it is Molly who did not rise from bed until

twelve o'clock and who has not eaten all day. Watching
Molly picking at the skin around her nails, her ath-
letic physique is growing thin, the outward self is turning inward, a shadow gnawing on her heart. Simon is
griping about the menu, Molly does not know what
she wants. The waitress comes by and slips a pencil
from behind her ear, her hooped earrings like dangling
grins. We are still waiting for my son, Eilish says, we'd
like to order some drinks. She is watching where Mark
will pull up on his bike, he will chain it to the railing
then hold back a moment wishing in his heart to be
elsewhere. The waitress returns and Eilish tries ringing
Mark again while Simon looks as though he is going to
devour the waitress with his eyes, Eilish trying to smile
as she orders food, a bald man peers through the front
glass and comes to the door, he takes a look inside at
the near empty restaurant and leaves again. The food
arrives and Simon and Bailey fork mouthfuls of pasta
without taking breath. They eat like ravening animals,
she thinks, their lips and teeth smeared with blood,
thinking of the body's needs, that which tends towards
nature satisfies most, food, sex, violence – orgy and
release. The ice cream is soft in their bowls when Mark
steps through the door with a wet and windblown look.
Eilish stands up out of the booth without speaking a
word and lets him slide in. It is Molly who slices him
open with a remark but Mark will not explain himself
and reaches instead for the garlic bread. Your hands
are blue, Eilish says, taking his hand and pressing it
between her palms. The waitress brings Mark a plate of

pasta and Eilish watches him as though it were possible to absorb an exactness of him, the resting expression of the body, the mind's inner light voiced in the fine, full-grown hands. She seeks to be at one with his blood, to soften the hardened heart, to warm the gaze grown cold before the world, seeing how he has adopted the inscrutable mask of his father. The couple in the other booth move towards the door, they put on their coats and the man leans out and watches the sky as though afraid. Eilish watching the faces around the table, she summons them to lean in and speaks in a low voice. I have some news that will affect you all, she says, it is something I discussed with Mark last night, I have decided to send him to a boarding school across the border, I cannot let what is happening affect his school-ing, he is simply too young to be called up for national service. Molly's face begins to crumple while Simon rolls a paper napkin into a ball. This will have to be our secret, Eilish says, you're not to say a word to anybody outside of this family, Bailey, do you hear? She watches him turning circles with an empty glass, Mark resting down his knife and fork, he begins to shake his head. I've changed my mind, he says, I don't want to go, I have the right to refuse service anyhow, there is a tribu-nal, others are going to go before it, if I go across the border I might never be allowed back, I'll be arrested for sure—— Molly covers her face with her hands and Bailey begins digging into the table with a knife. Eilish takes the knife from his hand and places it down before her. But, Mark, she says, we agreed last night, I am still your mother, from now on you will do what I say until you are eighteen years of age and then you can do what you like. Mark's face sours and he pulls his hands from the table and shakes his head. It would appear that I am owned by the state and not you, I don't have to go if I don't want to. It is then that Simon places his fist down on the table and leans towards Mark. There is a line in a poem you would do well to remember, he says, it goes something like this, if you want to die you will have to pay for it. Mark sneers at his grandfather. What do you mean by that, Mam, whatever does he mean? Simon leans back without lifting his eyes from Mark. It means, son, that if you want to hang around, see how that works out for you. Mark turns towards his mother and how quickly he is ten years old again, a look of boyish gloom on his face. Mam, why is he speaking to me like that? She looks to her father then watches onto the street thinking about what is quickening outside, moving unchecked, gathering in power. Watching them all now with this feeling of the moment vanishing, knowing she will remember them like this, her children seated around the table, sensing the wheel of disorder coming loose into spin. One day you are a house of six, then you are five and soon you'll be four. The kitchen door hinges open and the waitress backs out and turns to reveal a birthday cake, the candles veering to the point of expiration as she moves across the room forcing them all to sing, Mark looking away.

It is some other version of herself she puts into the car and sends out onto the road, hardly seeing the way, sensing her son's restlessness in the passenger seat, he has not looked up from his phone. There is a breach, she can see this now, between things as they are and things as they should be, she is no longer who she was, no longer who she is supposed to be, Mark has become some other son, she is now some other mother, their true selves are elsewhere – Mark is cycling to football and he will ring her later saying he will eat dinner at a friend's house while she is seated at the table with the laptop open reading through a clinical trial, Larry shouting for his slippers. She does not see the traffic slow until it has stopped and she hits the brakes a touch too hard and Mark turns with a scowl and she will not acknowledge him, watching instead the red light, watching the London plane trees that line the long avenue, how each tree stands alone and yet their shadowed selves are thrown onto the road in an ornate, entangled silence. The light greens and she looks at her son and they are met and returned to one another, his eyes softening and then he closes his mouth and looks down at his phone. Carole Sexton's house is a large semi-detached red-brick, Jim's BMW parked in the driveway beside Carole's compact Toyota, for a moment she expects them both to be at home. Mark leans down to Carole's car and runs his hand along the side which looks as though it was clawed by some metallic talon, Eilish ringing the doorbell. She thinks about how they must look, two people call to a house on a Sunday afternoon, a casual visit to a friend, nothing untoward in that and yet she tells Mark to face the door, better safe than sorry, she says. Fear attracts the very thing it is afraid of, he says, don't you know that? They are walking back towards the car when the front door opens. There is Carole in dressing gown clung with shadow and sleep, the look in her eyes of some cautious, bewildered animal. She casts a fleeting look up and down the street then waves them into the house. They follow through a dim hallway into a mustard kitchen that smells of mixed spice and cinnamon, Carole wiping down the table with a tea towel. She pops the lid of a biscuit tin and shows the contents to Mark. I made a boiled fruit cake for you this morning, it's still a little warm. Mark hesitates then looks at his mother. How can a cake be boiled? he says. Eilish is standing by the window looking out at the yellowed grass and wintered plants, an inkling of blue in the undergrowth, she is watching the small flat at the end of the garden in need of paint. None of this is real, she thinks, not this kitchen nor the flat in the garden, she will open the back door and instead of outside there will be the blind and monstered dark of dream, she will wake and turn onto her side and find Larry lying beside her. Carole is watching her as though she has asked a question. I'm sorry, Eilish says, turning around, I didn't hear what you said. Carole drags a long knife through the cake. She asked if you want some, Mark says. I don't know, she says, I suppose so, just a small slice. They drink coffee and eat cake and Carole wants to know about the new solicitor. Eilish begins to wring her hands then pits a thumbnail into her skin. Anne Devlin, she says, she's supposed to be very good, I haven't heard anything in a while, she says she will call when she has some news, she is under terrible pressure to put the cases aside, she is getting anonymous calls in the middle of the night. They will wear her down, Carole says, they will squeeze her to the pips and when that fails she will be arrested, I'm sorry to sound so negative, but that's how it is. She stands up and opens a cabinet door and slides a key into her hand. This is yours, she says, giving it to Mark. You must be careful not to be seen, you can enter by the alley at the back, go through the red door, I've left it unlocked, we are being made to behave like criminals don't you think? Mark fondles the key and looks at his mother. Can I go down now and look? Not now, Carole says, you must come and go when it's dark, I put a blind on the window so the neighbours won't see. Eilish looks discreetly at a photo of Jim Sexton on the microwave, a big-boned, hardy man in rugby green, she looks out upon the flat. He'll cycle over tonight before curfew, is there anything else he needs, is the place warm, I keep thinking there is something I've forgotten. Carole lifts up the knife. Do you want more cake? she says, watching Mark with a smile. I'll bring him down his dinner when it gets dark and some breakfast in the morning, just tell me what you want, you have a microwave, a kettle, as well as a storage heater, I was talking to my brother, he'll come down in about two weeks, he'll wrap you in carpet and stow you in the back of the van, he says they never check his van anyhow going across the border.

Eilish asks for scissors, she reaches into her bag and produces two cheap pre-pay phones and cuts the packets open, copies the number of each phone into the other then hands a device to Mark. From now on, she says, we'll use these phones to speak, you cannot use your old one anymore, I'll take it off you this evening. Mark is looking down at the second phone, he shakes his head and pushes it away. And what about Sam? he says, how am I supposed to speak with her, do you expect me to just disappear without word? Let me speak to her and when you go across the border you can give her a call. He bites his lower lip revealing the top incisor teeth, one of them is shorter than the other, he is staring at the floor. I don't like this, he says, it is all happening too quick, I want to talk to Sam before I go. And what are you going to do, just ring her up for a chat, do you want to get us all arrested? Eilish sighs and looks down at her hands, the wrinkled folds of her knuckles, she watches Carole in the chair, the long slippered feet, the drawn and ghosted face, she is seeking inside to the woman's grief and measuring it against her own. She turns again to face her son, thinking about how much more she has to lose, not just a husband but a son as well, grief upon grief is still yet more grief, watching her son as though suspended in time, his image graven to memory, he is moving towards the boiled cake and cutting himself a third slice.

Eilish goes to hang her coat on the stand and sees that
Rohit Singh is not at his desk. He was not at his desk all
last week, without fail he is among the first into work
each day. She is still holding her coat when she looks
again to where Rohit sits and sees his desk has been
cleared, nothing remains of his personal effects but for
a stapler and some push pins in the partition. She asks
around her what happened to Rohit and Mary Newton
looks up with a flustered face and nobody can answer.
She stares blankly at her screen, she picks up the phone
and dials Larry's number. I'm sorry, he says, I'm not
available to take your call right now. She finds Rohit's
number in her contacts and dials his number and
meets a disconnected tone. Alice Dealy walks through
the office fumbling at a golf umbrella, her hair dishev-
elled, she steps into her office and closes the door and
Eilish follows into the room without knocking. Where
is Rohit Singh? she says. Alice Dealy looks up but does
not answer, she is rooting for something in her bag,
she places a hairbrush onto the desk and stares at it a
moment. Please close the door, she says. Eilish folds
her arms and takes a step towards her. Do you think
closing the door will make any difference? Alice Dealy
stands up with a sigh, walks to the door and closes it.
I've instructed Michael Ryan to handle the account
for now. So Rohit is gone. There was no reason to tell
you. No reason to tell me? I don't see any reason why I
would have to inform you. Eilish closes her mouth and
becomes aware of being watched through the glass.
Eilish, it hasn't been announced but I've been placed

on indefinite leave, the bastard has got me out, this will
be my last day here, one by one we all fall down don't
you think? Colm Perry is watching Eilish as she goes to
her desk, they are all watching her, her hands in a fury
as she hunts for her cigarettes, her bag falls onto the
floor and Colm Perry picks it up and follows her out
into the lift. When she steps outside onto the street the
cigarette is already lit. Rohit Singh has been arrested,
she says. Colm Perry makes a wincing face and shakes
his head then gives her a warning look. I have a bastard of a hangover this morning, he says, we went for
a quick one after work and next thing you know it is
past curfew, took the devil's work to get home. He is
nodding past her shoulder and when she turns she sees
the ground-floor window open beside them.

Bailey is whining about his shoes, she is trying to watch
the TV, a security forces patrol was targeted this afternoon in the city, two soldiers are dead, a circuit court in
Cork was petrol bombed during the night, she wonders
what else doesn't make the news, the government says
it will extend the curfew. When the contact phone rings
from the kitchen, Bailey and Molly follow her into the
room, everybody wants to speak with Mark. Molly's
face has brightened, she grabs the phone from Bailey
and runs into the hall, stands regarding herself in the
mirror, Eilish watching from the door. She motions for
Molly to pass the phone then takes it upstairs to her

room. Are you still cold? she says, the last few nights weren't too bad, C said you can run the heater as much as you need. For a moment he does not speak and she does not know how to read his silence. I couldn't sleep last night, he says, I don't want to be here, there's other places I can go. Where else can you go, look, we've already been through this, it's only for a short time, everything will be alright. You're not listening to me, Mam, why won't you listen? I am listening to you, you should have seen your sister's face right now, the children really miss you, Bailey talks about you all the time, you're really important to him don't you know? Have you heard from Sam? I said don't use any names. I asked have you heard from her? Yes, I've heard from her. What did she say? What do you think she said, she's upset, the poor girl, she doesn't understand. She is silent for a moment thinking about what she will not say, how Samantha called to the door looking lost in a large overcoat, how she knew the girl had not slept at all and will not sleep and that what was being done to her is what has been done to her also, the taking away of her man into silence, and yet she stood before the girl as though wearing a mask and did not invite her in. Mam, are you there? Yes, I'm here, I spoke with her and told her you'd be gone for a while and that you'd phone as soon as you were able. She finds herself motionless by the door to the boys' room, her breath suspended, the bluing light through the blinds, this light that hurtles at maximal speed yet falls in an illusion of stillness. Mark's presence in the room, the humped duvet and rifled drawers, his dirty clothes on the floor. She gathers the clothes then sits on the bed with the laundry on her lap, seeing Mark as he was in Carole's kitchen, seeing his hand on the knife, knowing now what she has done, how she has drawn the blade on her son in order to save him.

She sits before the laptop on the kitchen table adrift and unbecome, the night borne through the open window, the city murmuring to the dreaming trees. She looks to her son in the highchair, the eyes that smile are from a world of pure and ecstatic devotion, his blond hair fingered with mashed apple and rice. Her awareness drifts towards her hands, the fine almost imperceptible grain of the skin, these hands have aged and will age yet still, they will sag and speckle and she pulls at the flesh and watches the skin smooth back around the bone, Molly shouting something from upstairs. There are thundered steps across the landing and Bailey is shouting from the hall. When she goes to the window she sees by the front gate a Garda car luminescent in yellow and white, two gardaí in dark aspect approaching the door. For too long she has heard their knocking in her dreams and she will not give them the satisfaction now. She moves quickly for the front door sensing her triumph, watching two faces bloom into light as she slides open the patio onto the wettish night, a man and a woman of equal bearing, standard issue gardaí

in waterproof jackets. The woman's manner is monotone and matter-of-fact. Good evening, she says, I'm
Garda Ferris and this is Garda Timmons, we are here
to speak with Mark Stack. Eilish allows a helpful smile
and glances across the street. Yes, she says, Mark Stack
is my son but I'm afraid he's not here. She is watching
the woman's eyes for something that has not yet been
shown, the stolid face that gives nothing away, wisps of
shadowy hair curling from under her cap. Can you tell
us when he'll be back? My son is no longer living in this
house. Garda Timmons wipes a hand across his mouth
then slides a black notebook from his back pocket,
nods past her into the hall. Might we come in for a
moment, Mrs Stack? Without thought she has taken a
teething ring from the radiator and walked with it into
the kitchen, the gardaí following behind, she puts the
ring down on the table then picks it up again, places it
into the sink and asks the gardaí to sit down. I'm just
making coffee for myself, she says, or perhaps you'd
like some tea? The gardaí rest their caps on the table
and Garda Timmons smiles at the child then opens his
notebook. There was a summons sent out, Mrs Stack,
your son did not turn up to answer for himself in court,
we have a duty now to speak with him. She is standing
with her hand on the kettle and takes a moment to
answer, telling herself she shall be unwritten before
them. A summons, she says, turning around, is that
what it was, I saw the letter and didn't think to open it,
would you like milk with your tea? Just a touch for me,
Garda Timmons says. Garda Ferris nods. I like a good

pour, good and milky, she says, tell me, is this the legal
address for your son? Yes, he has lived here all his life
but he is no longer resident. It would be helpful, Mrs
Stack, if you could tell us where we could find him.
Molly has come barefoot into the room, she stands at
the sink taking too long to fetch a glass of water then
stands behind Eilish and puts her arms around her
shoulders, Bailey listening from behind the door. Eilish
reaches across the table for the sugar bowl and Garda
Timmons slides it towards her, she is spooning sugar
into her coffee when she looks down at her cup, she has
never put sugar in her coffee before. Mark left home
two weeks ago, she says, he will be doing his schooling
across the border in Northern Ireland and will remain
there while the trouble here continues, he is just seventeen years old, he had wanted to study medicine for
the longest while but he has changed his mind after
what the state has done to his father, he wants now to
study law. She is being regarded closely by both gardaí
and stares back, separating each face from their uni-
forms, it is the uniform that speaks not the mouth, it
is the state that speaks through the uniform, seeing
what each would be like in civilian clothing, you'd pass
them by on the street without taking a second look.
Garda Timmons inhales slowly and places his notebook
down. So what you are saying, Mrs Stack, is that your
son is no longer living in the state? Yes, she says, that
is what I'm saying. She watches the man's hand relax
and a smile soften his face. Well then, he says, rubbing
his hands, there is nothing for us to do. Garda Ferris

picks up a spoon and plays with it then puts it down. Just between ourselves, she says, there's a lot of people whose sons have recently left the state, you need to know what that means, youngsters like your son are being handed down sentences in absentia by the military courts for refusing to join the security forces, if your son were to return home, or if he is found to be resident in the state, there is a warrant for his arrest and we would have to hand him over to the military police, but look, in the meantime, it would be of benefit if you could come down to the station in your own time and make a statement giving account of the facts. Garda Timmons keeps turning the mug in his hand then makes a sighing sound that signals it is time to go. He leans sidewards and stows his notebook in his pocket. Might I ask, he says, what happened to your husband? My husband was arrested by the GNSB, she says, he was denied access to a solicitor and remains in detention without recourse to the courts, he is a trade unionist for the TUI and was just doing his job, we haven't heard from him since he was taken, we were supposed to be going to Canada for our family holidays next week, it has been very difficult for the children. As she speaks she feels herself outside of time, feeling herself the carrier of some ancient burden, everything has happened before so many times, a look of silent outrage growing upon the Garda's face, he makes a rueful shape with his mouth then shakes his head. I'm afraid you are not alone, he says, but this is how things are now, and if I can speak between ourselves, it makes a right mockery of our oath, but look, as regards your son, what my colleague here says is correct, it would be the case that if you were to come and make a sworn statement, the department would be informed and we can wash our hands of the matter, the file would remain closed until such a time as your son decides to re-enter the state, and sure who knows how things will turn out, there might not be any problem by then. She is being carried forward as though in a dream, looks into the faces before her afraid to speak in case the spell is broken. She stands from her chair with her hands open, feeling herself without weight, a distant church bell striking the hour.

She is struggling to free Ben from the car seat, his coat is snagged on the buckle's tooth while he shrieks and beats the air with an impoverished fist, her phone ringing from the dashboard. She sees in the child's eyes that she is no longer his mother but some malefic witch and she turns and snaps at Molly as she combs her hair in the front seat. Who is that on the phone? she says. She looks up and sees herself unfamiliar in the rearview mirror, the witch in unpainted face, Molly leaning across the seat as the phone goes quiet. It was only Grandad, she says, do you want me to ring him back? The slanting cold rain as she carries the child across the street into the crèche shielding his face with her hand. She hurries back with lowered head and waves an apology to two cars waiting behind the Touran double-parked on the narrow street, she indicates and moves off as the phone again begins to ring. Mam, would you ever answer the bloody phone, Bailey says. Watch your tongue, she says, I don't have the energy to deal with him right now. It is Molly who reaches across the dashboard and answers the call. Hi Grandad, it's me, Molly, what's going on? Eilish watches the road without word while her father goes silent as though listening to them all in the car. Is your mother there or are you driving yourself to school? Eilish gives Molly a funny look and they both stifle a laugh. Yes, Dad, I'm here, I have the kids in the car and you're on speaker phone, are we still OK for Saturday? The laboured intake of breath that tells her he has forgotten, she might have to remind him what day this is, she stops for the lights and closes her eyes, she could rest like this all day. Have you seen the paper? he says, I'm presuming you haven't. Dad, I'm up since half past five with Ben and have just dropped him into crèche, his teeth are at him again, right now I'm dropping the children to school, no, I haven't read the paper. She hears a single crisp bark from the dog. There's no need to be snappy, he says. Are you talking to me or the dog? You need to stop on your way to school and get *The Irish Times*, page seven. What is it, Dad? Simon is shouting at the dog, she hears the clack of the phone on the console and the slamming of the kitchen door, he is out of breath when he picks up the phone. That damn dog is after chewing through the rug, he says, I'll call you back later. She slows into a line of grudging traffic watching the sunless sky, Bailey is pulling again at Molly's seatbelt who turns and slaps him away. I've told you, Bailey, to leave her alone. Molly is pointing ahead to the right. Mam, there's a petrol station ahead. She would rather not stop, she will not be told what to do, she swings the car across the road and pulls up in the forecourt. The humming hydrocarbon air, the teller does not even look her in the face while he takes payment for the newspaper, he is watching soccer on a phone. She stands outside the shop and slides the sports supplement into the bin and opens the newspaper onto page seven, there is nothing to read but a full-page advertisement from the state, the harp emblem at the top of the page, it is a public notice, a list of hundreds of names and addresses in small print of the people who absconded from military service. She looks up from the paper and sees Bailey sucking his mouth on the glass of the Touran, she is holding her breath as she scans the list and reads her son's name and address. She thinks of the sworn statement she made to the gardaí, she reads her son's name again and sees in the black print the dark night to come, seeing how they have damned her son and how easy it was after all, it is there on page seven for all to see in the form of an advertisement.

She is standing before her desk without memory of having walked from the car, this feeling of her heart in her throat. She turns and hangs her coat and goes to remove her white chiffon scarf but fixes it straight instead. Watching now about the room for anybody reading the newspaper, the door to Paul Felsner's office is closed, Sarah Horgan comes over to talk, she can finish the woman's sentences if she wants to. Yes, she says, but no, I'm sorry, I have to meet someone for lunch. Watching for anything untoward, a twitch in the mouth, a gesture of solidarity that must be conveyed in silence. It is then the contact phone rings in her bag and she chooses to ignore it, Sarah Horgan is watching the bag, her mobile phone is on the table. Oh, it's just one of the kids, Eilish says. When the phone rings again she turns it off. She lunches alone at a terraced café wearing her winter coat. She does not want to eat but drinks coffee, training blue cigarette smoke through her nose, thinking how Molly has noticed the smell, stopped her by the patio door with the alert suspicion of a parent. Don't be so silly, she said, laughing an untrue laugh while turning to hide her mouth. She is watching the screen of the contact phone underhand on her lap, she has tried ringing Mark but the phone rang out. Watching the grey ghost of a man take seat at a table beside her, the willowed fingers that place a lighted cigarette in the hole of his mouth, the fingers prising open the newspaper. She turns to face the street, watching the world pass by in strange pretence, the pale and stolid faces hurrying back to work, they are mostly civil servants, every day another international firm closes its doors and makes its excuses,

soon the city will be emptied out. A woman nearby
slides back her chair, neon pink runners under a grey
office skirt, and she remembers that Bailey needs new
shoes, remembers awakening last night from a dream
where she had been sitting down to eat food from one
of her shoes, it was the red loafer that squeezes her
toes, she was alone before the shoe with a knife and
fork. When she returns to her desk, people are gathering in the conference room, Paul Felsner has called a
strategy meeting for 2pm, she checks her email, there
is no invitation. Watching them gather inside the room,
watching Paul Felsner step into the room holding a
newspaper. Something has woken inside her body, it
creeps outward from her solar plexus into her arms and
legs, she is walking across the room and feels her hands
go cold, hearing the hollow sound of her knocking, she
clears her throat and leans into the room. I didn't get
any notice about the meeting, she says, do you need me
here? The blinds half-drawn and Paul Felsner is sitting
with his arm draped across the back of a chair reading
the newspaper as the room begins to fill, he turns and
regards her as though from within some shadowed
interiority and what she sees in his eyes is that he has
her pinned and wriggling. No need to concern yourself
with us right now, Eilish. He leans forward in his seat
and motions her away with his hand. She is standing
useless by the door, she wants to say, yes, but this is
my account, you can't go ahead without me, she cannot
open her mouth, she finds her hand touching her scarf
and lets the hand drop, the white bloody scarf, she

wishes she had not worn it now, seeing the trace of a smile that creeps along Paul Felsner's face. She moves aside to let her colleagues through and finds herself in the kitchen with an empty cup in her hand, a woman from HR is giving out about people dumping plates in the sink, she puts the cup in the sink and walks out.

She moves about the house listening to her son speak from across the city, stands by his bedroom door, the streetlight that falls into the room is the ghost of some wintered moon. It falls upon the bed and makes a translucent white sheet and she lies down, glossed and held, happy in his voice, hearing the thinking mind in the long intake of breath. The gas boiler shudders and clicks off into silence and Mark murmurs something, he says, I no longer know who I am, I'm stuck in this room but it isn't a room, it's a prison, Mam, that's what it is, how am I supposed to sleep— twice now I've had the same dream, I see myself being led up the street as though on trial, I'm walking through a crowd and the charge is read aloud that I'm guilty and the charge is cowardice and falsehood, I woke last night in the middle of the night and lifted the blind and saw the lights on in her house, guess who was standing at the kitchen door in her wedding dress, watching down upon the flat, as though she knew I was awake, Mam, she creeps me out, the other evening she came down with my dinner but didn't say a word, she just stood there for a minute looking out the window as if I wasn't there and then she turned and said to me, everything in this world is but a shadow, and I asked her what she meant and she looked at me and then she smiled and said, sooner or later, you will see for yourself. Eilish is pinching the bridge of her nose, she has an ache at the base of her skull. She opens her eyes and sits up, swings her feet onto the floor. She has no right to talk to you like that, she says. Mam, I can't do this. What do you mean you can't do this? Mam, I miss him, I miss Dad, I tried to do what you asked me but I can't stand by and do nothing anymore, there are people I know who've gone to fight, they've joined the rebel army. Mark, she says, but then she is silent, she is reaching but cannot find the right words. Listen to me, she says, you are still my son, my teenage son. And what is that supposed to mean? he says. I don't know what it means, it means I can't let anything happen to you. She hears a long sighing breath and then static silence as though it were a darkness of rain that could be felt, a rain falling from the darkness and washing them all, the dark rain entering into the mouth of her son.

She stands up from her desk and takes her coat, wraps her white scarf about her neck and tells a colleague she is taking early lunch. When she knocks on Simon's door she is met by a growl, then a high voice calling out, who's there? Simon is wearing navy pyjamas, the hall

light is on, it has just gone past one o'clock. He casts
her a derisory look then goes into the kitchen. I don't
know what you're doing here, he says, I can manage
fine on my own. Dad, I've only come to say hello, I've
grabbed an extra hour for lunch. She turns off the hall
light and stands arrested – within the old jumble of
smells is a novel smell woven through, she thinks it
is stale tobacco smoke, she isn't sure if it is her own.
She watches her father with narrowed eyes, Spencer
whining and circling his feet. Dad, when was the last
time you fed the dog? Spencer turns and regards her
with a hanging mouth and she sees what is told in the
obsidian eyes, a mercilessness that belongs not to the
dog but to the wolf. What are you having for lunch? she
says, pouring water into the kettle, Simon rummaging
with quick hands through a pile of papers on the table.
Lunch? he says, I hadn't thought about lunch. She finds
herself softly crying, she pulls a seat and wipes her eyes
then looks to her father and smiles. I'm sorry, she says,
it's just that I have been sidelined at work and I don't
know what to do, everything is happening much too
fast, that notice in the newspapers and Mark is getting
so difficult, you always know the right thing to do. She
looks up and sees in his eyes a drifting inattention, the
eyes rooting about for something, Simon rising slowly
as though lost in thought. He goes to the sink and
runs the tap without washing anything then turns it off
again. He turns and regards her as though she has just
appeared before him. Dad, what I said just now, were
you even listening? What do you want? he says. I said

I asked you a question, about my job, about Mark. She watches the mouth wobble as though struck, he shakes his head and bats at the question with his hand, turns and points towards the counter. That thing there, he says, the what-do-you-call-it, I can't get it to work. Dad, do you mean the microwave? She stands up and places her cup inside and presses the start button, watches it whirr. It's working just fine, she says, I don't know what you're talking about. This sudden sorrow as she climbs the stairs, seeing how time is not some horizontal plane but a vertical plummet towards the ground. She stops outside his bedroom struck again by stale tobacco, pushes open the door and sees an antique brass ash-tray on the bedside locker that belongs to the parlour room, it is half-full of ash, beside it a pack of cigarettes. She grabs at the ashtray and counts the smoked butts, runs her finger along a scorch on the carpet. When she steps into the kitchen she is holding the ashtray aloft, then places it on the table. What's this? she says. What's what? Dad, since when do you smoke, you're after burn-ing a hole in the carpet, do you want to burn the house down? He looks away and folds his arms. I don't know what you are talking about. Dad, I cannot put up with you like this, if it isn't one thing, it's another, I will have to go and speak to the doctor. The way he sours in an instant, his eyes taking the same blackened look as the dog. I've told you I'll quit when I'm good and ready. She has missed a breath, she is staring into his face and feels her hands tremble. Dad, you don't even smoke, it is thirty-odd years since you last smoked a pipe. She watches his mouth open and close and then he looks to the window as though searching for something outside. Dad, can you tell me today's date? She watches him remain very still, then he turns his head in sly movement reading the watch on his wrist. He looks up with a triumphant scowl. It's the sixteenth, he says. Yes, she says, but what month is it? He will not meet her eyes but looks about the room, regarding the wall and then the dog, he meets her with a pettish look. I don't have to tell you anything. He turns again to face the window and she looks onto the garden and recalls tearing her knee on a jag of metal, being carried in his arms to the car. About Mark, he says, we were talking about Mark and your job before you distracted me with this non-sense, you need to consider the situation as it is, armed insurrection is growing around the country, soldiers are defecting from the Defence Forces and joining the free army or whatever you like to call them, defectors are being shot on sight, the rebels are growing in size and will continue to grow and that is where Mark is going to go, that is what he feels he must do, and regarding your job, there won't be an economy in three months' time, so really, I wouldn't worry about it, now is the time for you to act before they tighten the border, you need to go and get the children out, go to England, Eilish, go to Áine in Canada, they printed your address in the newspaper, your son has been publicly shamed and is a target for arrest. He is looking down at his hands then slowly shakes his head. You cannot put a stop to the wind, he says, and the wind is going to blow right

through this country, but please don't worry about me,
I'll be fine on my own, no one is going to make trouble
for an old man.

She is inching through traffic alone in the car when she
answers the phone, it is five to nine, she turns down
the radio and hears Carole's voice. Eilish, are you there,
hello? Yes, Carole, I'm here, I'm driving to work, I've
just bought a pastry and my mouth is full. Look, I don't
know how to tell you, Eilish, but Mark did not come
back last night. The pastry lumpen in her mouth, she
makes herself swallow and feels as though something
malign is crawling down her throat. Do you hear me,
Eilish, I'm really sorry, I don't know what to say, I fell
asleep yesterday evening and woke early this morning.
OK, let me think a moment, I'll ring him now, I'm
sure it's no cause for alarm. She hangs up and reaches
into her bag for the contact phone, rummages about
then tips the bag out onto the seat, lifts the phone and
dials, a voice says the number you have dialled cannot
be reached. She looks for somewhere to pull over but
there is nowhere to stop along the canal, the traffic pulling her along until the car in front reddens to a stop,
gulls swooping onto the path by the water. On the rear
window of a car in front she reads a sticker that says,
The Best Defence Is An Armed Citizen, and beneath it
another sticker says, End Judicial Dictatorship. At the
junction she turns and drives northwards to Carole's

house, telling herself the simplest solution is most likely the right one, he went out on his bike to who knows where and missed the curfew, it would be too much of a risk to cycle home, a patrol car would pull him over, he would be arrested on sight. She looks out onto the widening sky seeking some kind of release, seeing her wrath fly before her, watching it fly into cold defeat. The front curtain wrinkles as she parks outside Carole's house and a moment later Carole stands strange before her with folded arms. In the light of the kitchen she looks as though she has aged overnight, the bones pressing through the face, water welling under her eyes. Without a word, Eilish walks down to the flat and finds the door unlocked, seeing the neatness and finality of the act, how Mark has made the bed and taken his belongings and left the room as he found it but for his bike left against the wall.

The phone is silent in her bag throughout the evening and into the night, it is silent throughout the night's passing. Waking in the dawn from a sleep that was no sleep at all she is met by a silence that has become some roaring abstraction. She must call herself up into the day and stand masked before the children, harrying them through breakfast, hurrying them into the car, telling herself there is no reason to alarm them. Her awareness coming to be in the car as though she has not been driving at all, some automaton is at the

wheel driving by rote while she sits outside of time
altogether, finding herself dim and distracted at work,
the day passing by without her as though she were
seated alone in some anteroom awaiting the opening
of a locked door. Soon it will be evening, the evening
passes, the phone sits upon the kitchen counter, it rests
in her hand, watching again and again as though at
any moment the phone will grow bright with his call,
watching the second night come down. She sleeps with
his phone by the pillow and hears its phantom ring in a
dream, wakes with the phone silent in her hand. She is
standing halfway down the stairs with Ben in her arms
calling for his shoes when the phone begins to ring
from the bedroom and she has to hear it twice before
she believes, shouting for Bailey to get out of the way
as she pushes past him on the stairs. She closes the
bedroom door and stands the child in the cot. Mark,
she says, hearing the blear of low music, the murmur
of voices, hearing the slow intake of breath and then
the breath's release, knowing he is afraid to speak, she
wants to smite him down and assert her power over
him. Why has it taken you so long to call, we have been
worried sick, Carole is beside herself, you had no right
to leave her place like that after all that she has done for
you. The phone is silent and then he allows a sigh and
clears his throat. I thought we weren't supposed to use
any names. Never mind that now. Mam, he says, do you
want me to hang up, is that what you want? The world
has fallen away taking with it her sense of the room,
the house, she is in some dark space sensing only his

breath, sensing the mind behind the breath, cursing herself for having rebuked him. Mark, she says, I'm sick with worry, anything could have happened to you. Look, he says, I'm sorry, but I can't do it. Something solid has begun to come loose, it is her heart sliding like gravel. You can't do what? she says. What you've asked me to do, run away, I can't go along with it anymore. So what do you think you're doing now? Mam, this is different. How is it different, we made an agreement, we decided this was for the best, what do you think is going to happen if you stay in the country and are discovered by the authorities, they'll put you before a closed military court where they can do what they like with you, they'll take you away just like your father. She thinks he is chewing on something, hearing the fizz of a soft drink and then the gulping mouth. Look, he says, I'm in a safe place. I want to know who you are with. Mam, everything is fine, I promise I'll keep in touch on this phone, I'm sorry I took so long to call. She closes her eyes, recalling a feeling from a dream, how she walked from room to room calling out but there was no answer and she could not wake even though she knew she was dreaming, she opens her eyes and sees her hand reaching across some blind and widening gulf. Mark, she says, you are my son, please come home so we can sort this out, I cannot sleep knowing you're gone, I still have a legal right over you. And what law would that be, Mam, seeing that there's no longer any law in the land? His voice has risen and she withdraws into silence. You're in denial, Mam, you won't admit to yourself what's going on. Really, she says, I don't think that's fair at all and it's entirely beside the point, you made an agreement with me, an agreement you did not keep. There, that's more of it, he says, why can't you see, you just won't see it until it comes to our door and marches us all out one by one. Ben is standing to the bars of the cot with his hand held out, his babble rising into whinge. She goes to him and swings him up into her arm, soothes the roaring cheek with her thumb. I can't sit by any longer, Mark says, the whole thing is making me sick, it is making Molly sick, I want to have my old life back, I want to have Dad back in the house, the way we used to live. Mark, I want you to listen—— No, Mam, you need to listen to me now, I want you to hear what I have to say, I no longer have my freedom, you need to understand, there is no freedom to think or to do or to be when we give in to them, I cannot live my life like that, the only freedom left to me is to fight. She has fallen down some blind summit, her words scattered and dissolving into the ground, she picks herself up, she is hurrying through darkness seeking for sight of her son and can see nothing but will, his will as though it were some disembodied light passing before her. She opens her eyes and places Ben back down in the cot, walks about the room pulling at her hair, seeing how it has come too soon, the giving up of her son to the world, the world become some underworld. Mark is silence and then he is breath and she does not know how to speak to him. She says, stay safe, love, do you hear, don't do anything stupid, and keep your phone on, I want to be able to talk to you. He says, can you put Molly on? She is downstairs, I don't want her to know what is going on, how do you think she is going to take this, it's bad enough that your father is gone. Look, Mam, I have to go, tell her— look, tell her I miss her as well.

There is memory in weather. In the sky the height of spring, the agile swallows, the swifts all dark, seeing in the return of the birds the years gone by, the time of innocence when she presumed the fruit, this is what she thinks, she took the fruit from the giving hand and bit into it without tasting, discarded the pit without thought. She walks alone in the Phoenix Park seeking to escape her thoughts but can see only her thoughts before her, the broadleaf trees watching down. She looks up thinking of the time that has passed beneath them, how the trees keep count of the years by ringing time in their wood, the days passing by and she cannot keep a hold of them, the days passing on and on and yet it is not time that is pulling away, it is something else and she is being carried along with it. Further down the Khyber Road she sees Larry in the broad back of a man holding the hand of a child and when the man turns around by the boot of his car she sees the same reddish beard, watching him as he helps the child into their seat, thinking she has been tricked, that Larry has been leading a double life all along and invented his arrest to deceive her. She walks up the hill by the Magazine Fort wishing this were true. She wipes rainwater off a white bench and sits down with a view onto the Liffey, the college rowers no longer on the water, the giving air, it was here on one of these benches that she sat with Larry and felt the quickening of the child that would be Mark, the first flutterings as though the child were growing wings to take flight from inside her.

# 5

The noise blooms into sleep, upward and adrift through two worlds hearing footsteps sound on gravel, a laugh beneath the bedroom window as though a shadow had been let fly from dream. She is suddened into the dark room, the awareness cold and quick in the blood that something has struck the glass door downstairs, hearing the sound carry in hollow shock through the house, the slow weight of the body as she runs from the bed. What she sees outside are three men in the driveway, a white SUV parked with a running engine. Something is thrown against the porch glass and there is a bang behind her as the bedroom door meets the wall, Molly tumbling into her arms shouting about men trying to get into the house, she covers the girl's mouth with her hand and moves back from the window. How an instant can slow and open upon some field of other time, she is wading without light through a compounding darkness fearing the surroundment of wolves, she is calling out to herself from a distance but cannot hear her own name. Something large strikes off the glass again and Molly is stricken, grips fast to her body, lets sound

a low groan. Without thought Eilish has gone to the
cot and lifted the sleeping child, she places him into
Molly's arms and ushers them out of the room, Molly
coming to a stop on the landing, she begins to breathe
in sawing exertions, her eyes loose with panic. Eilish
shakes her by the shoulders. Stop it, she says, there is
no time for this, go into the bathroom and mind your
brother and stay quiet. Bailey has come to the bedroom
door rubbing his eyes and Eilish sends him into the
bathroom telling them both to lock the door, do not
come out until I say so. Moving towards the bedroom
window she can see ahead to all outcomes, hearing the
laughter outside, if they want to come in you might as
well have left the door unlocked, her hand searching for
her phone in the dark, she does not remember having
left it by the window, the emergency dispatcher speaking in a slow and firm voice. Through the curtains she
watches a man climb the Touran, tattoos emblazoning
arms and throat, another man bent to the side of the
car. The man brings down a bat upon the windscreen
then takes out his sex and urinates on the car, the apish
laughing teeth as the man zips up and jumps down
onto the gravel. Across the street a bedroom light turns
on and then off again as the SUV powers away.


She watches the moon pass through the house, the
bruised light of dawn reaching for Ben in the cot, the
spoiled light reaching for Molly who is woven in sleep

like a young child to her body. The dawn has come
and yet the day has fled, she can see this now, how the
light that makes insubstantial the dark is false and it
is the night that remains true and unshaken, seeing
how she called the children into her arms knowing her
comfort was false, this house no place of shelter. She
slides free of Molly and goes to the chair and dresses
quietly, turns to see Molly's face caressed in satin light,
a frown on her face while she sleeps. Looking through
the door to the boys' room where Bailey lies on Mark's
bed dressed in his clothes and asleep on top of the
duvet. She goes downstairs and steps out front and
picks up a rock from the driveway, stands before the
Touran's shattered windscreen, reading what has been
written on the bonnet and on the side of the car, on
the walls and the windows and the patio door of the
house, the same single word sprayed in red paint. She
is speaking all this to Larry as though it is already some
past event, a story worked into shape from memory,
they are in the Touran and she is collecting him from
wherever he has been released, seeing him grown lean
in his clothes, seeing him pull on his beard with his
hands, knowing what will wake in his blood, what lies
dormant in the blood of all fathers, a primal violence
that awakes to find it has already been silenced, something breaks inside the man who learns he could not
protect his family, it will be best if he doesn't know. A
front door opens across the street and Gerry Brennan
steps outside with a black refuse bag. He drops it into
a wheelie bin and takes a quick look at the house and

knows he has been caught, he waves his hand and puts
the front door on latch and steps towards her, a nimble
old man in slippers tying a knot in his gown. My God,
Eilish, what have they done, you must have had a terrible fright. He bends down and picks up a rock and
rubs it with his thumb. Scum of the earth, he says,
Betty called the guards but we must have been asleep
when they came, 'twas an awful racket. She is watching
his eyes take read of the word TRAITER sprayed again
and again in red paint, he begins to squint down upon
the word then meets her with a puzzled look. Is it just
me or is that not spelt right? I don't know, Gerry, how
would you spell it? Hold on a moment, I can't think
without my glasses, yes, there should be an O not an
E—— It seems to me, Gerry, they spelled out exactly
what they wanted to say, spelled it out loud and clear,
I called the gardaí, too, but nobody came, I waited up
half the night for them. She watches the growling eye-
brows rise in disbelief and then the brows sink down
as though a thought were blurry before them on the
concrete. This country has gone to the dogs, he says,
the gardaí must have had a busy night of it with vandals
like that, illiterates, you wouldn't have been the only
house. He runs his hand along the side of the car. This
will have to go to a body shop, he says, but the walls
of the house will clean up nicely, I've got some white
masonry paint in the shed that will do the job, I'll nip
across now and fetch it out, it will take me just a few
minutes. She folds her arms and looks across the street.
Oh, let them see it, Gerry, let them see what has been

done to our home, an ordinary family minding our own business, isn't it a great advertisement for life now in this country? The sun breaking through a gap in the houses as Gerry turns and watches his own house. Sure I'll go anyhow and dig it out. The dressing gown cord has fallen loose as he crosses the road and he doesn't bother to tighten it. She sets her face against the street, seeing the shut doors in line and length, counting six houses that have hung the national flag from their windows. She is wrath as she steps into the house, wrath searching upstairs for acetone, it used to be in the bathroom press, she is looking under the stairs for the paint scraper but meets instead her humiliation as though it were on the shelf before her, the shame and pain and grief moving freely through her body. Seeing now how everything shall be known, how they shall be judged within the community, they watched what happened last night and will not say a word.

The children are dressed and ready for school but will not go out to the car. Bailey follows her into the kitchen and watches as she takes the lunchboxes from the press, the bread and cheese and ham on the counter. Mam, he says, can't we take the day off, I don't want to go to school. She pulls a knife from the drawer and closes it with her hip. Did you pick your towel up from the floor like I asked? Mam, did you hear what I said? You don't want to go to school. Yes, I don't want to go to school.

Well, what do you propose to do instead, you're not going to sit about here all day, watching the TV until you're goggle-eyed, go and get your coat. He refuses to go to the car, stands in the hall with folded arms. She goes outside and puts the baby in the Touran, stands in the hall before her son, picks up his schoolbag and puts it into his arms and marches him outside. When she goes back inside Molly is slumping on the stairs with her eyes cast down, her knees knocking together, she looks like a child who went to sleep with something in her arms and when she awoke it was gone. Eilish lifts her coat and bag. You've eaten no breakfast, she says, you're going to pass out from hunger, will you not eat some toast in the car? Molly is looking past her onto the street, her voice barely a whisper. What if they come back, Mam, they might come back, what if next time they come into the house? What is in her daughter's eyes pulls Eilish down onto her knees, she takes Molly's hand and strokes it with her thumb. They won't come back, love, why would they come back, they've had their fun, that's all it was for them, they saw Mark's name and address in the paper and wanted to give us a scare, other houses would have been targeted as well, I'll speak to the gardaí later today and let you know how I get on, I promise we'll be alright. As she speaks a voice inside her says, do not tell the girl lies, and yet when she stands up she is certain what she has said is true, she is impatient now, motioning for Molly to go outside, taking her by the arm. We are going to be late, she says. Molly will not sit in the front and so Bailey climbs from the back through the space between the seats and slides down into the front seat facing a web of broken glass. Eilish slides the porch door closed and locks it, stands taking a look at the house, Gerry Brennan has been and gone and done a nice job with the walls and in quick time too, he has wiped down the windows with acetone, looking at the house you'd never know they had been judged, branded in blood-red paint as enemies of the state. When she gets into the car Bailey is leaning down to pull at a sock, he gives her a severe look. Don't you dare go anywhere near the school gates, he says. Eilish starts the Touran and sets out onto the road watching fiercely through the glass, meeting the faces agape in each passing car, the cyclist who stares by the traffic lights, the schoolchildren who gawk and point. She drives feeling her rage in her hands, the car advancing through traffic as though powered by the cruel surging of her blood. She drives and takes satis-faction in the summary judgement and publicising of their crime, let them beat us with their eyes, she thinks, let them see what sort of traitors we are, what kind of world they've brought into being. Molly will not take her hands from her face and when she speaks Eilish does not hear her. What was that, love? she says. Bailey staring at his mother in rage. Mam, he says, she says she doesn't want to go to school, she says she wants to die.

She is unsettled about the house and ill at ease in her body, lying awake each night with her ear cocked to the street. The passing of a car can be many things, a reveller home late or an early bird to work, she turns and finds Molly asleep on Larry's side of the bed and has no memory of her coming. She puts her arm around her daughter wishing for sleep, wishing to wake into a different world. The gardaí did not call to the house, she rang the station three times and then called again asking to speak to Garda Timmons only to be told he has been reassigned. She knows now there were other attacks, that what happened to their home happened across the country, the windscreens of cars slugged with pipes and bats, shop windows smashed in and home fronts vandalised. There are rumours that some of the men were members of the security forces, that some of them belonged to the gardaí. It is some coincidence isn't it, Áine says, that it all happened on the same night, some kind of collective telepathy, we're watching you every night now on the news, I've started whispering little prayers, I can't help it, even though I haven't a religious bone in my body, I can't stop thinking about Mark. Áine, please, do not speak of him on the phone. This feeling now of quickness, of pressure giving to movement, it is as though some sensing equipment in the body can read the feeling of force in the air, telling herself that heat flows from hot to cold, that gas flows from high to low, that energy gives to disorder and what no longer has sufficient strength is dispersed. A car slows to a stop outside the house and she lies very still holding her breath, a door opens and closes, her hand reaching under the bed, she brings Larry's hammer into her grip and has it by her side as she goes to the window, a neighbour walking from a taxi to his front door searches his pocket for keys.

She strips the wet sheet from Bailey's bed and finds herself searching his bedside drawer, she does not know why. A mess of pens and stickers and plastic toy soldiers in various poses of war, one of them is throwing a grenade while others are taking aim on one knee, they used to belong to Mark. Her hand reaching to the back where she touches a lighter, she finds two more, she takes them out and sees they have been taken from her bag. She picks a hoodie up from the floor and holds it to her nose, it does not smell of cigarette smoke, who knows what he is up to, she thinks, perhaps he is trying to put a stop to your smoking. She walks with him down Connell Road, the air humming above the trees, watching the change taking place in his carriage, the bold and forward manner in his walk as though trying it on for size. She touches the lighter in her pocket and wants to speak as they both look up at a military helicopter passing overhead. The worm is turning, he says, are you afraid of the worm? She is silent, watching him carefully, trying not to frown. The worm? she says. Yes, the worm. What are you talking about? I'm talking about the worm. What is the worm?

I don't know, it's hard to explain, I thought you would know. There is a crease in his face as he speaks, the tips of his fingers trailing against walled ivy. The worm is turning, he says, it is gaining in power, the worm does what it likes. They have stopped outside the Alamode café and she falls quiet seeing the lacework of shattered glass, she counts three strikes of a bat or a rock, the window taped with an X. There is a mandatory closure notice on the door dated for next week. The lights are on but the café is empty, a man pouring beans into a coffee machine turns to meet them with two expressions on his face, the faltering smile that cannot hide his grief. Oh, Issam, she says, what have they done, I thought perhaps you were closed. They speak quietly for a moment while Bailey chooses a seat and then Eilish joins him by the window, she lowers her voice and leans in. I want you to stop with this worm nonsense, she says, I don't like it. But the worm is a fact, he says, it doesn't care whether you like it or not. Look, I'm going to be frank with you, things are going to be difficult over the next while, I really need your help right now. Bailey is spinning the salt cellar and she snaps it out of his hand, places it before her on the table. You're still wetting the bed, she says. My feet hurt, he says, I want new shoes. We'll go and get new shoes tomorrow, I want to know what we can do to make the bed wetting stop. I am not wetting the bed. Bailey, I want you to take this seriously, do you want to sleep in Mark's bed from now on, you can do that if you like, you always wanted to be by the window, he can have his bed back when he comes home. She studies the boyish open face, the simple fact of his presence, seeing him as he was as an infant and how he might be in old age, a particle of light suspended in a timeless dark flickering but for an instant, the freckles constellated around the nose, the eyes so familiar and yet unknown as though the looker behind the eyes had changed, how he must rise each day into a fatherless house, the brother gone from his room. And what if he doesn't come home? I want you to listen, she says, your father and brother are going to come back. And what if they're not? Don't be absurd, where exactly do you think your father is going to go, and your brother, too, when this is all over? The worm does what it likes. I asked you to stop this worm business, you must believe me when I say it, they are coming back, I have never known anything more true in my life, but for now, we have to carry on with things as best we can, do you understand? Yes, he says, but the worm does not care what we do. Then fight back, she says, take the worm by the throat and wring its neck. She watches Issam step towards them with soft scuffling shoes. She orders eggs and coffee while Bailey orders a large breakfast and Issam looks down at him and smiles. What do you want, milk, cola, juice, water? I want coffee. Eilish frowns across the table. Coffee? Yeah, I'm old enough now. OK, Issam says, coffee for the young man.

She is summoned to a meeting by human resources without notice fifteen minutes before lunch, the message appearing onscreen while she is talking on the phone. She looks across the room, the lights are on in the meeting room, the blinds are drawn, Paul Felsner is not in his office. Without speaking another word she hangs up the phone and takes her cup and walks towards the kitchen, seeing her colleagues abstracted before their screens, thinking of the sudden round of appointments, the party types brought into the firm, how the regime has tightened its grip. She watches the coffee machine spurt liquid into her cup and then drops the cup into the sink. She will make them wait a few minutes longer, she returns to her desk and takes the contact phone from her bag and sends a message to Mark, she has tried to ring but his phone is off, he has not answered a message in three days. An unseen hand parts the blinds in the meeting room and her desk phone begins to ring. She can see herself fetching her coat and exiting without word, calling a solicitor, but what solicitor now is of any use, she walks towards the meeting room seeing herself strung into movement like a puppet. There is Paul Felsner seated in the room at the oval table beside some nameless brunette from HR, she steps inside and pulls a chair and stares at the woman's faltering smile and then Paul Felsner says, thank you, Eilish, for coming. She will not look into his eyes seeing instead the narrow mouth, the crooked mandibular teeth, the small hands resting on the table beside the document that will sign her release. For an instant she is adrift on her anguish watching by the window, the recessed artificial light where it washes with the borrowed light from outside, a feeling of unreality as she looks down at her hands, how she is both sad and angry and wants to laugh that nine years of her life should come to this. It is then she looks the brunette up and down, smiles and says, shall I tell you how to begin? She looks into Paul Felsner's eyes and sees in the face an abyss.

The mirror holds the shadowed room. It holds her face as though she is passing through night and not the afternoon, the curtains drawn, the child asleep in the cot, Bailey shouting in the garden. She looks into the mirror and does not know herself, her hands reaching for the past in the drawer, her mother's gold wedding band, the pear-cut diamond engagement ring. She weighs both in her palm searching for an image arrested in the vanishing of her memory, Áine's face livid before her and then like a phantom it is gone. The pain she felt after her mother's death when her sister would not take one of her mother's rings. She closes her eyes seeking the past in movement but the past moves only as feeling, sensing before her mother's mocking look, something once said that fell from her bitter mouth, it suited your father better to be married. She looks down at the rings counting their value, her hand passing over the other items on the bed, the lead glass vase, the anniversary silver oval tray that belonged to her grandmother, her own baptismal spoon. An instant of feeling comes from each object and yet they contain nothing in themselves and she is done with them all, what are they but heirlooms, ornaments that live in darkened drawers, Molly standing by the door. I don't want you to get mad, she says, I got a message last night from Mark. The glare of her own eyes in the mirror as Eilish looks away from the door. I said you weren't to get mad. For goodness' sake, Molly, what did he say? He sent it at ten past one last night, he said he was fine, that I wasn't to worry, that he was doing this for Dad. Eilish watches the corner of the room as though watching her son in some soundless space, she turns as Molly sits down on the bed and fondles the lead glass vase. Have you told Bailey about work? she says. I'm not sure that he needs to know just yet. Why don't you ask Áine for money? I told you, Molly, everything is going to be fine. Are we going to have a lamb for Easter? Yes, we'll have a lamb though I have no idea why we still celebrate it. She finds herself watching the mirror across the room and sees her mother staring back, this mirror belonged to her also, no doubt Jean saw her mother too and her mother saw her mother before her. The sudden vertigo of time and yet when she opens her eyes the mirror continues to speak its truth that there is only this moment now. She slides her mother's engagement ring onto her finger and draws back the curtains onto a dullish afternoon.

The solicitor Anne Devlin is walking up the street in the manner of someone used to constant motion, her hands lightly balled and her eyes faced forward as Eilish waits for her to walk past. She follows across O'Connell Street Bridge, the woman slim in a dark suit, rings of reddish hair tied back, follows into a clothing store and out through an exit onto Prince's Street and then into a shopping arcade, following her onto Henry Street where the solicitor waits for Eilish to come alongside her. So many shops are shuttered and yet the street is busy enough, the sports store is open, the aroma of Italian ice cream drawing a queue. My assistant went missing, Anne Devlin says, he went home last Friday and hasn't been seen since, a wall of silence from the GNSB, he lived alone and I have to deal with his parents, my husband and children are terrified—— A female junkie in a tracksuit steps between them shouting into a phone, Eilish taking a sudden look at Anne Devlin's neglected face, the haunted eyes staring down the street are fixed upon the Medusa. I'm safe, I think, because I'm a face on the international news channels and write for the international press but some day soon they will come for me, my colleagues at the centre have asked that I go on leave, my husband has asked that I walk away, he says, what use can I be if I disappear other than to see with my own eyes where all my clients have gone. She takes Eilish by the wrist and squeezes. I'm sorry, Eilish, but I have no news for you, I will keep trying, of course, I've made extensive enquiries, I have back channels I can use but nobody can tell me where Larry is, I just don't know what to say to you, we must hope he is still in detention, there's nothing to do now but keep on hoping. The wrist is squeezed once again and let go. This bottomless feeling within the body as though the earth has dropped away, she watches the endless oncoming rush of people strolling along the street, thinking, how many people have been made to disappear? What I see now, Eilish, is a black hole opening before us, we have passed the boundary of escape and even when the regime has been overturned the black hole will continue to grow so that it will consume this country for decades. Eilish walks towards her car hearing the woman's voice, seeing the counterfeit streets and feeling breathless, scared and alone, she has to think for a moment where she left the car, she parked it on the street close to the Centre for Legal Studies, watching the Touran as she approaches sensing that something is wrong, seeing the tyres slashed, the front light kicked in, the wing mirror lying on the ground.

Bailey grabs at the remote control and turns off the TV, flings the remote across the room where it strikes the arm of the couch and lands on the floor. She has tried to smile while telling him the news that she has sold the car, the smile remaining dead on her face. How are we supposed to live now? he says, how will we get to school? Look, she says, the cost of petrol has gone through the roof, we simply can't afford it, you can go to school on the bus like everybody else, we will get by. He turns upon her with a savage look and Eilish stares into the face and does not know it, the hands brought to his side as fists, he looks as though he wants to strike her. You've made us look stupid, he says, what am I supposed to tell my friends? Molly comes up out of the chair and stands before her brother. Shut your mouth, she says, it's only a stupid car, none of this is Mam's fault, don't you understand what's going on? Eilish is looking for something but doesn't know what, stands as though caught in sudden nothingness, she picks up a magazine and puts it down. What did you do with my fountain pen? she says, staring at Molly, how many times have I asked you to leave it alone? A wrinkle of pain shapes Molly's face. Why are you speaking to me like that? She flings her arms and rushes for the door, Bailey still fierce before his mother. See, he says, this family is a joke, and I'll tell you something else for nothing, you're a fucking joke as well, I wish I never had you for a mother. She has fled into the kitchen feeling sick in her body but he has followed scenting blood. She stands to the sink dreading the unknown face, the eyes knifing at her back, looking outside to the rain, the trees surrendering to the rain and to the coming dark. It is then she knows that the worm has swallowed her son, or her son has swallowed the worm, she will pull the worm right out of his mouth, turning around to face him. How dare you speak to me like that? she says, lifting her chin so she can look down over him. Things are going to change around here, you stand there shouting and waving your arms but you're twelve years old and still wetting the bed and soon you'll be thirteen, you don't have a bloody clue, if you had any idea about what was going on you'd quickly hold your tongue. For an instant she is holding the worm in her fist, holds it wriggling before him, a skitter of fear alighting his eyes and then the baleful mask slips. She sees before her a child and wants to take him in her arms but the face of her son hardens into contempt. There you go, he says, that's just more of your stupid talk. The flat of her hand has struck his face before she has had thought to do so and he looks at her astonished and then he touches his cheek as though to test the slap were true. He smiles falsely and lets the tears run from his eyes and then his eyes narrow as though daring her to hit him again. She is dissolving before him, she stares into his eyes search-ing for her son without seeing him there, seeing how he is reaching blind into some inner obscurity and taking hold of something there, some new and for-bidden aspect of boy and man coming into meeting. It is then that Bailey's face folds and he cries like a child, he shakes his head and will not be held but she takes him in her arms and will not let go, feeling from within her the whole of her love. When he pushes her back he goes to the door and steps outside and takes Mark's bike, wheels it through the house. Where are you going with that? she says. I'm going outside. No you are not, look at the time, it's almost curfew. He

continues to wheel the bike into the hall until she hears
the closing of the front door.


The queue for the blue-tiled butcher's shop carries out
the door. It is quarter past five and she stands in line with
Ben asleep in the buggy, seeing all kinds of weather in
the sky. She looks towards leaden cloud in the east that
speaks to a feeling inside her, looks through the glass
to the butcher Paddy Pidgeon and his son Vinny who
works without chatter, a long white wrist reaching into
a tray of meat. She is thinking of the people she must
call in search of a job, tries to shut her ear to the talk in
the queue, the man beating a folded tabloid newspaper
against his hand as he speaks with an elderly woman,
the protuberant eyes and restless manner, he might be
the guy who trained Mark at football. Time has run out
for those rebel bastards, he says, we will rout them like
rats, what happens now will be decisive. She looks to her
feet, thinking about what she has heard on the BBC, how
the insurrection continues to grow around the country,
the rebels have gained a foothold in the south, the queue
shuffling towards the door as she takes out her purse and
counts her money. This tiredness throughout her body,
she would like to wake without dream, to reach in and
lift this feeling of the night from within her, for something of the night remains each day, a residue accreting
in the blood, it is there in her shoulders, in her back and
hips, one day she will wake from a sleep in which the

body has not slept at all. There was a woman standing behind her in the queue but she is gone as Eilish comes through the door, an elderly man with a trembling hand fingering a box of eggs while Vinny pulls an empty tray from under the glass. I'll be with you, Eilish, in just a moment. Paddy Pidgeon looks over his shoulder and lets his gaze pass over Eilish to something behind her, the plastic tubs of chicken curry, the open freezer, he places some change on top of the counter and puts a word in his son's ear. She watches them exit through the cooler strip leaving her alone in the shop, hearing a saw start up, she will lie herself down and ask to be sawed open, her marrow will be black as pitch. An elderly woman comes into the shop and Paddy Pidgeon steps out front again and addresses himself to her. Mrs Tagan, he says, and how are we today? Eilish directs a sharp look towards the butcher who watches the elderly woman as she points with a gloved hand to the glass. He leans on the counter and says, I only have what I have, Mrs Tagan, supply is short everywhere, though I might have some next week. He spins a bag of sausages then necks it in the tape dispenser, places the bag on the counter and takes the woman's change, Eilish stepping up to the glass but Paddy Pidgeon turns and steps out to the cooler. The lagging motion in the plastic strips, the faded religious calendar hanging on a nail beside the saw rack, the page that belongs to the wrong month, the wrong year, she tries to remember what they were doing at that time but no memory serves her, they were driving to school and to work and back home again, a nothing month giving

to a nothing year. She is pressing her fingers into the
serrated edge of her keys when she calls out. Don't leave
me standing here now, Paddy, I haven't got all day. From
the cold room she hears the sound of a heavy box being
dragged and dropped to the ground. An ample woman
steps breathless into the shop and stands with bulging
hands watching Paddy Pidgeon as he steps through the
strip with a flourish of his arm. He slides his gaze past
Eilish to meet the other woman with a smile. Mags, he
says, I'm just about to close up, quickly now, what can
I get you? She feels her heart grow sick, watching the
hanging meaty face of the butcher, the blunt red hands,
the way he stands before her with no face. Come off it,
Paddy, she says, I've been standing here all this time,
are you not going to serve me? The woman turns with a
skittish look and then frowns at the butcher who turns
his back and spins a bag of sausages. Sausages, he
says, everybody wants their sausages today. He fetches
some change and places it on the counter, watches the
woman exit the shop and then he leans into the glass
and pulls at an empty tray with a sigh and carries it
out back. From the street comes the running steps of a
child consonant on the blue tiles, the sound dying into
yellowed light, the smell of the shop entering Eilish's
body, the odour of fat and blood commingling with the
blood and fat of her own body so that she stands full
of the feeling of death, a lime delivery truck slowing
to the kerb outside.

She studies the lamb, bastes it with a ladle and closes
the oven door, hearing somebody step into the living
room, she looks past Molly and sees Samantha standing with her hands folded before her. Mam, I invited
Sam to dinner. Oh, she says, forcing herself to smile,
Molly meeting her with a defiant look. She hangs the
oven gloves and goes to the sink, hearing the girls on
the couch talking about who knows what, this feeling
of dread for her son brought by sight of the girl, this
fear that knows every part of her. She closes her eyes
and when she opens them she is met with the evening
light yellowed almost to an aroma, seeing a blackbird
plump under the tree, watching the bird absolute in
its moment, to live like that, to come and go under an
open sky. She removes the tray of roast potatoes from
the oven and calls them to dinner, Samantha standing
languid by the door still meek with her hands yet happy
to be among them. She studies the girl still sensing
her own scorn, this feeling she is an intruder, it is then
she seeks Samantha's eye and smiles, motions for her
to sit down, seeing how they are both flung, how they
are both caught in the same unknowing, knowing they
both seek the same thing of her son. Bailey is peering
through the oven door. Mam, he says, you left the meat
in too long, you're going to dry it out. She watches his
face seeking for Larry who has spoken through the boy's
mouth. The oven is off, she says, why don't you take it
out yourself? Bailey places the meat on the counter
then stands back and surveys it, pleased with himself.
Molly says, Mam, I thought you said you couldn't get a

roast in the butcher's. I had to walk to Kilmainham to get it, there's shortages now don't you know. The yellow light goldens and the dusk falls throughout dinner and she has forgotten to turn on the overhead light, watching them fall into shadow, watching Molly as though she were a different child, how her spirit has brightened beside Samantha. Bailey takes a drink of milk and asks if the country is now at war and Eilish studies the milk moustache and the question in his eyes. They are calling it an insurgency on the international news, Molly says, but if you want to give war its proper name, call it entertainment, we are now TV for the rest of the world. Samantha places her knife and fork down against her plate. My dad calls it terrorism, that's what he says, these people are nothing but terrorists, they are going to get what's coming to them, he shouts this at the TV. Eilish looks away and Molly is silent watching her plate. This lamb is lovely don't you think, Eilish says, such a pity Mark is not here. She moves the knife about the meat without cutting, stands up and turns on the light, Bailey watching as she sits down again. So is that where Mark's gone, he says, to join the rebel army? An obscure anguish passes across Samantha's face while Eilish pretends at the salt, Bailey wiping his mouth with his sleeve. I don't know what you're talking about, Eilish says, I told you, Mark has gone to school up North. So why can't I talk to him, do you think I'm stupid, why are you always talking shite? He stabs at the meat with his knife and then knifes it into his mouth. I heard the other day that three defectors were executed on the street, a gunshot to the back of the head, bang, bang, bang, he says, pulling a gun with his finger. Eilish puts down her knife and fork and pushes back her chair. I don't want to hear that kind of talk, she says, Bailey, you can fill the dishwasher, Samantha would you like to stay for dessert, we can watch a film in the living room. Molly and Samantha step inside and Eilish follows, Molly going upstairs to the bathroom, Samantha moving from photo to photo. I didn't mean to— you know, she says, her voice adrift, it's just that I don't like my father very much, I think he's a conspiracy nut. Eilish is searching for something that remains hidden in the girl's face, the orthodontic teeth, the warm yet inscrutable manner. And your mother? she says. I don't know, Samantha says, I guess she just goes along with him, tell me, how long have you been living in this house? Oh, let me think, we bought it just before Mark was born. Their eyes meet and of a sudden she knows. She says, you have heard from him, haven't you, it's written all over your face. In an instant she can see straight through to the girl's grief, seeing it tremble as though watching a naked flame, the girl folding her arms and looking to the door as Molly steps into the room. She looks to her mother then looks to Samantha, puts her hands on her hips. What's going on? she says. Eilish stepping into the kitchen. Who wants dessert? she calls, we have canned fruit and ice cream, Molly you can choose the film.

She is waiting for the tram on the canal embankment when the air begins to swell. They are in the sky night and day as though the city were beset by a plague of insects, military helicopters glutted and dark, she hardly notices them anymore. An elderly man standing beside her shields his eyes as he looks up. You never can tell whether they are coming or going, he says. She looks across to the waiting faces and sees only a sedate indifference, eyes glazed before phones, two women have resumed their chat while a young girl hopscotches the paving. Ben frowns against the sun and she lowers the hood and meets the elderly man's smile and drops her gaze to his worn black shoes seeing a lace undone, the tram belling as it approaches the junction. The man continues to watch the sky and says something in a mellow voice, and she says, I'm sorry, I didn't catch what you said, she is pointing to his shoe, your lace is undone. The man leans towards her and points to the sky. Five for silver, six for gold, seven for a secret never told. She turns from the man's strange smile and looks behind her onto the canal before embarking the tram, a swan gliding whitely through wrinkles of sun.

When Carole Sexton comes up the stairs of the old café, Eilish pretends she has not seen her. She studies the stained-glass window then feigns surprise. The sombre hand that pulls the chair, the pained smile that pulls the mouth is the painted smile of a clown.

Carole rests her bag on the floor and takes a cautious look around the mezzanine, the murmurings and absorbed chatter, the waitress drifting between tables, the smooth long white hair of an elderly woman who pecks with finger and thumb at a crumbled scone while reading a newspaper halved on her lap. I always liked this place, Carole says, though I've hardly come here since I was a student, it hasn't changed at all has it, one does feel preserved don't you think inside a time that does not exist anymore, those stained-glass windows, it is as though nothing else exists outside—— Eilish is studying a woman in a red gown in the decorative glass and has no idea who she is supposed to be, an icon of some false and mythical maiden singing out her freedom. She summons the waitress to the table asking Carole what she wants, thinking she should have chosen somewhere else to meet, St Stephen's Green under the cooling trees, Carole is twisting her wedding ring. What zone have they put you in, Eilish? We're in Zone D, it all seems arbitrary to me. I'm in Zone H, they're like postal districts, arrondissements, no doubt they will become fashionable after a while, I tried to cross the city on the motorway to visit you but they've put concrete girders across the lanes at M7, armoured vehicles, troops, they're clearly nervous now aren't they, the rebels are so much closer to the city, I was sent back, told to take the lane for the turn-off, he was very civil about it, I know someone who can get me one of those letters for essential workers, I'll be able to go where I like. Eilish is trying to see how Carole might have looked at twenty, long-necked and arch, a swan superior among the male students, seeing now the restless hand nicking at the thumb's cuticle, the rumpled blouse run with stains, the eyelids red and inflamed, the outstaring eyes wired to some engine of thought that keeps her awake all night. The woman has brought something with her, an undulant dread that passes from her body into the room. I managed to get a letter as primary carer for my father, Eilish says, but it took me a while, he's in decline and has no awareness of his illness, sometimes it seems that he suspects something is wrong but cannot see his own mind so he turns that suspicion outward, if he's not false then it is the world that is false, there is always someone else to blame. Carole looks up as the waitress steps towards them with a tray and places the drinks on the table then smiles and steps quickly away. You look as though you haven't slept in a week, Eilish says, are you sleeping at all? Sleep, Carole says, her voice distant, far off in time, she looks across the table at Eilish without seeing her. I don't sleep much at all, she says, I dream each night of a soundless sleep but that is impossible now, it took me some time before I understood that I was already asleep in a manner, you know, that I was sleeping all the time I thought I was awake, trying to see into the problem that stood before me like a great darkness, this silence consuming every moment of my life, I thought I'd go mad looking into it but then I awoke and began to see what they were doing to us, the brilliance of the act, they take something from you and replace it with silence and you're confronted by that silence every waking moment and cannot live, you cease to be yourself and become a thing before this silence, a thing waiting for the silence to end, a thing on your knees begging and whispering to it all night and day, a thing waiting for what was taken to be returned and only then can you resume your life, but the silence doesn't end, you see, they leave open the possibility that what you want will be returned some day and so you remain reduced, paralysed, dull as an old knife, and the silence does not end because the silence is the source of their power, that is its secret meaning. Eilish folds her arms and leans back in the chair, watching Carole reach into her bag, she brings a folder to the table. It is clear now they've been lying to us all along, Carole says, that the silence is permanent, that our husbands will not be coming back, they will not be returned because they cannot be returned, everybody knows this, even the dogs on the street know it, so I'm taking matters into my own hands—— She opens the folder onto a stack of photocopied paper, an image in colour of Jim Sexton with the words ABDUCTED AND MURDERED BY THE STATE, the small print beneath the photo detailing the facts of the case. Eilish has quickly pushed her chair back and closes the folder against Carole's hand. Are you out of your mind? she says. Without thought she is looking about the room, the waitress leaning over a table placing cups and saucers onto a tray, the elderly lady folding the newspaper. You've got to stop this, Carole, you're going to get yourself arrested, you're going to get me arrested too, I've got the children to think about—— Carole brings a cup to her lips without lowering her eyes, a look of secret knowing contrary to the facts. I know that you know, Eilish, there's no point trying to hide it anymore, we all know it, they're not in the Curragh, that's what the rebels said when they took hold of it, they were never there to begin with, so where do you think they are? Eilish has nowhere to look and so she closes her eyes, her heart beating strangely. It is not what she sees in the dark of her eyes but what she feels, the shadow of something colossal about to break over her, the terror of being forced down into the darkness, down and down, she opens her eyes looking upward for air, looks towards the stairs then turns towards Carole invoking her anger. It is then the day expresses in sudden brightness through the decorative glass, falling upon Carole in flowered colour as though she were lit from within, her face radiant with the memory of loving her husband. Look, Carole, I've heard enough of this, I won't listen to rumours you can pick up off the street, they do more harm than good, nobody knows anything, there is a total absence of facts, you've ceased to believe, that's all, but you must continue to believe, there cannot be despair where there is doubt and where there is doubt there is hope. Her hand is searching for the sleeve of her coat but the sleeve is turned inside out and she remembers Larry by the door, she looks again towards the stairs feeling her panic, grabs at the coat and opens her purse, places a note on the table. Here, she says, that should cover us both. A nail-bitten hand reaches across the table and pushes the note away. So, Carole says, how is he getting on, your eldest son, is he doing you proud? Eilish stops zipping her coat, sees in Carole's face an indefinable smile. What did you say to my son? she says, what did you tell him? The eyes agleam with hidden knowledge, the long hand coming up into the air to bat dreamily at Eilish as though to dismiss her. Your son is going to do you proud, she says, the rebels won't be stopped, they'll drive the murderers out and put a stop to this terror, the blood of this country will be cleansed once and for all, you mark my words, it's going to be a beautiful war.

# 6

She places a refuse bag on the lid of the wheelie bin and looks up and down the street, the black bins have not been collected for three weeks, a gull is feeding from a black bag left against a wall, its side torn open by an animal, perhaps a fox during the night, its contents spilling onto the path. She shoos at the bird and claps her hands while the gull studies her with a stony look then opens its bill to reveal a dark swallowing gullet. She will go upstairs and run a bath for Molly, she heats a cup of milk and searches the press for cocoa while listening to the foreign news, the rebels have pushed the Defence Forces into retreat, the fighting will soon reach Dublin. She stands by the bedroom door watching Molly propped on a pillow with her knees to her chest reading her phone. It is as though she has become separate from them all, foreign almost, like some other child in some other house, the girl hardly saying a word anymore. Eilish places the cocoa on the dresser and picks up an old teddy, seeing it blinded, its eyes replaced by buttons, she does not remember sewing them on. Drink up your cocoa while it's still

hot, she says, I'll run a bath for you now. Molly lifts
her face from the screen and meets her mother with
a look of clear water. Mam, she says, I want you to
listen, we need to go, we need to leave before it's too
late. Eilish is looking down at her right foot freeing
itself from the shoe, the weight of the body borne by
the legs, the weight of the world borne by the ball of
each foot, the absorbent metatarsal bones, the soft toes
beaten all day long, she wants for Larry to rub her feet
and then she'll take a bath. And what about your grandfather? she says, who is going to mind him, he's getting worse all the time, and what will your father do
if he's released without warning, you haven't thought
any of this through. Molly reaches for the cocoa, wraps
two hands around the mug then takes a sip closing
her eyes. People from school have left for Australia,
Canada, others have gone to England—— And where
would we go, we have nowhere to go, it costs a lot of
money to go someplace else. We could go to Áine and
wait for Dad to be released, you could apply for an academic visa. Molly, the government will not give Ben a
passport, they wouldn't renew Mark's passport either,
you know all this. She finds herself in the bathroom fit-
ting the plug into the bath, she runs the hot water and
tests it with her finger and enjoys the stinging rebuke,
returns to Molly with folded arms, begins to smooth
the duvet. Look, she says, I haven't been an academic
for a long time, and anyhow, this is not going to go
on much longer, we don't live in some dark corner of
the world, you know, the international community will

broker a solution, there are talks going on right now in London, this is how it goes, first there are stern warnings and then there are sanctions and when the sanctions don't bite they bring everyone around the table, they'll broker a ceasefire any day now. Something in Molly's look enters freely into her mother's thoughts, she is roaming around, sifting truth from falsehood, Eilish is forced to look away. Mam, what's going to happen to Mark? Eilish is turning for the door and stops. Mark? she says, I don't know, how am I supposed to answer that, he'll be fine, I just know it, I have to take your grandfather for his scan tomorrow, it's going to take forever to get him out of the house, you know what he's like. Mam, I tried his phone, Mark's phone, the number's been disconnected. Something has rolled across Eilish's mouth, she is moving through the room bending to collect the clothes on the floor, she is standing in the bathroom staring at the steaming water, what rises and dissipates, what comes into expression moment by moment yet cannot be known, this feeling always of possibility giving rise to hope. She wants to go into the bedroom and take Molly's hands and say everything is going to be fine, she remains before the wicker basket and drops the clothes and feels herself falling from her arms, this feeling they are all falling towards something that cannot be defined by anything she has known in her life.

She knows the room beyond the door, the efficient, bird-like movements of the consultant, her father seated beside her smoothing the creases from his trousers. She wants to run her knuckles down the white-stubbled cheek, to take his hand but doesn't, twice now he has said he would rather be at home. She reads the ticker on the state TV news, the headlines speak of ordinary things, a world that belongs to the past or to a present that lies in strange parallel, in one world there are announcements about new appointments and budget cuts, in another there are rumours of a mass killing by government forces, civilians rounded up and executed, the receptionist behind the glass sips at tea from a takeaway cup. Dad, she says, I want you to come and live with us until this is all over, I don't want you to be on your own, it will be good for the children too. I'm perfectly happy where I am, he says, I've been living on my own since your mother died, next thing I know you and your sister will have sold the house from under me, I know what the two of you are like. Dad, what are you talking about, who's going to buy a house right now with so many people leaving the country, you can take the dog with you, we can put a kennel out back—— I just told you, I'm managing fine as it is, I have supplies, if I need anything I'll drop into Mrs Doyle's on my walk with Spencer. Dad, Mrs Doyle's shop has been gone for at least twenty years. She stands from the chair looking down at him. I need a coffee, she says, I saw a drinks machine in a corridor back there, do you want some tea? What time do we get back? he says, I told you I don't like the bus. She is watching the painting behind Simon's head as he scowls at her, the sudden rupture of peonies into flower. Dad, I asked if you want some tea. Simon shakes his head as she squats down to the sleeping child in the buggy, pressing the back of her hand to the puffed red cheek, the jaw tucked under the upper lip. I'll be gone just a moment, she says, take his hand if he wakes up. The red door swishes closed behind her as she walks the long corridor, the drinks machine is not where she thought it was, she stops by the security desk and asks for directions, she had it all wrong, the machine is close to the hospital entrance. She is standing before the machine searching for coins when her phone begins to ring. Yes, she says, this is Mrs Stack, the female voice introducing herself as somebody from Bailey's school, she doesn't catch the name, a secretary no doubt. Mrs Stack, your son has been absent from school on an irregular basis these past two weeks, we put a letter in his bag for you to sign and he gave it back with what looks like a forged signature. A man standing behind her begins to huff, she turns and mouths an apology and steps away from the machine. I'm sorry, she says, this is news to me, I had been dropping him off to school but of late he's been taking the bus, I will find out tonight what is going on. Mrs Stack, there was an incident at the school last week involving your son. An incident, what incident, please, call me Eilish. It occurred in the classroom, your son was in clear violation of the school's speech and harassment policy. I'm so sorry to hear this, what did he do? Your son was engaged in inappropriately directed laughter and—— I'm sorry, I don't understand what that means. It means, Mrs Stack, that Bailey was mocking the teacher, disrupting the class, this kind of behaviour goes against the school charter. Yes, of course, I understand, though I find that strange, Bailey is very fond of Mrs Egan, she doesn't strike me as someone to put up with any nonsense. Mrs Egan is no longer teaching at the school, Mrs Stack, she was placed on extended leave in March, I am handling all principal duties for now. Eilish is silent a moment watching Mrs Egan being escorted from the classroom, trying to form a picture of the speaker on the phone, sensing some vague outline of the woman, a smallish mouth and pinching face. I'm sorry, she says, I didn't know about Mrs Egan, Bailey didn't say, I didn't catch your name by the way when you introduced yourself at the start of the call. My name, Mrs Stack, is Ruth Nolan—— Please, call me Eilish, so who is Bailey's teacher now? I am teaching Mrs Egan's class. Oh, so you are the teacher he laughed at. Unfortunately, yes. So why did he laugh at you? I want you to understand, Mrs Stack, that his laughter was inappropriate and goes—— Yes, yes, I know, but I have to ask, were you a teacher for long, Miss Nolan, before the party put you in charge of the school? I don't see what this has to do with anything. If my son was laughing aloud then I'm sure he saw something to laugh at, as though that were a crime, for goodness' sake, I'll speak to him when he gets home about the truancy, but for now, if you don't mind, I have to go.

Her hand is shaking as she coins the drinks machine, she folds her arms and watches the machine growl coffee, she pays again and selects tea for her father, he said he didn't want tea, he'll have some tea anyhow. Seeing her son's face before her as she walks the corridors craving a cigarette, she has taken a wrong turn, the sign for the memory clinic is the other way. When she shoulders through the red door she sees Ben alone in the buggy, Simon is not in the waiting room. She knocks on the reception glass and asks if her father has been called inside, perhaps he went to the toilet? she says. She places the hot drinks down on the seat and unlocks the buggy and wheels it backwards through the doors. She leans into the men's room and calls inside, speaks with a security guard by the hospital entrance, the man speaks into his radio, a second security guard arrives and asks for a description of her father, as she speaks she is making excuses for Simon, look, he probably just went for a wander and got lost, he might find his way back. When she finds him he is in the canteen seated under the television before a sandwich. He picks up a stainless steel jug and pours milk. She glides into the seat across from him and places her hands on the table and looks into his eyes while he leans back and puzzles at her. So you decided to have some lunch, she says. I'm having a quick bite to eat while your mother sees the consultant, he says, you should get yourself a sandwich while we're waiting. He is smiling now and for an instant she is a child, watching him eat, the pink tongue lolloping an escaping prawn, a smear of mayonnaise on the corner of his mouth. He is looking for a paper napkin when she hands him one and he wipes his mouth then reaches out and touches her cheek. Don't worry, he says, everything is going to be alright. She watches his face trying to return the smile, she watches his hands, like sand the wrinkled skin as though the tide had gone out past his knuckles.

Another decree is announced on the news, the listening to or reading of any foreign media has been prohibited, news channels from abroad will be blocked and an internet blackout starts from today. That's ridiculous, Bailey says, how can they just turn it off like that? I don't know, love, they can do what they like, they want to control the flow of information, they don't want us to know what's going on. So what am I going to do now, how am I supposed to live? You need to get ready for school, I'm coming with you on the bus, your jumper is on the chair, the internet might not come back for a while. Bailey is leaning into the fridge. There's no milk for my cereal, he says, is there a ban on that as well? There was plenty of milk there yesterday, you're the one drinking it all the time. In the evening she takes the stepladder and stares blind into the attic, pulls herself up, the narrow beam of her torch searching for an overhead light, there appears to be none. She will have to have a word with Larry, chief bearer of items up and down, the attic is your concern, you can't expect me to climb up here with only a torch when you're not around. The torchlight shows where Mark shoved the Christmas tree and the boxed decorations. What a mess he has made amidst the refuse bags full of old clothes, the children's toys in boxes, suitcases full of oddments and clutter she was afraid to throw out. She pulls at an old suitcase and unfastens the clip realising she does not want to see in, looking in she meets what she does not want to see and shuts it, stands motionless amidst the hanging smell of dust. This feeling the attic does not belong to the house but exists in its own right, an anteroom of shadow and disorder as though the place were the house of memory itself, seeing before her the remnants of their younger selves, the self folded, packed into boxes, bagged and discarded, lost in the disarray of vanished and forgotten other selves, the dust laying itself down upon the years of their lives, the years of their lives slowly turning to dust, what will remain and how little can be known about who we were, in the closing of an eye we will all be gone. It is then she is met with the feeling that Larry is beside her, she turns to look and meets her grief, she is balling her hands and shaking them, telling herself over and over that what Carole said cannot be true, nobody knows what is true anymore, telling herself that what she feels isn't grief, it has to be something else, grievance is grief dressed in the clothes of hope. She must escape down the hatch into daylight, she opens the suitcase taking out what she saw, a leather bracelet belonging to Larry. She is standing very still sensing the bracelet with her

fingertips, seeking who they both were, Molly is calling
out from the base of the stepladder and she remembers
what it was she came up for, the portable radio is in an
old plastic bag, she hands it down through the hatch.
She takes the radio to the kitchen table and wipes it
with a cloth, Molly watching behind her. What are you
doing with that thing? she says. I want to hear the
news, the real news on the foreign service, not the lies
we are told here. No, not the radio, that thing on your
wrist. Oh, it used to belong to your father. She touches
the bracelet and pulls the aerial to its length and turns
on the radio, she cannot believe the batteries still work,
the room filling with warm static as she dials through
the long-wave frequency, a strange electric pinging
descends into a swish that belongs to her childhood, to
distant cities sounding at night in alien tongue. Molly
fingers the chrome edge of the radio. I suppose we're
going back in time now, she says, soon we'll all be
riding bicycles, washing our clothes by hand and speaking of having tea when we mean dinner, we'll no longer
know who we are, I can't conceive of myself as a person
without the internet. There is light in Molly's eyes, a
glimmer of happiness hiding in her heart. Eilish slides
the leather bracelet from her wrist and holds it out to
her. He'll want you to have it, she says, just don't tell
your brother, where is he anyhow, it's almost curfew,
he knows full well he's been grounded. I don't know, he
went out soon as you went to the attic, I told him not to
go but he warned me not to tell you. She finds herself
watching by the front window, she tries to call Bailey

again but he doesn't answer. At seven o'clock she walks
out onto the street watching a white van go past, she
waits a moment watching the road and then sleeves her
coat and calls out to Molly. I'll be back in a few minutes,
ring me if he gets back while I'm out. She walks with
her hands tensed listening for any approaching cars,
the roads silenced as though by a switch, whispering to
herself the words she will say in case she is stopped by
a patrol, I'm sorry but my youngster didn't come home
on time, he's only twelve, I'm just taking a look around
the block. Bailey is not in any of the usual places, the
wall by the corner, the playground near the school, she
is returning home when she sees him kicking a ball off
the kerb, he is chatting with some kid she doesn't know,
he waves goodbye then dribbles the ball and lifts his
eyes absently before her. She cannot speak her fear, this
fear that blackens like ink the blood and misshapes the
mouth into rage, seeing the soured look before her. So
what if I'm late? he says, I'm home now, aren't I, don't
be an old fussbag.


The queue outside the supermarket carries around
the corner to the bottle bank, two soldiers are waving
people through in groups of three or four at a time, the
queue shuffles forward a little then stops. She parks
the buggy and frees a trolley, tries to place Ben in the
seat but he bucks and kicks his legs as though she has
just pulled him feral out of a hole, he screams so much

she lets him stand inside. A woman pulling on a trolley beside her nods at Ben with a smile. He'd buy and sell you in an instant, she says. Eilish returns the smile without looking at her face, scowls at her son bouncing up and down in delight. She should have made a shopping list, people are panic buying but she cannot think what she needs most, everybody wants the same things, bread and pasta and rice, all the bottled water is gone. She stops before the tinned food section and sees the stocks are low, she is speaking to Ben who is seated now, playing with the contents of the trolley. We need powdered milk for you and condensed milk for the rest of us in case the ordinary milk runs out, you just don't know what's going to happen, it probably doesn't matter anyhow, you stock up on one thing and it's always another that runs out. She is standing at the deli counter when she sees a man in shirt and tie moving sidewards through an aisle nosing a clipboard. Excuse me, she says, are you the manager? She follows him to an office door painted the same off-white as the wall, she wouldn't even have noticed the door but for the fact he has opened it and gone through. He emerges again fixing a sheet of paper to the clipboard. So, he says, you want to apply for a position at the store, did you bring a CV? No, she says, I just saw the ad on the noticeboard outside, part-time work would suit me right now, though I haven't worked in food retail before. OK, the man says, let me take your details and we can get back to you, soon as I can get this damned pen to work, what did you work in yourself? She waits a moment while a discouraged voice calls out over the intercom for a teller, the music resumes that is not music at all but a pleasant, smearing noise. I have been in full-time employment for almost twenty years, she says, I was in senior management in biotech until now, I am a molecular biologist by training, I have a PhD in cellular and molecular biology, but there's not much work the way things are right now. The man has stopped scoring the pen and meets her with a look that makes her feel like a fool, she thinks she is overdressed. The manager turns his eyes towards Ben who is revving his knees up and down in the trolley, he rubs at a half-grown moustache and tries to smile but gives up. Well, OK, he says, let me just write your name and number down, it's only part-time work stacking shelves in the evenings, we've had a few others applying for the job, quite a few actually, but we'll get back to you anyhow. She will not remember this face, already it belongs to the plain and sorry faces that have looked away, seeing how this face has already been told, seeing how all faces have been told, this face that speaks of all creation, the terrible energy of the stars, the universe smashed to dust and made over again and again in deranged creation. She lifts her son and stuffs him into the trolley seat and does not give a damn for his shrieks as she fills the trolley then joins the long queue by the checkout, staring at the contents of the trolley, the two-month supply of tinned food, baby milk, toilet roll and detergent, it is then she is struck with the feeling that what is occurring is implausible, she wants to laugh out loud, watching the moist, hairy neck of the fattish man before her nudging a trolley filled with beer and toilet roll, watching the people in line around her and despising what she sees, the common run of mankind, what are they all but animals in docile servitude to the needs of the body, tribe and state. When she steps outside past the soldiers Ben is licking a stick of cheese, she is afraid to take him out of the seat and put him in the car, she cannot remember where she parked the Touran. She walks the length of the car park then circles back and sees the buggy in the trolley bay. You stupid fool, she says, what were you thinking, how are you going to get all this home? For a moment she stands watching the shopping and then she folds the buggy and puts it in the trolley and begins with it towards the exit, stepping out onto the path along the main road, recalling what she forgot to buy, washing up liquid, treats for the kids, the crackers Simon likes, the trolley wheels catch on the pavement and then one of the wheels begins to drag. She kicks at the wheel and looks at her watch then begins to walk home, the shadows beginning to define the edges of the afternoon.

She wakes to the sound of war come like some visiting god, a hammering fury that brings out a hammering in her heart, she cannot find the light switch, her hand padding blindly until she finds it fallen behind the bedside table. There is nothing to see outside but a lone gull pearled in blue light on a chimney top, a gauze of fine rain. Every dog in the area is baying at the noise as she pulls the window closed, looking down at Ben, the puckish smile on the sleeping face, the small fists surrendered above his head. She cannot find her dressing gown and unhooks Larry's from behind the door, her hand is caught in the sleeve and cannot push through. She moves through the house trying to see ahead, the world branching into impossibility, the dread thing visible in the growing light from the kitchen window, two columns of dark smoke adrift over the south suburbs, a helicopter gunship nearby, she cannot guess how far, perhaps three or four kilometres away. She turns on the radio awaiting the news and steps outside to the washing line, watching the trees in roseate light and wondering what it is they can know, perhaps it is true what they say, how the trees sense the air and speak their terror through the ground, letting other trees know that peril has come, what sounds in the sky like some all-consuming fire chewing wood in its mouth. She drops the clothes in the basket and looks down at her hands and does not know why she remains so calm, another door has been opened, she can see this now, it is as though she were looking out upon something she has been waiting for all her life, an atavism awakened in the blood, thinking, how many people across how many lifetimes have watched upon war bearing down on their home, watching and waiting for fate to come, entering into silent negotiation, whispering and then pleading, the mind anticipating all outcomes but for the spectre that cannot be directly looked at. The electricity stutters and the lights grow dim and a fluttering sickness passes through her belly. The worm is turning, Bailey says, and she watches his face thinking he is too tall for his age, in the past few weeks he has bolted and stands taller than Molly, a shadow growing over his lip. Molly's eyes are fixed upon her, they are waiting for her to declare something, she does not know what to say. We need to get ready in case the power goes, she says, you guys need to eat breakfast and get ready for school. School? Bailey says, I'll eat breakfast but I'm not going to school, there's no way the schools will be open anyhow with all this going on, I just don't see the point. She places a box of breakfast cereal on the table and turns on the state television news. The government has issued a series of new decrees, all schools and third-level institutions have been closed with immediate effect, citizens have been ordered to stay at home except to buy food or medicine or to provide care to the elderly or sick. When she turns around, Bailey is standing behind with his hands on his hips. See, he says, I told you the schools would be closed. Wipe that smile off your face, she says, I want you to go around the house and find whatever batteries we have, gather together the candles. She has errands to run, she needs cigarettes and alcohol, she must get her boots reheeled, post some medical forms for her father. She rings Simon and gets through on the fourth call. The dog has gone berserk, he says, he thinks it's Halloween outside. Dad, she says, did

you see the news, is everything alright? He is shouting again at the dog. Sorry, he says, I didn't hear what
you said. Never mind, she says, I can see dark smoke
from here. There's somebody knocking on the door, he
says, hold on a moment—— She hears the clink of the
phone put to rest on the console, the opening and closing of the front door, Simon bellowing again at the dog.
There's nobody there, he says, bloody messers outside.
Dad, I want you to stay inside, please don't take Spencer
out for a walk, do you hear? The line goes silent and
she can hear the dog growling as though sanctioned
to speak for her father. I need topsoil for the garden,
Simon says, can we go later this week in the car? When
she hangs up the phone she does not move but stares
at the base of her thumb where she has scored a series
of erratic moons with her thumbnail. She goes upstairs
and changes into jeans and a black sweater and brings
the baby down and slides him into the highchair. I'm
going to nip out to the corner shop as soon as Ben is
fed, she says, I need money from the ATM, we need
some other bits and pieces. Molly's face aghast before
her. What's wrong? Eilish says. Leave Ben here, she
says, you don't need to bring him. I told you, love, it's
safe for now outside, anyhow, I'm only going around
the corner. She watches Bailey go to the fridge and take
a look inside. Make sure you get some more milk, he
says, we're almost out again.

She walks listening to the sky, the unknown muddled with the familiar, the periodic release of gunfire and a percussive booming that leaves behind a strange and shattered silence. Only an odd car on the road or passer-by, the brake cable on the buggy is causing the wheel to click and she wonders if she'll be able to get it fixed, she has not noticed the rain has ceased until she is standing before the ATM and lowers her umbrella, the machine is not even out of order but out of power, the screen cracked as though struck by a brick. Across the street a man is shading his eyes as he watches the sky, three helicopter gunships moving southwards like a slowly fragmenting arrowhead. The saddler's is closed and the shutters are down on the fruit and veg shop where somebody has scrawled in blue paint HiSTOrY iS THE LAW OF FOrCE, a fist drawn beside it. She follows the road seeking another ATM, recalling something her sister said, the self-satisfied voice on the phone, history is a silent record of people who did not know when to leave, the statement is obviously false, she is telling this to Larry, seeing him seated across the kitchen table trying to hide his I'm-not-listening face while playing with his phone. History is a silent record of people who could not leave, it is a record of those who did not have a choice, you cannot leave when you have nowhere to go and have not the means to go there, you cannot leave when your children cannot get a passport, cannot go when your feet are rooted in the earth and to leave means tearing off your feet. The ATM at the bottom of the road shows a letterbox of broken light on the screen, a sign on the window of the corner shop in sharpie pen says, No Dairy, No Bread, a sad face drawn beside it. The shelves inside are half empty, she grabs some bruised bananas, a roll of bin bags and batteries, selects two chocolate bars and points to the cigarettes, regards the items before her with a frown when the teller tots them up. I'm sorry, she says, how much did you say the cigarettes are? The teller opens his hands and takes a sleepy look towards the door. What am I to do? he says, everything is at a premium, see how you get on someplace else. Her rage has clouded all before her, she places the bin bags down on yesterday's newspaper and cannot choose between the batteries and the chocolate, she puts the batteries to the side and says how much for the chocolate and the bin bags without the cigarettes? She slides the change from her hand and the words fly from her mouth and carry her to the door. You're going to look like a right dickhead when this is all over, everyone will know what you are.

Ben is whining to be free of the buggy when she turns onto St Laurence Street and sees a heavy military truck blocking the road, government soldiers in full combat gear, other soldiers with open jackets and black T-shirts piling bags of cement into a checkpoint fifty metres or so from the house. A soldier standing at the corner bends to his knee and readies his weapon while another begins towards her with a flat, gloved hand asking her to stop. She has ceased to breathe as though the gloved hand were upon her throat, she wants to make a signal to say that nothing is untoward but is afraid to move her hands. I'm sorry, she says, I live on this street, I'm trying to get home. The soldier circles his hand in the air as though instructing a car to turn around. This street is closed for now, he says, no pedestrians are allowed. For an instant she is met with some sense of expansion as she watches the soldier's face, the angry brow aslant over the green eyes, the weaponed body that speaks of absolute force, and yet what she sees in the soldier's eyes is a skite of uncertainty, she is speaking with a boy no older than her son. Look, she says, I live at number 47, I have a child to take home for his lunch. She finds herself pushing the buggy towards the soldier and meets a look of panic in his eyes, he speaks quickly into an earpiece radio while a second soldier calls for her to stop, an officer in a dark beret stepping crisply towards them. I'm sorry, she says, I just want to go home, my house is there. The officer does not follow her pointing finger but asks for her ID. Let me just get it from my purse, she says, the purse is in my bag, I have to take it down off my shoulder. Two civilians are helping to build the checkpoint and she knows one of them, an odd-jobs man from the flats nearby, an ex-junkie with hardly a tooth in his mouth, she cannot recall his name, last year Larry gave him twenty quid to clean the gutters. She is told to place the bag on the street and hold it open, her hands shaking as she unzips her purse and takes out her ID, the officer's eyes tracking from her face to the child's. This is a war zone, he says, my men are under strict orders to shoot, stay at home until further notice. Yes, of course, she says, bowing her head, she begins to walk quickly away and sees a cement bag fall off the truck, it splits on the ground and the breeze takes hold of the dust and disperses it around the soldiers as though a dervish had come among them from some foreign war with its eyes closed and its arms held out.

War shapes itself around them, gunfire that sounds like pneumatic drilling, shelling that drums the earth and sends shudders into the house, the windows and the wooden floors rattling while Bailey watches the TV with the volume turned up, the radio beside her reporting the movements of the rebels, the areas within the south city under siege. It's such a beautiful day outside, she says, how many days a year do we get like this? There should be ice-cream lemonade in the garden, Ben plashing in the paddling pool, Molly and Bailey wrestling over the hammock. Instead she is looking out upon a broken colonnade of oil-dark smoke rising from multiple sites, the June heat trapped in the house as she keeps the windows and French doors closed, she will only open the windows at night. She tries again to ring her father but the networks are down and his landline makes a disconnected tone, counting the days since they last spoke, seeing him taking the dog for a

walk into who knows what, she is standing at the door
to Molly's room. The girl will not get out of bed, she
picks at her food and will not look at her mother. Come
on, Eilish says, please, I need you to snap out of this,
the fighting will soon come to a stop. She pulls the girl
into a slack embrace then lets her go, watching her as
though her mind can be seen, this mind that has drifted
slowly into absence. The electricity begins to stutter and
then an outage dissolves in an instant the constant of
electrical hum to an elemental quiet, the piercing and
steady irruptions of war entering freely into thought.
She tells herself it is the sound of pebbles rolling on
a tin roof, the sound of a nail being hammered home,
the exhaust of an old car giving out, the house alarms
in the area ringing until one by one they fall silent.
Bailey goes upstairs and sits with Molly on her bed
watching a movie on a laptop with a pair of earbuds
shared between them while Eilish tries to read a novel
downstairs, a sudden noise outside sends her upstairs
holding the book in her hand, she is standing in the
bathroom and flushes the toilet without having used
it, she cannot remember where she placed the book. In
the afternoon she sits by the bedroom window waiting
for a detailed report on the BBC while Ben naps in the
cot. The news comes on and she turns it off shaking
with rage, thinking, this is not the news, this is not the
news at all, the news is the civilian watching the soldier
outside her home as he lolls on a sandbag playing with
his phone, the news is the assault rifle resting against
the sandbag, it is the soldier's laughing mouth, it is the

fast-food wrappers and coffee cups strewn about the asphalt, it is the retired couple from up the street who have decided that they want to go, the news is their quarrel in the driveway, it is the woman flapping her hands about what cannot be taken in the car, it is the husband who shuts his face to his wife, it is the black bag the woman holds in her arms like a child, it is what is inside the bag, the news is the entire contents of the car, it is the boot the man has to sit closed, the news is the driveway gated for the last time, the house dark at night, it is the traffic light stuck on red for a week before it goes dark, it is the car that will not be allowed through the checkpoint, the news is the shrinking air on the streets, it is the shuttered shops, the windows ply-boarded, it is the hoarse dogs woofing throughout the night, it is the eldest son who does not call anymore because it's too risky to call and nobody knows if he is dead or alive. She watches an army officer riding down the street on a nodding black horse, the build of the thing, she thinks it is a Friesian sport horse, the rider's hands quiet on his lap, his dark boots gleaming to the knee. How he moves within some serene and regal bearing as though he were but an emissary of the law of force, the soldiers at the checkpoint come to standing and the officer does not dismount but waves his crop as though casting incantations into the air. She watches the horse rotate an ear without turning its head, it is listening it seems to something beyond the uneasy stillness, the whisperings of a tall conifer, the radiation from the sun upon its leaves, it can hear the death that awaits with open arms all over the city, the death that waits to be let drop from the sky. Of a sudden the house begins to hum and the bedside light has come on, Bailey shouting with joy downstairs, the TV is back on in the living room. For a moment she is met with the feeling there is no war but some military exercise outside on the street, the horse committing a smooth turnabout, the rider dressed not for combat but for an equestrian outing it seems, the brown leather band across the chest and the emerald green tie, the hooves clicking a military tattoo on the asphalt. A smiling buddha in a T-shirt leads a cooking demonstration downstairs on the TV, the microwave clock blinking neon-green, the fridge humming a low and steady tune of the always-was. So much to do now that the electricity has returned, she stuffs laundry into the washing machine and selects a short cycle and recharges the laptops and phones and reheats rice and a casserole, trying again to reach her father, seeing him eating his dinner cold, reading by candlelight, shouting at the dog. She calls Bailey to the table and spoons casserole into a bowl and brings it upstairs to Molly who won't come down, the electricity stutters and is gone again as she reaches the landing. She smacks the bowl down on the bedside table and stares at the face that will not look at her, pulls a headphone bud free, pulls her into sitting by the arm and puts the bowl in her lap. Look, she says, I've brought you your dinner, I'm not even going to ask that you eat with us downstairs but please make some attempt at eating this while it's still hot. She goes downstairs and Bailey watches her across the table while Ben smacks the food tray and lets fly the spoon. What are we going to do about Molly? Bailey says. I don't know, she says, I just don't know, can you get me a fresh spoon from the drawer, look, your sister is unwell, I think she's depressed, it is very hard to get an appointment right now. Bailey makes a thinking pout with his mouth. She needs to spit it out, he says, that's what she's got to do and then everything will be alright. Spit what out, can you get me a spoon? The worm, he says, I'm talking about the worm.


This airless heat and how it gums the sleeping mind and sticks to dream, she is outside in her nightdress and bare feet, she must tell the soldiers about her son, standing before the horse agleam in the true and deepest colours of night, the animal's heat passing into her hand, knowing this smell not of the horse but of the man, the voice that belongs to the detective inspector, John Stamp, the eyes watching down at her. You have come to me for the truth, he says, let me show you something of that. He holds in his hand a mirror and what she sees is a face that is not her own but that of some old hag, John Stamp withdrawing the glass and when she looks again there is nothing in his hand. It is impossible to see the true self, he says, you can only see what you are not or what you want to be—— The horse gently drifting backwards, it lifts its head and snickers at some knocking noise behind it. The real is always before you but you do not see, perhaps this is not even a choice, to see the real would be to deepen reality to a depth in which you could not live, if only you could wake up—— The horse is bowing, moving away, I forgot to dress, she says, looking down at her feet, I'm cold, I need to go into the house—— Bailey is standing at her bedroom door yelling for her to wake. I am awake, she shouts, hearing a whistle and then a violent vibration as though something had burrowed by explosion into the earth. It's getting closer all the time, Bailey says. She is afraid to look out the window, tells Bailey to stand by the door. The street in early light, the checkpoint empty but for a youth who stands alone at the junction and looks as though he is awaiting command to place his weapon down and go to school, a Toyota Land Cruiser slowing past. It stops at the checkpoint and two heavily armed soldiers step out leaving the doors open and call towards the youth. Bailey is sitting on his father's side of the bed rooting through the bedside drawer. What's this? he says, holding up something she can't see. Put that back will you, she says, come on, we need to get this mattress downstairs. She strips the duvet and sheet off the bed and is talking quietly with Larry as they bend the mattress out the door onto the stair-case, the trouble we had getting this into the room and the fun we had after, she is pulling the mattress down the stairs but Bailey cannot bend it around the newel, he has just got it through when the mattress asserts itself straight again and smacks a picture off the wall,

the photo tumbling past her until it strikes the hallway
floor. She is bracing against the weight of the mattress,
Bailey is pushing too hard or not holding on at all, slow
down will you, she says, you are going to knock me
down the stairs. I'm not doing anything, he says, the
mattress has a mind of its own. They walk the mattress into the living room and place it against the front
window, a pall of dark smoke winding slowly over the
rooftops, the soldiers and the Land Cruiser are gone.
What do you think? Bailey says. I think it best if we live
downstairs for a while, she says, the fighting might not
come too close but it's probably best if we sleep down
here. Her phone is ringing upstairs and she runs to get
it. Dad, she says, I'm so glad you got through, I've been
trying to ring you for ages, we've had no electricity for
days, is everything alright where you are? I was just in
the garden, he says, there's an infestation of English ivy
coming from next door, he's doing it on purpose, you
know, I cut it back last year but it's coming in over the
walls and the shed roof, it's going to strangle everything
I planted, I've called over and knocked on his door but
he won't answer, tell me, I can't find the long-handed
shears, I suppose you took them without asking. She is
holding her breath trying to summon the face she has
known all her life, seeing instead the broken likeness
of an image on water. Dad, she says, I've been so worried, I don't know when I can get across to you. Don't
worry about me, he says, I'll be fine. Oh, she says, I've
just remembered, I think I have them in the shed. Have
what in the shed? The shears, you gave them to me

when I was cutting back the fuchsia, look, are you sure everything is alright, do you have enough food, is there anything you need right now? When she hangs up the phone, she is standing before the photo lying face down on the floor. She picks it up and sees Mark as a child with his thumbs up emerging from the mouth of a waterslide, the wooden frame loose though the glass is still intact, she cannot recall where the photo is from. Saint-Jean-de-Monts, she says aloud to herself. What was that? Bailey says from the living room. What was what? she says, looking at his face and seeing Mark, there is a likeness there after all.

A quick cold shower, the last perhaps for days, she calls for Molly to go downstairs then locks the door, stands before the water with gritted teeth then steps in. Her hair is coming loose in her hands as though she were dreaming it. It washes by her feet like some dark aquatic plant and when she steps out of the shower she fishes it out and flushes it down the toilet. The sudden exchange of heavy weapons fire and she goes to the window and tries to see out, it is impossible to know how far away it is, the warm blue sky over the trees, how many days have passed since Molly last tied a ribbon, it must be two weeks. She finds herself standing before Molly with her hands on her hips. I asked you please to go downstairs, she says. Molly watching her strange-faced and then she begins to shout, we're

going to die, we're going to die, Eilish yanking her by
the hand, she pulls her out of bed, telling her enough
is enough, walks her into the bathroom and runs the
shower and undresses her, puts her under the water
without regard for the cold, watching the slight, white
body make no resistance but for the lifting of an arm to
cover her breasts. You are not going to die, Eilish says, I
just want you to go downstairs, the fighting is not going
to come near the house. Eilish steps into the shower
and begins to wash Molly in hurried strokes with the
flannel, she bends to her knees to wash the girl's feet,
Molly is shivering, Eilish still wearing her clothes, her
knees are sodden, the arms of her blouse wet through.
You have to snap out of this, she says, who is it you
want your father to meet when he comes through the
door, the daughter he left behind or a ghost? She looks
up towards Molly and sees a smiling, vacant look. But
Daddy isn't coming back, Molly says, he isn't coming
back because he's dead, didn't you know, did they not
tell you he is dead, I wonder why. The hand stopped
upon the body, the breath caught in the throat, the
flannel falls from her hand as she hinges slowly to
standing. She has taken Molly's chin between finger
and thumb and lifts her face the better to see into the
eyes that swivel in refusal to look at her. Don't you ever
say that again, she says, don't you ever even think such
words, your father is not dead because nobody said so,
I don't know what you might have heard but none of
it is true, right now there is no truth, you don't know
and nobody knows, the truth of anything cannot be

known. What has been stored in the body, what has been locked in the heart gives release through Molly's mouth into sobbing, her hands squeezing the air, Eilish pulling her into a hug, whispering to her, stroking the back of her head. We have entered into a tunnel and there is no going back, she says, we just need to keep going and going until we reach the light on the other side. She lathers Molly's hair, softly palpating the skull, sensing the mind through her fingers, what it is she must think about life, this mind that was so full of the world but now that world has gone, the world poured from her eyes. She dries Molly with a yellow towel then wraps it around her and sits her on the chair. What is it you used to say to me about hockey, you never lose, you either learn or win, we are learning now don't you think, I need you to come back to me, I need you more than ever. Molly lifts her face but the face is empty and unguarded as though all the pain had gone and there is only looking now, looking out from an uninhabited body, the voice whispering. Why do I feel this way if he's not dead? she says, why do I feel it in my chest all day, it's there when I'm asleep, it's there when I wake in the middle of the night, I feel as though something's dying inside me, that's what it is, I'm afraid that what's dying inside me is the part of Daddy I hold in my heart, that's what makes me so afraid, I want so very much to keep him in my heart but I don't know how. Eilish moves to take Molly's hands but Molly puts up her hands to stop her. I dreamt the other night he came back, she says, it was nine o'clock in the evening and

he just came through the door and kicked off his boots
and put his slippers on, he was at work all along and
couldn't find his phone, it was as simple as that, he took
his dinner and sat down beside me on the couch and
put his arm around me and then I woke up. Eilish is
stroking Molly's hand, watching the eyes wide open and
stricken with the heart's burden, seeing the heart flutter
in the pit of her throat. Your father is with you all the
time, she says, even while he's gone, that is the meaning of the dream, your father came home to remind you
that he is always here with you because your father is
always alive in your heart, he is here with you now with
his arm around you, and he will always be here because
the love we are given when we are loved as a child is
stored forever inside us, and your father has loved you
so very much, his love for you cannot be taken away
nor erased, please don't ask me to explain this, you just
need to believe it is true because it is so, it is a law of
the human heart.

She wakes into living room darkness unsure if she has
slept at all, the time on her phone says twenty past one,
Molly cradled in her arm, Bailey asleep on a mattress
beside them, the cot pushed to the wall. For how many
days the shelling and gunfire has continued, the fighting
stopped for the night but her body does not believe the
silence, a sensory prickling in her nerves, the banging
deep in her skull. She turns to Molly inhaling from her

hair the fading scent of jasmine, sensing the mind at peace beneath the sleeping breath, to reach in with her hand and pull the terror out by the root, to caress the mind back to its old shape. Something has winged from the dark of her mind and she holds very still, then turns from Molly, gets up and goes into the kitchen. The sky in astronomical twilight, watching the trees rooted in the earth, thinking, there will be goodness again, there will be high and happy voices, the sound of feet seeking for slippers and the clicking of bicycle wheels through the porch. She watches a flare search the night sky like some bioluminescent fish drifting absently through an ocean dark and is met again with the thought she left behind in the other room, it has followed her into the kitchen, it is standing before her now and she doesn't want to hear, the thought that says it is her son who is helping to bring upon them this destruction, the thought that says her son cannot return until the destruction is done. When she wakes again it is to a storm of heavy weapons fire, the baby standing in the cot calling out mama, she holds him in her arms shushing him, rocks him back and forth on her knees, the involuntary pinching of her shoulder blades every time a blast sounds nearby, the children like drugged sleepers to the noise. The dawn reaches into the house through the kitchen window, the light falling over the flung shapes of the children asleep on the floor where the coffee table used to be, the table pushed against the wall with the children's schoolbooks and the cups and plates from last night's dinner on top of it. Male voices call out to each other in the lull between gunfire, for a moment she imagines Sunday morning football, overweight men shouting for a pass of the ball, another voice starts up and something catches at the base of her throat as she listens to the flat, unceasing monotone of a government soldier on a megaphone. Everybody in the area can hear, he could be a manager at the supermarket announcing cost reductions at the meat counter. We are sending someone to find you, when we find you we will know who you are, when we know who you are we will identify your families and then we will go get them. A shell detonates and sends a wrinkle into the earth and the man's voice is gone. She tells herself to take a breath, she lies down with Ben in her arms and tries to sleep but cannot, she must have dozed because when she opens her eyes she sees that Bailey has gone from the room, he is not in the kitchen, he has gone upstairs to the bathroom and locked the door. Come down here right now, she shouts, how many times have I told you not to go upstairs? She has followed him with Ben in her arms, she bangs on the door, open up right now. She can hear him trying to flush the toilet, he unlocks the door and meets her with a sheepish look then points towards the cistern. It won't flush properly, he says, there's no cold water in the tap either. She looks at the sink as though she does not believe him. How many times have I told you before not to go upstairs, use the bucket in the kitchen if you have to. The sullen face turning away as though she were at fault. There's no need to give out, he says, I forgot, that's all, there's a reason why a bear shits in the woods you know and not in the fucking kitchen.

She watches him slump downstairs dragging his hand on the railing and then she checks the tap in the sink, the kitchen tap has no water either, she has been saving water in plastic bottles just in case but they might not have enough. They toast bread for breakfast on the gas fire in the living room and watch cartoons on a laptop, Bailey eyeing a slice of cold toast that Molly has not eaten, his hand slides across and in instant it is gone. Eilish beside the radio listening to the reports, the government forces are in retreat, she says, the rebels have advanced through the south city as far as the canal. Past twelve o'clock Bailey touches a finger to her wrist. Do you hear that? he says, it sounds like the fighting's stopped. They eat a cold lunch of tuna, olive oil and bread disbelieving the silence as it continues into the afternoon, the silence growing dense and disquieting, it is the silence that speaks of gathering force, it is the silence that awaits the next round of shelling, it is the silence of the wolf before the knock on the door of the house made of straw. She tells the children to hush a moment hearing an engine slow on the street, there are male voices, nothing can be seen from the front window when she pulls the mattress back, she does not want to go upstairs, the trembling air as she peers through the curtains in her room and sees two unshaven men beside a Nissan pickup truck stopped alongside the checkpoint. A man in improvised battle fatigues and tan running shoes stands with an assault rifle strapped to his chest, it looks as though he is trying to get a signal on his phone, another man in T-shirt and jeans and a weapon slung from his shoulder, he lifts a baseball cap to scratch at the nape of his neck. A Jack Russell with pointed ears watches from a window across the street, four weaponed men arriving on foot with dust and dirt on their faces, their clothes a motley mix of civilian dress and army surplus clothing. They begin to pull the checkpoint apart, dragging sandbags by the ears to the side of the road and stacking them, the toothless ex-junkie has returned offering out cigarettes and lends a hand dismantling the barrier he helped build. So this is freedom, she thinks, but her heart cannot free itself, watching the rebels she cannot call out her joy, it is not joy but relief, it is not relief but something that awakens her deepest fear, the cold she cannot warm away, the thought that circles every other thought, what if her husband and son do not come home? Watching down upon these men as they stand on the street lighting cigarettes and trying to get a signal on their phones, she is overcome by loathing, seeing not men but shadows parading the day born from darkness, seeing how they have made an end of death by meeting it with death. How quickly the flags have been taken down from the houses, not a single one remains. In half an hour the soldiers are gone and the road is clear and people are stepping out of their houses, Gerry Brennan sweeping his yard while an enormous balding man in a blushing pink T-shirt stands by a poodle with its leg cocked to a tree. I want to go out, Bailey says, seeing a youth passing down the street, I want to go and get ice cream.

# 7

The fighting has passed through Connell Road like some ferocious grabbing water pulling the walls and the house fronts into rubble, the hull of a Toyota minivan burnt to the colour of bone lies in the road as though deposited by the onrush, the asphalt full of pockmarks and spatter. She is speaking all this to Larry as though he would never believe it, a commercial building off the main road is still expelling smoke however many days later, the cement dust and the ash that lies upon the leaves and upon the cars with their windows and body-work shot out, the white dust faint in the air and still falling it seems upon the sycamore that stands unvan-quished outside the school with half its trunk scorched to the neck as though some vandal had tried to set fire to it. Windows along the street are sealed with refuse sacks or plastic sheeting while an elderly man in front of a B&B hammers plywood over a bay window, this street that looks like two places at once as though some filmed transparency of a foreign war has been placed upon an image of the city, the summered colours fused with the ashen hues of destruction passing through in a rush. The queue for the water truck will take who knows how long, she stands in line with Bailey watching people swinging jerrycans and containers, children jostling in the slant evening sun. We can't get enough water home with just these plastic bottles, she says, we need to find something better. This false sense of the city at rest, a lawnmower's droning daydream of summer, the birds feasting in the gardens, everyone is talking about inflation, everything has gone up ten, twenty times in price, there is a man at the top of the street who will charge your phone on a generator for a tenner, you'd be afraid to turn anything on in the house when the electricity returns for fear of the size of the bill, if it continues like this the currency will be worthless. A pickup truck with rebel soldiers passes by and she searches for Mark's face among them, seeing the rebels standing guard at the water truck, seeing her son as he would be among them chatting and smoking and staring into his phone, they seem to be enjoying themselves, not so long ago they were employees of all kinds, students and trainees and the unemployed who in the blink of an eye became seasoned to bloodshed. Bailey wants to know why Mark hasn't called, we should have heard from him by now, he says. She is studying his face seeing the soft hair on the upper lip beginning to thicken, she has not the heart to tell him he should shave it off, it is not a mother's job to tell him so, Larry or Mark can do so later. I don't know, she says, I just don't know anymore, we might not hear from him for a while yet, there's fighting still going on in different parts of the country, it might be too dangerous for him to ring my phone, you never know who is listening in, give me your shoulder a moment, there's something in my boot. She rests her hand against him and slides free the boot, feeling about her sock, it is not even a stone but the seed of a stone, a pip growing slowly, steadily into sharp rock, she turns the sock inside out and shakes it then puts it back on, testing her foot, the pip is gone until she leans forward, it is there again on the ball of her foot.

The city breathes itself into being as she pedals Betty Brennan's old bicycle, the shattered glass glittering within the rubble swept to the side of the streets. How quickly posters have appeared on the advertising boards along the bus routes, pages handwritten or typed up on a computer with the photos of men and women who have disappeared, the people arrested, detained by the regime, one moment you are asleep in your bed and wake to see the GNSB standing in your room, they ask you to put on some clothes, help you find your shoes. She studies the faces on each poster and whispers the names, please help us find our brother, have you seen our friend, our beloved mother has dis- appeared, our son went missing on—— A helicopter hangs over the city as she swings free of the bike and wheels it towards her father's house, whispering words of thanks, everything is as it should be, the front door closed and the dog inside, the facts otherwise to what she has imagined. She lifts the peeling gate entire from the keep and wheels the bike through, swinging her eyes upon the house across the street without stopping to acknowledge Mrs Tully ghosting the window, the potted plants and hanging flowers in the veranda have neither bloomed nor died in twenty years. She is standing at her father's door when she hears her name called from across the street, Mrs Tully has stepped to the gate waving her arm. Oh hello, Eilish, I just want to see if everything's alright with your father, I saw him leave the house the other day with the leash in his hand but no dog in the collar, it trailed along the ground behind him. When she opens the front door she calls inside. Hello, Dad, it's me, Eilish. The smell of dog as she wheels the bike through, though the smell of cigarettes has gone, Spencer woofing from the kitchen. The smile on the face that steps into the hall belongs to her father though the white beard belongs to somebody else. I like the new look, she says, it gives you a dignified manner. I don't like it at all, he says, that damned thing, what-do-you-call-it, pointing to his face, I can't get it to work, where did you get the bike? I need to get someone to look at the gears, she says, they keep getting stuck, I'll have to get back home before curfew as the children are alone in the house, I got through two rebel checkpoints and at the third I was told to turn back so I just circled around them, they're making up the rules as they go along, they're just as bad as the regime, there's a van going around our area with a megaphone blaring out a list of restrictions as long as your arm, nobody is allowed out past 7pm. I suppose you'll want tea, Simon says, I haven't got any milk, the electricity comes and goes but at least I have the gas. At least you have running water as well, she says. She is watching him carefully, the soiled dishes resting on the counter and piled in the sink, seeing him go without knives and forks, plates and cups, she looks to his hands as though he has been drinking from them. What are you doing with the stove lit? she says, it's the middle of summer. The face before her takes a wondering look then turns to study the dog. There's no heat from that sun, he says, I can feel the damp in my feet, let me tell you about that bloody dog, he ran off on me in the park the other day, one minute he was on the leash and then he wasn't, when I got home he was in the garden waiting for his dinner, he thinks this is a five-star hotel. She is watching her father with sadness and wonder, seeing the old commander at his perch, the unyielding mind looking out upon a vanishing world, Spencer giving them both a sullen look, he winks his eyes then lowers his head onto his paws. The tea tastes of must, she washes the dishes and cleans the counter while talking to Simon over her shoulder. I should have known Mrs Taft would not turn up, it will be impossible now to get any help, if you were to come and live with us for a while you wouldn't have to worry about anything, you'd get all your meals and there'd be no cleaning up, you could do as you like until this is all over, it'd be good to have a man about the house again. She's still taking things from me, he says. Dad, the cleaner hasn't been here in weeks, look, I really need your help with this, I don't see how you can manage on your own, the supermarkets are closed, you have to queue for hours to get supplies, it'd be easier if we could get through this under the one roof until it's all over, I could call a taxi, there's still one or two about, we could pack a bag and have you over today. Did you pay her? he says. Pay who? Mrs Taft, you stopped paying her, that's why there's trouble with the help. Dad, of course I paid Mrs Taft, look, I want you to listen, it's difficult now to even cross the city, the roads are still a mess, there are roadblocks everywhere, the situation is unstable, I might not be able to visit you for a while—— I've told you already, I'm perfectly fine as I am, isn't that right, Spencer, I'd only be a nuisance in your house and anyhow, I have my supplies, let's talk about something else, you're starting to sound like your mother.


A woman, a stranger, is seated in the kitchen, Molly moving quickly from the chair, she shapes her hands into some semaphore of apology as Eilish wheels the bike through. The woman turns and greets her with solemn green eyes. Mrs Stack, she says, I'm sorry to intrude like this, might we have a word? Eilish parks the bike outside and goes to the sink, washes her hands in a basin of water. This house is very quiet, she says, turning around to look at Molly, is your brother

upstairs? Bailey went out an hour ago when I was putting Ben down to sleep, I don't know where he went. I
thought I told you both not to leave the house. Molly
shrugs and looks away while Eilish dries her hands on
her jeans, she motions for Molly to leave the room then
pulls the glass door closed and straightens her back.
Are you here about my son? A swift clean smile, fine
hands and fingernails, a confident urbane manner. I
was sent here by your sister. Áine? she says, I was afraid
you were going to bring me news of my son, I have no
coffee but I can make some tea if you like. She gestures
with her hand to the pot on the camping stove while the
woman declines with a smile. The shadow of Molly
listening by the door. Come with me outside, Eilish
says, motioning with her hand to follow. They step
through the garden to the shade under the trees, the
young woman reaching for a strip of ribbon, she
touches it a moment and lets go. Nobody can hear us
talk out here, Eilish says, you didn't tell me your name.
I am part of a small organisation, you don't need to
know who we are, we are hired by people like your
sister, people who are living outside the state and who
are in a position to help their loved ones. The young
woman is watching the backs of the houses facing onto
the garden, she reaches into her coat and takes out a
manilla envelope and a cylinder of rolled banknotes
secured with an elastic band. Keep this document safe,
she says, it's a letter signed by a senior official bearing
the seal of the Department of Justice, it will allow you
to cross unimpeded to the government side where you

can buy fresh meat, vegetables, dairy for your children without paying end of the world prices, look, Mrs Stack, I'm here because your sister has arranged for us to help get you out, your children and your father also, we need to move quick. She is watching the woman standing in the garden yet seeing her sister at home in Toronto, Áine speaking with her husband, arranging this over the phone, she hasn't spoken to her sister in weeks. Out? she says. Yes, I'm going to need photos, personal details, so we can falsify passports and identification documents, we can get you out of the country and your sister will arrange transit to Canada. Something has crashed silently to the floor of the self, she looks away, watching the walls frowzy with ivy, the flower beds that should have been replanted in the spring, this garden needs so much work, she closes her eyes and sees it all vanish, sees the time to come like some dark mouth and looming from that darkness her unspeakable failure. Out? she says, whispering the word again, squeezing the roll of banknotes in her hand, sliding it into the pocket of her jeans. Yes. Just like that? She cannot look at the woman's face as she speaks. There is some degree of risk but we do this all the time—— The hollowed eyes in the bark of the tree are witness to this, the eyes that watch without sight do not blink at the wind and meet the world wide open, she is looking down at the woman's black ankle boots. This is a lot to take in, she says, what I mean to say is, no, I don't think so, no, this is not what I want. There is no trace of emotion in the woman's face, the lips coolly breathing before her, the clear, green eyes reading her carefully. You didn't tell me your name, Eilish says. You can call me Maeve. I'll bet that's your mother's name, Maeve, tell me, how does my sister expect me to leave just like that, without even speaking with me, do you know what happens to a house like this when it's abandoned, my eldest son could return any moment, he'll slide open the patio door and slouch into the kitchen as though he had never gone, he'll go to the fridge and give out that there is no ham then pull a chair asking if there's any news of his dad, my husband was taken, you see, we haven't heard from him since he disappeared—— Summer nights in the garden, the rust and scald of the fire pit in ashes before her, she closes her eyes seeing Larry pour wine into a glass and when she opens her eyes the tree is hung with grief, the ribbons on the breeze rising like pointed fingers whispering for her to go. The young woman lifts her eyes and smiles. Prunus avium, she says. I'm sorry? Your cherry trees, she says, wild cherry, my grandmother was a botanist, spending time with her was not unlike having to take a degree in Latin at ten, they look old, have they been planted a long time? I think so, yes, they were mature when we bought the house, my husband thinks they will have to be cut down or risk having one come down during a storm, but I don't know, I'd rather wait and see, the flowers are a sight in the spring. Mrs Stack, your sister told me about your husband, I don't know what to say, I don't know what it is you know. She goes to speak but rolls her lips, Eilish watching the lips and the eyes that speak without speaking, she can hear what the eyes want to say but does not want to listen, the eyes are wrong, the eyes don't know a thing, the eyes cannot know anything when nothing has been proven. Mrs Stack, you have a difficult choice before you, leaving home is the most difficult thing to do, but I don't believe you are looking clearly at the situation, at what is about to happen, that spotter plane overhead, what do you think it's doing up there all day, this ceasefire is not going to hold, the rebels have run out of momentum and the military has begun to encircle them, the south of this city will be put to siege and the military will turn this place into hell, they will pound the rebels into submission, you'll be cut off from the world, from supplies, none of what I tell you is a secret, you have children to think of, you have an elderly father who is in need of medical care—— My father? Eilish says, snapping at a leaf with her hand, rolling it into pap. My sister has done next to nothing for my father, what my father needs is to remain at home, to be surrounded by his memories, to have the past within reach, in time there will be nothing left to him but shadows, a strange dream of the world, to send him into exile now would be to condemn him to a kind of nonexistence, I cannot allow that to happen. Mrs Stack, I understand, but I should explain that your sister has paid a lot of money for this. Yes, I suppose she has, you don't look much like a trafficker. Mrs Stack, I'm a medical student, I was a medical student, now I am this until I can be a medical student again, everything costs a lot of money, there are passports and documents to be forged, bribes to be paid, there are transit fees, this is not without risk, I believe you will change your mind but we really do need to hurry, in three or four days I will send a young man to collect what we need, here is a list of what you must give him, in the meantime, you can use the letter to get supplies, you have enough currency now to deal with the inflation, the Canadian dollar goes a long way. Bailey has come to the glass and for an instant she sees Mark as he was at the same age, what lies hidden in a face but is suddenly revealed by the turning of a head or a glance of the eyes that gives to the other face. She looks to the ground shaking her head. Tell my sister I'm sorry, she says, tell her I greatly appreciate the money, I really do, I'll tell her myself when I can, things have gotten so very expensive, as soon as I'm able I'll pay her back. She watches the young woman walk up the street and closes the hall door, Bailey standing in the kitchen smeared in dirt and dust holding two rectangular, off-white, five-litre drums. He puts them down on the floor with a smile and won't say where he found them. The smell of must inside the drums, she needs to wash them out with boiling drinking water bought from the water truck, she stares at him with pride and relief and then snaps at him in anger. I did not bring you up to be a thief, she says, watching his aggrieved, darkening eyes narrowing as though to reduce her in size. Why aren't you glad? he says, you're never glad about anything, I'm hardly going to put them back. The face before her has changed again, it is

Larry's face now, Larry deepening into anger, Larry's shoulder turning away.


They are twisted together in wakeful sleep, her arm around his waist, Larry rousing, whispering something and when she opens her eyes he is standing by the bed slowly shaking his head, a look of sorrow in his eyes. What are you shaking your head for? she says, watching him go to the door, the light from the hall finding his face and it is as though she does not know him, he is at once Larry but he is somebody else, a man made hollow by age and grief, when she looks again he is gone. She wakes sodden and bereft, thinking about what she would like to say, how dare you come to me in a dream as though you were dead. She is crying when she steps into the kitchen, taking a glass from the sink, she runs the empty tap out of habit. How alien the world in the blue hour of dawn and yet it is known, the rain murmuring in the trees, it is an ancient rain that speaks to the place where it has always fallen, the cherry trees rooted in the earth, a strip of ribboned light for every week he is gone. Amber light fills a bedroom window in a house across the way, she watches the light travel into the bathroom, somebody has risen as though for work, you go to the bathroom and splash water on your face and brush your teeth and make coffee, you call the children up into the day and get them ready for school, this is how we live. When the children are awake she tells them they must continue their schoolwork, the schools will reopen soon anyhow, I don't want you falling behind. Molly is content to study alone but Bailey will not do any work, she sits with him for a while then says she must go to one of the checkpoints and cross for supplies. Nappies, Bailey says, don't forget the nappies and the baby wipes and toilet paper and chocolate also, we're going to run out of batteries for the lamp as well. She walks towards the checkpoint at Dolphin's Barn, a line of double-decker buses parked on the path along the canal to shield the rebel soldiers from sniper fire. She stands in line before the Camac Bridge waiting for the ID check, watching the people come and go across no-man's land with wheelbarrows and trolleys and baggage, the rebels are demanding to search the merchandise of the people returning from the regime's side, everything has to be unpacked, an elderly woman with jet black hair throws up her hands and begins to shout at two rebels who insist at her bag, she won't let go until a soldier tears the bag from her hands and a chicken comes feathering out while the woman flaps after it along the road. Eilish holds out her ID to eyes hidden behind sunglasses, a toneless voice asking why she is crossing, the sound of a warplane overhead. She reads the sign hung on the traffic lights warning of snipers and moves into hurry as she crosses the bridge, looking ahead to the windows of the tower block watching down from the far junction, this feeling of standing before some authority that declares life and death by fiat. An older woman with a breathless, husky voice has come alongside her and begins to talk as though they know each other. Thank God today's quiet, she says, I've an elderly mother in the flats at Oliver Bond afraid to leave the house God love her, I could hardly get across all week, there's lots of people like that, what about yerself? Eilish does not even look at her face, she is watching the regime checkpoint two hundred metres beyond the bridge, cement blocks and sandbags and a national flag without lift on a pole, watching a man with lowered head crossing on a bicycle, he veers around a discarded boot in the centre of the road, it looks like one of the cherry boots she keeps in the press but never wears, a young woman at a half-run pushing a buggy with a sack of rice in the seat, an elderly woman with swollen ankles pulling on a tartan trolley, a tall old man leaning on a stick, a lurcher loping ahead without leash. She comes upon the cherry boot with its one-inch heel and sees it has slid off the owner's foot without having lowered its zip.

Simon is cursing the TV in the front room while she empties the rucksack of supplies onto the kitchen table, she steps inside and stands before him and puts her hands on her hips. Let me shave your beard, she says, we can do it here if you like. She goes upstairs and takes a towel, opens the bathroom cabinet, shaving foam in a can and a blue plastic razor, a packet of half-smoked cigarettes on the shelf that she slides into her pocket. Simon waiting in the armchair with his hands on his lap, the fingers spread and matted with dark marram grass, he exhales noisily while she lifts his chin and studies the face, two fields of snow fallen upon the old land, she has never shaved a man's face before. It's not going to hold you know, he says, the ceasefire, did you hear the news, the lies they're coming out with, they must take us all for fools, today they are saying the rebels have violated the ceasefire with twenty-eight attacks registered in the city in the past twenty-four hours, however many mortar shells and artillery shells launched at our positions, blah blah blah, you can hear for yourself that the rebels have been silent for days apart from the odd rifle crack, the regime is preparing another attack, just wait and see—— Dad, she says, holding the jaw in place with her hand, I can't shave if you won't be still, they're not going to break the ceasefire now with the threat of further sanctions, everybody wants it to stop. The beard is giving fight to the razor, the path she has shaved smooth continues to grow at an infinitesimal rate. That tall fella called over yesterday, he says, he had a good rummage about upstairs while he was here. The blade has stopped in her hand, she leaves it down in a bowl of water and takes her father's arm. Dad, what tall fella? You know the one. Simon watching her with a slant eye as though she were at fault. Dad, how am I supposed to know who you are talking about? The tall fella, one of your lot. My lot? she says, do you mean one of your grandsons, I hardly think so. Yes, he says, that's who it was, he called over about three o'clock. And what did he want upstairs? She watches Simon close his eyes, her gaze seeking past the translucent skin of the eyelids, seeking into his mind, she will shake the old man out of the skull, shake him into knowingness. She dips the razor into the water then pulls too hard on the blade, Simon's hand coming up in protest as blood makes a run down his chin. Do you mean Mark? she says, her voice sliding, she looks about the room without seeing, her sight coming to rest on the chairs around the table. So how did you know it was Mark? she says, hold on a moment while I get some tissue. Who else would it be, he says, I said are you one of Eilish's sons and he said he was and he came in and said he was here to help. Here to help, she says, help with what? I don't know, this and that, he said he would help with the garden. She has gone into the kitchen running cold water on her hands, cups it into her face, stands at the French doors watching the garden, the hedgerow shorn and cropped smooth at the top, the beds newly weeded, seeing Mark as he stood in the garden last summer in his work clothes helping out. She places a piece of tissue onto her father's face and continues to shave around the half smile as he closes his eyes. She is speaking to him when she realises he has fallen asleep, the chin smooth in the palm of her hand as she towels the rosy skin. She goes into the hall and lifts his coat and opens it at the neck, returns to the front room and sits in her mother's chair, takes from her pocket a white label inked with his name and address and her phone number and stitches it to the lapel. Listening to the empty house, hearing the old voices upstairs and her mother calling them to dinner, their feet booming on the stairs, the fire in the stove ticking as though it spoke to time like some deranged clock, as though the log in the stove were spitting out the time stored in its wood, thinking, time is at once addition and subtraction, time adds one day to the next and always takes away from what's left, the slow sleeping breath before her. It is the body that breathes the mind, this is what she thinks, it is the heart that beats the man until the man is beaten and she finds herself reaching out for his hand, whispering, I never wanted you to be anybody else.

Soft-foot she goes to the front door and puts it on the latch, steps out through the porch flaming a cigarette. Late twilight edging into nightfall, a light rain speckling the path, a figure is walking up the street in disregard of the curfew. She watches the youth's hunching walk as they both suck on cigarettes, the youth cupping his hand to his mouth. He has gone past but a moment when she hears a vehicle come around the corner, she steps back into the wall watching a 4X4 go by, seeing two rebel police in front, watching the brake lights hue the neighbouring windows as the vehicle comes to a stop. She goes to the gate whispering for the boy to run but he turns and faces the 4X4 instead, two men stepping down to surround him, she sees the boy shrug, a rebel policeman grabs him by the arm and turns him around, shoves him towards the vehicle to cuff him. She is rolling her sleeves as she marches up the street calling out, what are you doing to my son? She is upon them in the moment of their hesitation, the pair of hands on the youth have let go and the rebel policeman turns and meets her with a look she cannot read in the dark. She is no longer of the street but has entered into some part of herself where she is absolute, carrying a sword in her mouth, this boy is her son, she has pulled him by the sleeve and is shaking him, I told you not to go out after curfew, she says, go back now to the house. She has put herself between the youth and the two men, turns and sends the youth with a push down the street, standing with her hands open before them. I'm terribly sorry, she says, I understand there is a curfew, the baby is teething and I can't keep my eye on all of them, he thinks he can just sneak out as he likes, this will be the last time I promise you. The false quiet of the street as she is met and read by an iced glare, a two-way radio crackling in the jeep. She turns, afraid the youth will continue past the house, calling out to him, wait for me there. The men no longer see the boy and she folds her arms before them, one of the men clearing his throat, he speaks in a smooth city accent. Count yourself lucky this time, if I see your son out again past curfew I will take him in, do you understand? She meets the man's face with a sour look. You are asking me if I understand, yes I understand, but I want you to understand something as well, my eldest son left home to fight against the regime with you lot and here I stand now on the street being threatened, we wanted the regime out but not to be replaced with more of the same, that's all I have to say to you. She is walking down the street listening to the idling engine, the men are watching no doubt in the rear-view mirror as she takes hold of the youth's elbow and marches him into the house. The front door shut and locked as she walks him into the kitchen, Molly and Bailey looking up from a laptop, they want to know what's going on. She tells the youth to take a chair, he is only a boy really, sullen and flinching, braced as though before a beating. She can see now how he could never be her son, the quick eyes and feral manner of a youngster from the flats, she steps into the living room and watches through the blinds. Wait here a little while before you go, she says, they will circle again and then you can make a run for it. Something unpleasant grows on the youth's face, he goes towards the sink and spits into it, turns with a resentful look. What did you go and do that for, missus? he says, I was going to run away.

The hurry of explosions as she brushes her teeth by the kitchen sink, the shock of each round shattering the night's silence, a hand slides around her heart and tightens into a fist. When she looks down she sees the toothbrush in the sink, sees hope gone from her hands, hope held like cupped water in the hands of a fool searching across some great expanse, she knows it is Bailey who has come to the glass door behind her. That last one was a rocket, he says. She turns hearing the pleasure of knowledge in his voice, seeing him headless in the dark but for the pale long limbs in boxers and T-shirt. And how would you know? she says, shaking her head, turning again towards the window, a church bell tolling the hour in the blue summer dark and faint beyond it another bell tolling out of time as though it were but an echo of the first bell and then she hears the dull boom of another explosion. This rage she cannot wring from her hands, this sadness that comes upon her as she pulls the window closed and turns for the living room, a weight has been placed onto her chest so that she can hardly walk, she rests a hand on the counter and closes her eyes and takes a deep breath, her feet are cold, she does not know what she's done with her slippers, you were wearing them only a while ago. They huddle under a duvet while the rounds continue to fall on the city with the slow and steady beat of a military drum. She tells the children they are safe, that the regime is targeting rebel positions, she does not believe this herself, Molly making a strange noise in her throat each time a round strikes. Ben is awake and will not stay in the cot. She turns on the radio and waits for the world news, there is no news about what is going on. She tells them it will stop, that one thing always gives to another, in the morning I will cross to the government side and get more supplies, maybe I can find us some chocolate. A mortar strikes close by and then another and Molly makes that noise again with her throat but longer this time as though giving utterance to the opening note of some ancient and austere cry, she searches under the duvet for her mother's hand and Eilish grasps the hand knowing she is false before the children, false with nothing to offer, no comfort nor succour, only lies, distraction and evasion, telling them stories from her childhood they've heard before, the time her sister fell from a tree and instead of her back she broke her arse and had to sit on a rubber ring for weeks, the time her granny was struck by lightning while pregnant, how she was thrown across the backyard but remained unharmed and your grandfather was born with a scar behind his ear. At 2am the bombardment makes the foreign news, the military has launched a strategic offensive on rebel-held positions, it has launched an offensive against sleep, against the sanctuary of night, this wish now to close her eyes and seek a door through to morning but instead she sees the darkness of a tomb and the night slabbed over them, sees the house coming down on their heads. There begins a steady pounding that does not let up, her right hand has begun to shake, she holds it with her left hand and hides it under the duvet, seeing the faces of the men firing rockets and mortars down upon them, knowing they are sending death down upon friends and relatives, knowing they are men she has passed on the street. Ben wakes again with a cry and will not be appeased, the angry breath on her hand as she slides her finger into his mouth searching the gum, the poor fellow has a tooth coming down, she has nothing to give him for the pain. She rubs her thumb along his jaw wondering what it is a child this age can know of the world, the odour of fear on her body, the child growing to know the smell that cannot be wished away nor suppressed, the child absorbing the mother's trauma and storing it in his body for later use, the child become adult stricken by dread and blind anxiety, lashing out at those around him, she is holding a damaged man in her arms. Steady the beat of the military drum, steady the march of explosions, the shelling growing distant for a time as though it were a thundercloud passing out to sea, the radio reporting nothing new before she turns it off. She thinks Molly and Bailey are asleep, the sirens in the dark and woofing dogs, Ben shuddering as though to sleep more deeply his body must expel her fear. She closes her eyes and sees her father alone in the house with the dog pawing at the French doors, her father bedded under the stairs and asleep with his mouth open, her father bedded into the earth like rock, seeing the land, the sea, the mountains, the lakes all erased, the world become some void of darkness but for this death that comes from the sky, this death that seeks to enter sleep by explosion so that she is afraid to close her eyes.

She does not know the time when she hears the whistling of rounds pass overhead, she had been asleep

with listening ears, two blasts so close they shake
the house and something crashes onto the floor. An
animal sound has escaped her throat while Molly sits
up screaming. She cannot find the torch, Molly has
lost it under the duvet, it is found and when she turns
it on they see ceiling plaster in pieces before the fire-
place. Bailey has gotten sick on the floor. I don't know
what's wrong with me, he says, I must have caught
a bug or something, maybe I've got food poisoning.
The light from the torch is shaking in her hand as
she goes into the kitchen for disinfectant and a cloth,
standing for a moment by the window to watch the
pluming luminescence of white smoke. She must not
waste any water, places a basin beside Bailey and tells
him to get sick into it instead, scrubs the boards with
brutal strokes then returns to the kitchen and sees that
the shaking in her hand has stopped. She stretches
her fingers for a moment then lets the hand rest, a
mortar round brings the tremor back, she sweeps up
the plaster from the living-room floor then begins to
clean the countertops, the area around the sink, the
windowsill behind the sink, the splash area around
the cooker, an explosion close by shaking the ground
so that she must hold onto the sink with two hands,
thinking of the grime on the cooker hood that needs
to be scrubbed, she has been ignoring these things for
much too long, the amount of dirt that creeps along
the countertop and gets caught behind the microwave,
the food waste that falls into drawers and lies beneath
the knives and forks, the crumbs from the bread bin

and the toaster that travel all over the place, you cut a slice of bread and half the loaf ends up on the floor, the crumble rolls under the kettle, it drops into the cutlery drawer that's just been cleaned. Mam, what are you doing, Bailey is after getting sick again. She has gripped hold of Molly's hand, shaking it up and down but it is herself she has found again. When there is light outside, she says, we need to put tape on the windows in case the glass comes in, what time is it now, let us hope that Ben stays asleep.

Her fingers fumble at the buttons of her coat as she stands before the hall mirror. She has not brushed her hair for days, she lets it down and runs her fingers through. This tremble in her right hand as though something has burrowed under the skin to live off sinew and bone, she picks up the comb then puts it down and ties up her hair instead. She picks up the phone hoping for a dial tone then steps outside watching the sky, seeking to locate a source for the drift smoke, the sirens calling out, Gerry Brennan is hoisting a bin bag onto a mound of refuse black and tumescent along the path. Rats, he says, pointing his finger at the street, there's rats big as cats, I've never lived in such filth. She does not know what to say, she does not care about the bins anymore, hardly an hour's sleep in five days and nights and this feeling in her body that things are different now, this deep black fear that lives in the blood, this

sense of no escape. Gerry Brennan brings up his hand
as though to speak but they both look up to the sound
of a warplane that has already passed, a rumbling echo
as though the sky were a cave and then the explosion
from the drop-site a few kilometres away. It must be
7am, he says, you could set your clock by those mur-
dering jets, you don't hear them until they are about
to strike or have already struck. She is watching Gerry
Brennan's unshaven face, seeing him before a mirror
with a razor every day for fifty years and now his cheeks
sparkle with silica, his shirt and tie replaced by a soiled
vest, the gaunt arms and chicken elbows. Do you need
anything, Gerry? she says, I'm going to try and cross
the checkpoint, I can make room in my bag. He doesn't
answer, stands lost in a stare while she looks past him
to the front garden, seeing how the man has been dis-
commoded, how he chose for his retirement the potted
plants thirsting for the hose, how he chose the weeds
in the cracks of the paving bowing to the blade of his
hoe, how he chose to build the remainder of his days
out of footling tasks, balding the heels of his socks in
garden clogs, working the hanging fat off his elbows
along the raised beds out back full of blistered cabbage
and mid-season carrots, beetroot and turnip for winter,
stepping in and out of the house in silent devotion to
each summons from his wife. And now the fierce look
in the eye scanning the street for rats. It's plain as day
what they're up to, he says, they're trying to chase us
out like vermin, that's what they're doing, they want to
exterminate us like rats, it's just a matter of time and

effort, I used to work as a city planner, you know, there's a finite number of roads and buildings in this city, drop enough ordnance and after a time you'll have put a hole in every road, you'll have struck at every block of flats, every shop and house, then you keep going night and day, you keep dropping more and more until you've smashed every structure into the ground and you keep going until you turn the brickwork into dust and there's nothing left but the people who refuse to leave. He turns, momentarily taking a wild look at the sky. Why should we leave? he says, tell me that, they won't get us out, we will live underground if we have to, I'll dig a hole in my fucking garden, if you've lived in one place all your life the idea of living someplace else is impossible, it's what do you call it, neurological, it's wired into the brain, we'll just dig in, that's what we'll do, what else are you supposed to do anyhow, I don't know where else I'd go, they can drag me out in a coffin. She does not know what to do with her face and turns away, toeing at the concrete. Tell Betty thanks again for lending me the bike, she says, the gears keep slipping and I let my son take a look and now they're worse. It's an old bike, he says, you might have misshapen teeth on the back wheel, bring it round to Paddy Davey, he has a small bike shop on Emmet Road beside the chipper, I used to bring the kids' bikes round to him, tell him I said hello, he'll do you a good price.

She mumbles at Larry to answer the phone and cannot come free from sleep, her arm is trapped under weight and when she wakes she hears the phone belling in the hall, sirens sounding nearby, her arm is caught beneath Molly. She hurries into the hall thinking it must be near dawn, she is speaking with Mark before she reaches the phone, of course you bloody well lost my number, who can remember mobile numbers anymore but a home phone you can always recall, didn't I drill it into you as a child—— She knows her father from the way he clears his throat, the signature intake of breath and then a quaver in his voice. Are you there? he says, she's gone, do you hear, I was asleep and awoke and she's gone. Dad, she says, what time is it now, the phone line has been dead for days, are you talking about the dog? You need to listen, he says, I'm talking about your mother, I've looked all about the house but she's not here, she's taken all her things, her wardrobe is empty, I should have known this was going to happen, I should have known she would leave. The high voice becomes a fearful whisper and then he is sucking for air. I can't breathe, he says, I can't breathe—— Daddy, she says, oh my god, please, Daddy, will I call for a doctor? No, he says, leave me be, that woman is out to destroy me. Eilish is pinching her eyes with finger and thumb, she pinches the bridge of her nose, seeing a man who has woken inside a dream, knowing he cannot be told of his wife's demise when he has no memory of her death. A shiver of emotion passes through her body and she looks up and sees Molly by the door, waves at her to go back

inside. Down the dark and dusty phone line she seeks
her father's face, wants to hold him, seeing him standing
in the hall with every light in the house turned on, he
will have forgotten his dressing gown and slippers. She
tells him to take a breath and when she opens her eyes
she sees two pale cautious faces watching from the door.
Daddy, she says, whispering now, turning her back on the
children. Daddy, I really need you to listen to me, please
take a breath and listen, Mammy is not gone, she'll be
back soon, I promise, she has just—— You are lying to
me, he says, you are always lying, I knew you would be
complicit in this, you are always taking her side, snivel-
ling after her like a dog, this house is so bloody peaceful
without you all. She hears a great sucking sound and
then he releases a sob. I can't breathe, he says. Daddy,
she says, oh Daddy, please listen, everything is going to
be alright—— I should have known this would happen,
he says, I should have known but I shut my eyes, I loved
her once you know, I really did love her, I still do love her,
oh— tell me, where did the love go, tell me that, I can't
remember where things go anymore, where does all our
love go when once we held it beating in our hand? She
is aghast, whispering, writhing under the skin, pulling
at her hair. Daddy, please, Daddy, listen, this is not what
you think, please listen to me, I'm going to come over in
the morning, soon as it's light, soon as I'm able. No, he
says, I don't want you here, I don't want you to be kind,
I don't want kindness right now, your mother drove me
away, she drove you all away, that is what she is like, let
me be alone. She hears a ruffled noise as though he has

covered the mouthpiece with his hand. I didn't hear you, Daddy, what did you say? She is waving furiously at the children to close the door. Oh my dear, he says, what have I done, I did not listen, I did not listen to any of you, I have to go and look for her, I know where she's going, I should be able to stop her if I go now——— Dad, she says, please listen to me carefully, you can't leave the house, it's just gone past 5am, they are shelling the city and the airstrikes will start in two hours, please stay where you are and I'll find a way to cross later, I'm going to call for a doctor as well. She hears the receiver being placed on the console and is left in silence calling out his name.

She calls Mrs Tully's number to ask her to check on her father but there is no answer. The doctor's surgery gives only to answering machine with an automated message for an out-of-hours service that directs her to another message, the service you require is no longer in operation, the doctor on call has left the country with his family and may never return, he has taken his parents with him, if you need urgent attention, go directly to your nearest emergency room. The look of panic in Molly's face when she tells the children she must cross the city, Molly following her into the hall as she reaches for her raincoat, she turns around and Molly is standing before the hall door with her arms folded. Mam, she says, you can't go out in that, can't you just wait a while, Grandad will be fine, he'll have gone back to sleep and won't remember what happened, he's sitting in the kitchen now grumbling over an old newspaper, he's drinking tea with sour milk, his glasses are around his neck and he's searching about for them, you know what he's like. Eilish is watching Molly's face believing for a moment that what she says is true, she watches the girl's hand taking hold of her wrist, Molly whispering, pleading with her. OK, Eilish says, I hope you're right, I'll wait until there's a lull, the shelling does seem to go quiet for a time after lunch. This sense of having stepped into a dark room with the door locked behind her as the shelling and airstrikes continue without abatement, the day passing out of her hands, the afternoon giving to night. They eat a cold dinner while she listens to the BBC, the government barrage has intensified despite outrage from the international community, she listens to the state radio, the regime insists it is bombing terrorists. She switches off the radio but cannot sleep, lies turning circles in her mind, is woken by Ben who finally closes his eyes holding her face in his hands. In the morning she stands resolute before the children, her voice grave as she sleeves her raincoat. I cannot wait another moment, she says, I must go now, I'll be back as soon as I can.

The birds will always inhabit the earth, the birds calling the dawn in the rent and ruined trees as she cycles across the city. There is light now where there used to be none, the buildings folded into rubble, the solitary walls and chimney flues, the staircase that climbs to a sudden drop. The rear tyre suffers a puncture and she must hide the bicycle behind the wall of a school and continue on foot, shelling in the southeast of the city and a landscape of grey smoke, hearing sporadic gunfire, whispering to Larry, the border between the rebels and the regime has shifted or perhaps there is now no border at all. She hurries through quiet residential streets and loitering dust, the checkpoints belonging to the rebel soldiers have been abandoned while children roll tyres and burn them in skips that spout black smoke to blind the warplanes. The streets surrounding her father's house lie silent, hardly a car on the road. She calls out to Spencer seeing him seated on the mat outside the front door, he springs to his feet and turns circles waiting for her to let him inside then stops as she knuckles his skull. What are you doing out here on your own? She knocks on the door and listens a moment then keys it open, the cylinder is double-locked, she steps into the hall and knows the house is empty, the coat gone from the stand, the lights turned off, the cordless phone on the console has been returned to its base. The curtains in Simon's bedroom are open, the bed roughly made, his slippers paired before the wardrobe. She sends the dog into the garden then checks the phone but the line is dead. She pulls the front door closed and walks to the end of the street then follows her father's daily route along the main road towards the park, the local shops all shuttered, stopping whoever she meets, nobody has seen the man she describes and a wall-eyed youth on a bike just laughs in her face. The blinds are down in Mrs Tully's, the house locked up, the plants drying out on the veranda. Gus Carberry is slow to answer the door then rests a papyrus hand on the jamb and leans his white moustache outside, looking up and down the road while shaking his head. She crosses the street to Mrs Gaffney who asks her to take a breath and come inside, potpourri infusing the hallway and she follows into a dim kitchen and takes a seat at the table. You're going to have a cup of tea and then we'll see what we can do. The woman flames a gas hob and fills an old stove-top kettle with water from a container. I don't know what I'm supposed to do, Eilish says, there are no services to call, the gardaí don't seem to exist anymore in the south of the city, I'm going to try and call the hospitals. She looks to the kettle heating on the gas. Perhaps you can keep a lookout for him, she says, any moment he's bound to return, let me give you my number, you can give me a call if you can get through, in the meantime, I don't know what to do with that bloody dog, I knew he would only come to bother. The kettle begins a rising whistle and Mrs Gaffney stands up and clinks two cups from the press. I can take the dog, she says, if you've got some food but I wouldn't have anything here to feed him with. She is watching the creases in the woman's face trying to recall the faces of her sons running about the street, they are grown men now with children of their own that live in photos arrayed on the windowsill. And your sons? she says. Oh, they're long gone, both of them in Australia, they've been trying to get me to leave the longest while but I don't want to go. But why, Mrs Gaffney, why have you stayed? The woman is silent a long time. She puts a mottled hand to her chin and goes to speak but sighs instead and looks away. Why do any of us stay? she says. Eilish walks the roads searching for her father, cowers in a doorway then hurries homeward. She is crossing a junction when she hears behind her the blatter of hooves, turns to see three horses following the road at a canter, two dappled greys and a skewbald that pass by wild-eyed and berserk.

The days passing out of her hands, the house at night amidst the bombardment watching her father as though he were a ghost standing before her, Simon stepping away into silence. She has crossed the city once more and stood in the empty house and cowered in the streets and will not leave the children again, whispering to Larry, I should have known this would happen, what was I supposed to do, yes, I know, I should have known, this was all my fault. The phone network returns and she receives a call from Mrs Gaffney to tell her the dog has run off. Her sister tries to call from Canada and she turns off the phone knowing how Áine will respond to the news of their father, seeing her failure and shame placed before her, she has lied to the children hoping Simon will return, she has lied to herself about so many things, Áine sending multiple messages asking her to call. I can't get through, she says, we need to talk, please tell me you're alright. The south city besieged, night and day the bombardment, the BBC says the military is using helicopters to drop bombs stuffed into barrels full of shrapnel and oil, the children trying to sleep under the stairs while Ben wails for the pain in his teeth, the upper and lower canines are coming through. Something inside her body has tightened into a knot that cannot be released, her body alert at all times, this body that listens while sleeping and the eyes that watch through the top of the skull while she queues for the water truck and supplies. She is standing in line when she meets a man she knew in school and there is something in his gaunt smile that makes her consider for a moment what it is like to be held, to lie side by side with a lover, to escape the mind entirely and enter into the body, to lose the self entirely for a spell. She turns away ashamed of how she looks, she has stopped combing her hair for fear of the hair falling out. The man touches her wrist and tells her that a smuggler has opened shop in an electrical store on Crumlin Road, she might be able to find there some of the things she wants. She walks the half-demolished streets passing civil defence volunteers in their white hats combing the rubble at a block of flats, is ushered into the electrical shop by an armed guard and stands in a queue. Second-hand washing machines and tumble dryers, dishwashers and cookers and no electricity to use them, she is wearing the wrong shoes again, her summer loafers pinching her feet, she slides one free and regards her toes thinking how she used to love these shoes, her feet have changed since Ben was born, there is no doubt now, the arches fallen, the bones grown longer, they are not her feet anymore, her phone is pinging in her bag. She reads the message and stares at the screen then reads the message again. I want you to know he is safe. She writes back to her sister, who is safe? Sleepless eyes and an unshaven face watching from across the counter. She wants powdered milk and paracetamol for the child, the man stepping to a back room while a young man tots up on a calculator. She does a quick sum in her mind, they are charging twelve times the usual price for paracetamol, she looks at the phone waiting for Áine to respond, soon she will be out of money and will have to go begging to her sister. Áine is taking too long to answer, she writes back again, who is safe? She is hurrying home cursing her shoes when Áine responds and she stops and reads the message twice. Dad is safe, Áine says, our friends got him out, I've been trying for ages to get through.

# 8

Clicking tongues the back wheel of her bike as she lifts it through the hall door and puts it against the wall, the oven timer pinging in the kitchen. She calls for somebody to turn off the alarm and looks about for her slippers, calls out again then steps barefoot inside. Where's Bailey? she says, passing Molly at length on a mattress with her face before a laptop and headphones on, Ben dozing in the cot while gripping a wooden spoon. She has tipped the brown bread out of the pan onto the rack, tapped it on the base testing for a hollow sound before she thinks to turn off the alarm, the electricity is going to go off again any minute, she will try to do one more wash of clothes. The warm stillness of the crusted bread, she is thinking of Carole Sexton and her sour mouth, finds herself before Molly waving the oven glove, why couldn't you take out the bread like I asked? The wounded eyes that glance up from the screen belong to Carole and not her daughter, Eilish turning for the kitchen when she stops with a listening look towards the ceiling and in an instant she has covered her head with her hands, the sound of the world coming undone, a tremor passing under the house and the sound of raining cement. She is running for Ben and lifts him from the cot roaring for Molly to get under the stairs, Molly pulling her headphones off, Eilish's eyes wild about the room. Where's Bailey? she shouts, where's your brother gone? The look of panic on Molly's face, the mouth that opens for words that do not sound but have fled before her under the stairs, her hand pointing to the door. He went out, she shouts, he said he was going to get milk. Eilish places Ben into Molly's arms and shunts her into the recess, she is moving for the front door with Bailey's name in her mouth, her hand sliding open the patio door, her eyes reaching for the street thinking there is no milk to be bought when soundlessly she is raised from her feet and borne through the air rearwards with her arms held out in some counter-time of light and darkness holding pieces of cement in her mouth. She is lying in a mute darkness beneath an immense and flattening silence. Something rests inside her mouth that is not blood, blood rising around the bitten tongue, the blood building around what lies in the mouth, it is not cement but something else, her eyes opening to the hallway clouded with glass and dust and Molly leaning over her to lift the bicycle off her body while holding Ben in her arm, Molly shouting with a silent mouth and Eilish cannot understand as she is pulled by the wrist into sitting up. From silence there comes a rushing sound that gives to bawling voices and running calls for help amidst the ringing of house alarms as though everyone had just been belled awake into morning, Molly wiping at her mother's face, Eilish seeing her own blood dark on the sleeve of Molly's top, she has taken her daughter by the wrist but cannot shape her mouth, she tries to stand but the weight of her body has come to rest in her skull so that she dizzies against the wall. She leans her weight into her hand and forces herself to stand, printing the wall with blood, Ben wailing and clinging to his sister while Molly tells her to sit down. She must force the mouth to speak, seeking to work the tongue to sound the word that sits in blood beneath the bitten tongue, the name, there is only a name that must take shape in her mouth, the mouth a silent cave after she has whispered it. Bailey. She is stumbling through the doorway and will not be stopped, some rank amalgam smell coming to meet her, it penetrates the nose, the eyes, the mouth, it burns her throat as she steps out into a void of smoke and hanging dust that occupies the space between the houses. She walks shouting for her son as men and women come to be from out of the dust, glass and cement crunching under running feet, the white hats of the civil defence calling to each other as they move upon the site of the airstrike. Through the dust she can see the sudden rubble of houses to the right of the Zajacs' house, the cement dust suspended in the air and the smoke turning in an easy breeze that fans outward as though to brother with the smoke rising from the first airstrike towards the end of the street. She is met with some broken mechanism of thought, cannot recall who lived across the road, cannot put a face to anyone she knows as she walks alone in a silent world staring fiercely through the dust, somebody has taken hold of her elbow, a speaking face under a white hat asks if she is hurt, a blanket is placed on her shoulder and she is walked to the side of the street and made to sit on the path. You don't understand, she says, trying to force a smile against the pain in her mouth, my son is coming back from the shop, my son went out to get milk. Molly has come alongside her clutching Ben to her chest, their hair and their faces pale with dust and the lips of the child are white until he opens his mouth to cry and she sees the surprising pink of his tongue, Molly pleading with her to come back home, Eilish trying to see down the street while blinking the dust from her eyes. She looks across the street and sees a pair of curtains hanging outside a bedroom window. She begins again towards the site of the first airstrike holding the blanket in her hand, a rippling nausea as she walks, the lurking smell of gas, the brickwork and wood and cabling undone to a ragged and smoking demolition where a row of houses once stood, people massing upon the debris and feeding it through their hands while a man hauls a woman by the underarms on shoeless dragging feet, another man lifting the woman by the ankles, she is carried towards a hatchback car waiting with its boot open while a man puts down the seats. It is then Eilish sees her son, knowing him at once though he is bending with his back turned among the white hats and civilians pulling on the rubble with his hands, his hair and his clothes white with dust and her voice caught in her throat. He does not hear until she takes him by the arm and pulls him back onto the street, pulls him into her arms, the dust silting his long lashes as he blinks and then tries to wriggle free. It's alright, Mam, he says, would you ever calm down, I have to go back and help. She is shouting out of love and pain and stares at him with wounded pride and smooths at his hair then pulls her hand back staring at it, she turns Bailey around by the shoulders and sees the hair matted with blood. She is calling in a hoarse voice, her eyes casting about as she yells at Molly to find a medic, a woman in civilian dress with a surgical face mask and shoulder bag steps towards them and quiets Eilish with a touch to the wrist, the practised efficiency of her hands as she sits Bailey down on the path and leans him forward, pours bottled water over the back of his head, Bailey lifting his eyes to his mother. You see, he says, I told you so, I'm absolutely fine. The medic hingeing up out of a squat. There is a piece of shrapnel embedded in his skull, she says, I think he will be fine but he'll need surgery to remove it, the Children's Hospital at Crumlin was struck this morning but you should go there anyhow and if they can't see him you should try Temple Street Hospital if you're willing to cross the front line, find someone here to take you in a car. A rancid smoke seems to turn in the air and fly directly into her mouth so that for an instant she has become inhabited, she cannot breathe the smoke back out, what is held in that burning smell. The medic has already moved on to a man sitting alone on the path with his hands wrapped around his knees staring into space. She cannot think, the street full of people shouting and waving and pointing for people to be put into cars, it is Molly who is able to speak, it is Molly who looks down at her mother's feet and says, Mam, you forgot your shoes, your feet are covered in blood.

The must of leaves and tree resin, a hooding gloom in the landscaper's van as the sliding door is closed. She can see Molly's face before they were parted on the street by a phalanx of men carrying a woman on a bedsheet towards a taxi, the fear that pooled in her daughter's eyes and then a sudden look of strength as she agreed to take Ben home, seeing her daughter now as though she stood in the smoking dust outside time, knowing that what she saw in her daughter's eyes was the instant of her adulthood. Tools rattle and clink on the van floor as the passengers in the back try to make space around a youth who has been placed supine on a jacket. He is calling out in a high and broken voice and she cannot see who is with him, Bailey trying to see out front between the seats and she whispers for him to sit down, tells him to keep the blanket stanched to his head. The red flexing neck of the driver as he leans out the door to back up the van, he brakes then pulls the door closed and bends over the steering wheel shoving the gearstick forward, the van edging ahead until it brakes again, Eilish holding the blanket to Bailey's head as the driver lowers the window and begins to shout and wave his arm. Back up there will you, pal, so I can get this crowd out. The naked hull of the van transmits into the bones every bump of the road, she is trying to find a clear line of thought but the pain in her skull pinches on thought so that she cannot recall where the hospital is or what it is called, not a word spoken in the van but for the driver cursing at what he meets on the road, he hammers the horn with the heel of his hand and shouts at the traffic in front, lowers the window and waves himself through a junction. She closes her eyes seeing herself carried forward in the dark, seeing herself become a passenger to her own life, this present moment in the back of the van and there is only this moment coming into being out of what is now past so that the future does not exist, the future retreating into the silence of the dead idea and yet she seeks a small piece to hold onto, to coax the future back out of nothingness, to break its silence by advancing into the logic of events by counting on as many variables as she can, seeing how the van will stop outside the emergency doors of the hospital and seeing them step inside, seeing Bailey forced to wait a while and then finally being admitted and taken through for surgery, or if not that, then Temple Street, seeing them step outside the van, seeing her son forced to wait and then finally being admitted, feeling the future again in her hands. The name of the hospital comes to her, the features of the building, whispering its name to herself as though it could be lost again from her mind, Crumlin, whispering it to Larry, seeing the glass at reception and the admissions clerk behind the computer and the many hours she and Larry have both spent in the emergency room waiting for their child's name to be called. She is looking for Larry's face but cannot see it, she searches her memory and seeks to touch his hair but his face remains obscure to her, she opens her eyes and sees Bailey leaning forward again trying to see out front. She moves to pull him back by the T-shirt when the van strikes a speed bump and Bailey is thrown backwards on top of her, a gasp of pain from the boy on the floor and groaning inside the van, she roars at the driver to slow down and sees a repentant hand come into the air, the tips of the fingernails dark with earth. Sorry about that, love, he shouts, we'll be there in a jiffy. She cannot recall his face, seeing it obliquely in the mirror, the red neck shining with sweat, a head of dark hair turning grey in half an hour, one moment you are pruning trees and the next you are an improvised ambulance driver, wondering what it is the man will do with this when he tries to sleep tonight, watching the small child with the face full of shrapnel he helped carry into the van, watching it replay in his mind for the rest of his life.

The van comes to a stop on the street before the hospital ramp and advances no further, the driver beating the horn and then he climbs out and pulls the side door open and she sees a different face than what she has imagined, the sad shook eyes of a man whose certainty has gone. It looks like the hospital's been struck again, he says, maybe it's not too bad, people are still trying to get inside. A man with a child in his arms ducks out of the van and begins towards the ramp and the others follow while the driver shouts for help with the boy on the floor. She is standing on the ramp with Bailey watching smoke rise from the rear of the hospital, the forecourt in chaos, people shouting and crowding the entrance while two security guards and a nurse stand by the door calling for people to hold back, two ambulances blocked on the exit ramp blare their sirens in urgent plea for the vehicles before them to back out. She cannot meet a single thought, she takes Bailey's hand and closes her eyes to the pain in her skull and when she opens them she sees a line of nurses and porters and civilians carrying children in bedclothes or wheeling them down the ramp towards a red minibus pulled up on the path, a boy standing in the driveway of a house across the street watches the evacuation while rounding an orange in his hand. A corpulent clown in a neon green wig has come towards them in elongated feet and a doctor's gown motioning for them to follow, she looks behind to see who is being summoned while the painted mouth yells at them to hurry, Bailey pulling on her arm until they are seated in the rear of the clown's beaten Corolla. She clutches Bailey's hand and closes her eyes against the nausea that begins at the base of her skull, seeing how all of this has happened without thought, seeing how she been carried forward as though caught within some enormity of force, the body no longer at swim but carried by the torrenting water, the car exiting the hospital grounds to join a small convoy behind the bus. Bailey sits on the middle seat in the rear while she refolds the towel and holds it to his head, watching as they go past the old shopping centre, past the rows of shuttered shops towards the canal, watching the old clown in the rear-view mirror, his left eye pulled into melancholy droop as he cleans the grease paint off his face with a wipe. The wig on the seat, the newly bald head perspiring and the real mouth concealed inside the painted mouth as he tells them it won't take long to reach Temple Street, they know me in there, he says, everything will be fine. A sense of hush as the children's convoy approaches the canal, the mounted sandbags and barbed wire, the rebel soldiers waving the convoy through onto no-man's land where the bus and the cars slow to a crawl and hands emerge from the bus waving white paper tissues and what looks like a page torn from a book while the clown produces a white hanky which he waves slowly outside the window. It won't be too long before we get across, he says, and then it's a straight run, I didn't even think to ask you your names, I'm James, by the way, or Jimmy the clown, whichever you prefer, I didn't even have a moment to take off me shoes, they're a right bugger to drive in. He has lifted a knee to reveal a large red patent shoe with bows for laces then puts his foot down and brings his fist to his mouth and puffs a cloud

of red glitter into the front area of the car so that for an
instant the world has exploded into flickering blood, the
red rain falling onto the gears and onto the grease paint
sticks and into the hair of the wig on the front seat and
she can see now that the man is insane and that they
need to get out of the car, Bailey pulling at her sleeve,
Mam, he says in a whisper, what the fuck is going on?
That one always annoys the nurses, Jimmy says, somebody has to come and clean it all up, OK, folks, here we
go now, whoopy-do, whoopy-do. The clown lowers the
window and it is then she knows she has left the house
without ID, begins to feel at the pockets of her jeans,
she has not even a handbag nor money, whispering this
to Jimmy who pretends not to hear as he holds up his
hospital pass and shows his ID, points to Bailey in the
backseat, this kid has shrapnel in his skull and needs
to go to Temple Street. Eyes lean to the glass and study
Bailey and Eilish and they are asked for their IDs, the
clown begins a smiling remonstration, he points to the
bus and the cars that have already gone ahead through
the checkpoint. Look, he says, let's not delay, this kid
needs urgent attention—— She puts her arms around
Bailey when the soldier orders Jimmy out of the car.
I want to see what's in the boot. The clown leaning
stoutly out the door, he steps around to the rear while
the soldier demands he lift the spare tyre and when he
starts the car again he has taken off the clown shoes
and seems deflated, rubs at his half-painted face, pads
about blindly with his left hand for the wipes. The road
ahead is clear, the convoy has gone. Don't worry, he

says, we'll quickly catch up. He is leaning forward in the seat when he smacks the steering wheel and begins to slow. Goddamn it, he says. The blue flare of a Garda roadblock, two gardaí on the street waving the car to a stop. The clown lowers the window and is already explaining, holding up the hospital pass, pointing to the convoy that has gone ahead. The bald sweating skull, the hair wiring out his ears, the Garda leaning down while shaking his head. I've orders not to let any more through, he says, turn the car around now. For Christ's sake, the clown says, I'm only taking him to the hospital, can't you see this child needs medical attention. The clown muttering to himself as he makes a U-turn, he wipes at his mouth with his sleeve so that his grease paint becomes a vicious smear. Shower of cunts, he says, and I do apologise for my language. He is watching the rear-view mirror and then makes a sudden, sharp turn down a narrow street. I can't get you to Temple Street, he says, they've got my registration and ID, but don't you worry, St James's Hospital is over this way, you can tell them he's sixteen and they'll take him in and sure what can they do after they've fixed him up, he looks old enough, you can tell them to go fuck themselves and leave.

She cannot recall what day of the week this is, no sense of night or day in the bleached light of the hospital corridor, Bailey leaning into her half asleep while she sits against the wall probing her foot for glass. The emergency department at overspill, patients in various states of bloody undress on seats and in wheelchairs or lying on the floor, two nurses have stopped in the corridor to speak and a hushed laugh escapes between them, Bailey sitting up with a yawn. He folds his arms and fixes Eilish with an aggrieved, put-on look while she smooths the hair away from his eyes and fixes his dressing. I'm starving, he says, I've had enough of this, how are we supposed to eat if you didn't bring any money, why can't we just go home and come back later? She is watching a gaunt man lying dead or asleep on a blanket nearby dressed in a crumpled tan suit with blood discolouring the sleeve, his hand clutching a plastic bag filled with bread rolls, a lone black shoe on a foot. Another man she saw being carried into the emergency room was wearing just one sports shoe, so many shoes gone astray, she thinks, so many shoes dislodged while their owners are carried by the arms and legs or dragged by the armpits into the backs of cars and vans and dragged again into emergency rooms without a gurney, the orphaned shoes kicked aside in the rush or left to lie on the street or on footpaths like an unblinking eye awaiting the return of its owner. Bailey nudging her in the ribs as an ample nurse with a tired smile comes through the swing doors calling his name, the smirk on his face as he sits into the wheelchair and pats his hands on his lap. You're in fine fettle, the nurse says, you'll be right as rain before you know it. The nurse nods for Eilish to follow and then stares at Eilish's feet. My goodness, she says, let me see if I can sort something out for you upstairs. A stackable grey chair beside the bed curtained off from the ward and a sense of pleasure comes upon her, seeing the future has arrived in the way she had hoped, Bailey propped on a pillow in a paper gown with the dust and blood washed off his face, his head dressed and awaiting the razor before surgery, repeating to herself what was told by the scan, that there will be no internal damage to the blood vessels or tissue. She wants to hold his hand, she must try and call Molly somehow, watching Bailey's impatient face, the hands jittery for something to do, he looks fourteen, fifteen at most and then in another glance he doesn't, he looks like a boy who turned thirteen during a day-long bombardment. It's Tuesday, she says, clapping her hands, and he looks at her and puzzles. Never mind, she says, you are so bloody lucky you know, to think what might have been if that shrapnel had been any bigger. You said that already, Mam, the fact is, it wasn't, so there's no point going on about it, ask the nurse if she'll let me have a piece of toast or something, I'm going to starve to death, go and tell them I haven't eaten all day. The nurse from downstairs places into her hand some anaesthetic wipes and plasters and paper slippers in a see-through wrapper. The nurse manager has just asked that you stop by on your way out, she says, it's the desk at the end of the corridor. Eilish cleans and plasters the cuts on her feet and walks through the ward in paper slippers preparing a face for the nurse, recalling the lie she told the admissions clerk, the poisonous flower hanging from her mouth, thinking, they will have phoned our GP or found out his age somehow, why did you lie, Mrs Stack, your son isn't sixteen, this isn't a paediatric facility you know, it is against the rules to admit a child, she will touch the back of her head and feign surprise. She stands before the desk watching the nurse speak into the phone and receives a vacant, drifting look, the nurse puts down the phone and rolls her mouth as though making ready to spit, she is rolling a sweet with her tongue. I was told you wanted a word, I'm Eilish Stack, the mother of Bailey Stack on the ward. The nurse pulls a tray towards her and begins to search through it, slides a file free from the pile. Oh yes, we have a note here from downstairs, we are awaiting information regarding your son's admission, we just have a name and address and date of birth but we don't have your son's public service number and we need his security ID, I'm afraid the protocol is very strict. Yes, Eilish says, I explained all this already downstairs, I don't know my son's public service number off the top of my head, I can't even remember my own, I don't have my handbag or anything else with me, we didn't plan to come here—— Yes, of course, this happens all the time, look, don't worry about this tonight, you can give us the details when you come back tomorrow. Eilish is frowning, shaking her head. I'm sorry, she says, but I can't leave my son tonight, when is he due to go into theatre? Mrs Stack, visiting hours finished hours ago, you are not even supposed to be here right now, look, there's really no way of knowing when your son is going to go into theatre, the place is in chaos, the trauma team is working non-stop, the best thing for you to do is go home and get some sleep, I will have a nurse call you in the morning when your son is out of theatre and you can come back then. Eilish is looking at her feet in the paper slippers. I don't know how I'm going to get home, she says, I'm going to have to cross the frontline without ID, I'll probably get arrested. The nurse swings her mouth to one side. Let me see if I can get you a hospital pass, she says, it will say you were brought here by the emergency services, people do it all the time, you can use it to cross over. She is watching the nurse's hands without seeing them, seeing instead some interior space of mind, a sudden brightness of feeling that moves through her body, this sense that Bailey is going to be fine, seeing how life can stretch suddenly beyond you and then in a moment it snaps back to its old shape, she closes her eyes and feels the tension release from her body as though she has let it drop from her hands, a quick fatigue coming upon her, she wants to sit down and close her eyes, she looks up and sees the nurse frowning. I'm sorry, she says, what did you say? You look a bit pale, Mrs Stack, are you sure you're alright, would you like to use the phone to speak with your husband, you might be lucky and get through. She stands before the phone and cannot recall their number, what if Larry cannot recall it either, she picks up the phone and it is not memory that dials but a pattern stored in her fingers.

She is examined by torchlight at the military checkpoint
and must explain why she is trying to cross the front
line five hours past curfew, the hospital letter taken
from her hand, she points to her feet without shoes,
the paper slippers in tatters, she is made to wait before
she is allowed to cross alone in darkness towards the
bridge, a lifetime in each step, the windowless buses
parked along the road and the faceless eyes watching
her approach. She has no letter nor ID for the rebel
soldier standing guard and tries to explain, she cannot
see the face behind the torch, thinking that he sounds
too young to understand, too young to know the world
beyond black and white and regimental command, he
brings the torch down to her bloody feet and takes a
look again into her eyes as though asking himself what
does madness look like, it looks like this, not someone
waving their arms and yelling at the gods but a mother
trying to get back home to her children. The soldier
calls to a superior who asks her to step through, a man
about her own age, beard shadow and dark fatigues,
I'll take you home, he says, it's much too dangerous
to go alone. He points her towards a Land Rover and
rubs his jaw and yawns, drives without lights. I don't
suppose you need me to remind you that you are taking
your life into your hands being out here after curfew.
She knows from his voice the locale of his childhood,
knows the rugby school and the university that followed
and could take a guess at the career in the life that was
lived a lifetime ago. She is silent and cannot open her
mouth, to explain it all again is suddenly beyond her.

The road no longer a road, the driver slowing and then he stops and leans out with his torch and brings the Land Rover onto the path and weaves a way through. When he pulls up at the junction onto St Laurence Street he lets the engine idle, turns and seeks her eyes. I'm wondering, he says, why you chose to stay, there is nothing here for you now. And what about you, she says, why are you here? I am here because I have a job to do, he says, and I will remain until that work is done or leave in a box. She makes a shape with her mouth and cannot answer, pulls the handle on the door but does not move. I have a son who joined the rebel forces, she says, I haven't heard from him for a long time, do you think perhaps he is dead? It would be hard to know, he says, he might be holed up, he might have been arrested or perhaps he is just wise enough not to email or call, they trace the messages back to the families you know, I sent word to my wife that I was alright but I haven't seen my family in months. He watches her climb out and tells her to stay safe. It's not too late to leave you know, he says, this place is going to become a hellmouth all over again, the regime is about to agree to let the UN open a humanitarian corridor from Lansdowne Road stadium through the port tunnel to the north, you'll be allowed to leave like rats so long as the piper calls the tune, take care of yourself, alright? The paper slippers still in her hand as she steps through the street seeing the dust and the smoke have gone, half a house left standing across the street as though cleft by a butcher's knife, an upstairs window frame that remains within the brickwork reaching out into nothing, the other half of the house and the two houses alongside it are gone into a sliding of masonry and wood, a car on the street burnt out. She stands before her house seeing the front window sheeted with bin liner, the porch in ruins, Molly coming to the door with a torch in her hand as Eilish takes her into her arms, Ben asleep under the stairs. Molly shines the torch onto the damaged ceiling. The upstairs is worse, she says, showing where she has swept up the glass, the cement dust still suspended in the air, the dust upon the sideboard and bookshelves and in the eaves of the picture frames, Eilish gathers the pictures and sits them in her lap in Larry's armchair, the bin liners in the window sucking softly on the breeze. You'll have to go for water in the morning with Ben, she says, I have to go back to Bailey and check him out early from the hospital, I had to lie about his age to get him into St James's. She is too tired to eat the food that Molly has heated and too tired to sleep. She rests in the armchair cleaning the photos with her blouse, watching the past go by in mocking parade, whispering to Larry about the airstrike, watching the brow come down under the weight of his incomprehension, his hands pulling on his beard, his hands become fists overcome by a rage made impotent before the world's derision, this house no longer a house.

She goes to her son under an umbrella, birdsong calling the dawn and then gunfire quickens the world to
quiet, this fear that lives in her abdomen stretching
itself, it moves into her legs when a warplane scuds
overhead. By the checkpoint she sees more buses have
been parked along the canal and have been placed in
single file across the Camac Bridge and down into
no-man's land forming a protective barrier. She is told
to wait behind the sandbags, the soldier from last night
is gone. She watches an upended umbrella on the road
divide beyond the bridge, the asphalt strewn with shattered glass and a dozen people or so standing behind
the last bus on the other side of the bridge waiting for a
rebel soldier to give the command to go. A young man
is pointing beyond the sandbags. The sniper's up in that
tower block at Dolphin's Barn, he says. There is a shout
and then rebel soldiers make cover fire and the people
waiting at the last bus begin to run, a mother with a
bouquet of wildflowers pulling on the hand of a little
girl who cannot keep up, a youth running with his head
tucked into his shoulders, the discharge of a sniper
shot echoes like handclap and the mother shrinks and
yanks the hand of the girl while a greyish man covers
his head with a newspaper. An elderly woman makes
a lumbering run across the bridge towards the rebels
holding her hand to her chest. There follows a long
quiet filled with the slow revving of a bus being driven
by a rebel soldier who backs it over the bridge to extend
the cordon, he reverses it into place behind the last
bus while the sharpshooter tries his luck, one quick

handclap after another as a window shatters and the bus makes a pneumatic gasp as though the bullet had penetrated a lung. The doors open and a rebel soldier steps out and walks back towards the bridge. She stows her umbrella in her pocket and squeezes against the tremor in her hand. She will cross, she knows this now, she will empty her mind and become a running thing without thought, thinking, everything seems to be OK anyhow, it is only a short distance from the last bus to the safety of the shops. She walks single file across the bridge behind a soldier who tells them to keep tight to the buses while people continue towards the rebel checkpoint at a run, a round cracks the air and everybody flinches and still the people make it across unharmed, a youth with a small dog in his arms jogs across while a woman runs with a shopping bag, her face in a grimace as though tensing for the arrival of a bullet, for the shattering of bone and haemorrhaging of blood, for the release into darkness. It is then Eilish sees the wrinkled IV bag lying on the road, sees the residue of blood diluted by the rain, a youth from behind tries his luck and takes off at a sprint and makes it across, the hand of the rebel soldier remains in the air telling them to stay put. He sights binoculars through the bus onto the tower block and she wonders if the sniper by shooting reveals his perch, a puff of smoke or blur of movement, the soldier turning towards them with a lop-sided face. There's a stretch of about fifty metres before you get too close for the shooter's scope, keep at a run as you go across and stay close to those buildings, it's

very difficult to sight a running target and that shooter's just trying his luck. A man behind her is telling his
wife she is wearing the wrong shoes, there comes from
the canal a burst of cover fire and at the soldier's command she runs past the last bus onto the road behind a
man in a flapping black raincoat, a woman to her right
clutching a pink bag, she runs looking down at the road
seeing in the slicked asphalt the shadow shapes of the
runners in front as though they are not runners at all
but have taken flight beneath into some underworld,
telling herself not to lift her eyes as she flicks her sight
upward taking a glance perhaps of the shooter in some
anomalous contract, it is impossible to know if she has
seen him or not, she runs watching ahead to the junction, runs watching the Indian takeaway and the supermarket with its shutters down, the two cars passing
through the crossroads and then with a clap the man
in the black raincoat stumbles and his coat flies outward and he falls down and the woman closest to her
throws an arm outward to the sound of another clap
and the bag falls from her hand as she plunges sharply
before Eilish's running feet, the world wheeling as she
is tripped to the ground. When she opens her eyes she
is lying on the road with her hands covering her head,
running footsteps pass into silence while a sharp pain
gnaws on her elbow, she does not think she has been
shot. She must get up and run, the man in the raincoat
remains still and the woman behind her makes a congested wheeze as the rebel soldiers begin to shout and
then heavy gunfire commences from the bridge, of a

sudden there comes the roar of return fire from somewhere close by, she lies pressing her nose into the road
shuddering at the noise, it is the mouth of some ferocious beast let fly above her, she cannot move and then
she begins to see how there is no escape from this, the
gunfire continuing to traffic overhead in a stuttering yet
unceasing exchange and from her heart there runs a
cold sad feeling that says she is going to die, she opens
her eyes and knows she has crossed a border of some
kind, wet light on the asphalt and rusting green on the
railing that runs in unity along the path to the shops
and she knows she is lying not against the road but
against something endmost and is astonished by her
calm, death is waiting and she was not prepared, death
stood before her in brazen signal and she did not look
but ran into its arms without thinking of her children,
and it is grief that seizes hold of her when she sees her
children abandoned, seeing how she was told and did
not listen, it was your duty to deliver them from danger
but instead you stood your ground, such foolishness
and blindness before the facts, you should have got
them out, hearing the words her father gave in warning
again and again, to leave the country and make a better
life, seeing the missed opportunities grow before her
and how they could have escaped, all of it dust, all of it
a nothingness in a false past and she sees herself in a
hole in the earth and she sees the best parts of her love,
sees how one thing gives to another thing and how
her life has been consumed by some law of force that
governs all and she is nothing within it but a speck of

dust, a small mark of endurance, and in her sorrowing she turns her eyes and watches the man's blood travel in slow escape from his body, the blood still alive with cellular life, the red and white cells in strange oblivion seeking to do their work while the blood follows the camber of the road as though it had thought for the gutter to carry it down into the groundwater where it will find dissolution and return, she is squeezing her fists and toeing the ground, she wants to live and see her children, a profound silence opening overhead as the shooting stops and a rebel soldier shouts down at them and she is afraid to wave and show she is alive, and she lies very still in absolute contact with the world and meets the feeling she is going to live, watching the road-stone held in its bitumen, the stones of the earth formed by heat and pressure aeons ago but there is only this moment and she must go to it, some inward force moving through her body and she closes her eyes and can see the years of her life gone by and the time that is yet to live and of a sudden something has hauled her up into movement and she has become a running body.

She slips through the hospital entrance past the security desk without being stopped and goes to the lift and meets a different face on the nurse's station, clear blue eyes glancing up from a screen. Can I help you? My son went in for surgery last night, can you tell me where I can see him? The nurse allows a small smile then shakes her head. I'm sorry, she says, visiting hours are between two and four, or six thirty and eight thirty in the evening, you'll have to come back later. The phone is ringing on the desk and the nurse looks towards it then looks at Eilish who remains standing before her. Excuse me a moment while I answer this. Eilish folds her arms and looks down the corridor, three trolleys with patients are waiting for a place in the ward and she thinks of the man in the tan suit lying on the floor with his hand clutching the bag of bread rolls as the nurse hangs up the phone. I'm sorry, Eilish says, look, I just want to know how he is, he had surgery last night to remove some shrapnel from his skull. Yellow the tips of the nurse's fingers pushing softly at a ballpoint pen and then the hand reaches for the in-patient tray and pulls it towards her. I can check his file and let you know before you go, you would have been due to get a call anyhow. Good luck getting through, Eilish says, and the nurse smiles without looking up. Yes, I know, she says, everything has been an absolute nightmare, what did you say your son's name was again? She is watching the nurse's face as she searches the tray, the coating of make-up powdery in the overhead light, a blemish of skin running from behind the ear to the clavicle, it looks like eczema, the nurse sliding another tray towards her, she reaches the end of the files with a frown and returns to the first tray. I'm sorry, she says, Bailey Stack, that's his name? Yes, that's correct. I'm afraid we have no Bailey Stack here, are you sure you have the right ward, this is Anne Young Ward, people get confused all the time, they all look much the same. Yes, she says, Anne Young Ward, I stood here last night and spoke to the ward nurse, I don't remember her name, my son was in a room down that corridor waiting to go into surgery, she said somebody would call me in the morning. The nurse's eyes drift across the desk. Things are chaotic around here at the moment, she says, just let me go speak to the nurse manager. The phone begins to ring on the desk but the nurse steps through a door and pulls it closed, another nurse appears and answers the phone and speaks a yes and a no then steps away. Eilish watching the handle of the door turn slowly though it doesn't open and then it opens a crack and a different nurse looks out and closes the door again. She wants a cup of coffee and a cigarette, she wants to give Bailey fresh clothes and take him home, the nurse manager steps through the door and does not glance her way but walks down the corridor while the other nurse remains inside. Eilish turns and walks towards the multi-bed room where Bailey was last night, an elderly man with a sunken face is asleep in the bed space where Bailey was, she looks to the other faces and draws a curtain back, a male nurse has come behind her. Excuse me, he says, can I help you? She walks past him into the corridor and sees the nurse manager stepping towards her with a pursing mouth. Mrs Stack, I'm the nurse in charge on this ward, I'm sorry for the confusion, I was hoping the registrar could speak with you, your son was transferred last night to another hospital, he was signed out of here just past midnight, this sometimes happens I'm afraid. I'm sorry, Eilish says, I don't understand, what do you mean he was transferred to another hospital? As I said, this happens all the time, we have to make use of spillover hospitals during the crisis, your son was due to go into surgery but was transferred instead, the orders come from above and we have no say, I have all the details to hand at the desk, in the meantime, there are papers you need to sign. Just hold on a moment, Eilish says, I really don't understand this at all, you are telling me that my son is no longer in this hospital even though he was due to go into surgery and had a bed last night? Yes, that is correct, Mrs Stack, no doubt we tried to call you but—— I'm sorry, this is ridiculous, I've never heard of such a thing, my son is a minor, I did not give permission for him to be moved, I signed him into this hospital and not someplace else, I want you to speak to your superior and I want my son to be returned back here. I'm afraid there's nothing we can do about this, Mrs Stack, the decision was not taken at this hospital, they came for him just after midnight. Who came for him just after midnight? The mouth before her purses again and something begins to move in the eyes that looks like the glimmer of fear and then the eyes look away, the nurse casting a glance towards the desk as though searching for help, she folds her arms and releases them. Look, I don't know who makes these decisions, it has nothing to do with us here, he was transferred to St Bricin's Hospital shortly after midnight. I really don't understand this, St Bricin's Hospital, are you making this up, I've never even heard of St Bricin's Hospital. It's the military hospital in Smithfield, it belongs to the Defence Forces. Something slides down the length of her being and leaves in its wake a coating of sickness, she is trying to clear her throat. What is my son doing in a military hospital, why is my son in such a place? The mouth continues to speak because the mouth does not know and so the mouth asks and awaits an answer while the body speaks as though it knew all along, she thinks she is going to be sick, she finds herself sitting on a chair with a cup of water in her hand, she takes a drink and then stands up looking for a bin for the paper cup, she holds it out for somebody to take but they are afraid to go to her, she makes a quick motion of wrath with her hand. Would somebody write it down, she says, write down the address of the fucking hospital, and would somebody please take this cup.

Something is wrong on the street ahead, people are sitting under the awning outside a café having food and drinks, a man forking at an open sandwich beside two girls leaning into straws, two elderly women conversing over tea with their trolleys parked beside the table and she walks past them despising what she sees and then she corrects herself, thinking, people are entitled to live their lives, people are entitled to some small moment of peace. She stands in line before the security gate to the military hospital under the eye of a camera, rehearsing what she is going to say, seeking the right words and tone, speaking the words over and over, altering them, seeing herself before some faceless individual, there has been a mistake, my son was transferred here but he is just thirteen, he was sent to a general hospital when really he should have gone to a children's hospital instead—— She is searched and her phone is taken for collection on exit. A stern three-storey building with red-brick wings looms as she walks up a tree-lined drive, Defence Forces personnel and plainclothes gardaí standing about the courtyard while a paramedic closes the rear door of an ambulance. There is a small queue inside the door before the administration desk, an orbed camera watching down, people are being admitted through a further door where a soldier stands guard. She shows her security ID and tries to speak the words she rehearsed but they come out wrong, it does not seem to matter, the administration official types Bailey's name and address and security number but when his face lifts from the screen his eyes are all wrong. I'm sorry but your son is not registered here as a patient, perhaps you've made a mistake. She is frowning at the face as though it were unintelligible, her hands becoming fists as she leans on the desk. But I've just come from St James's Hospital, she says, I was told that my son was taken here last night for surgery, I saw the transfer document myself. Yes, but it says here he is not a patient, and anyhow, we don't do surgery at this hospital, this wing of the hospital has been reserved for overflow from the city's hospitals, perhaps your son was taken into custody and detained in the military wing of the hospital, it is sometimes the case that people detained in the city hospitals are brought there. The official is clicking at the screen, his eyes flicking back and forth. What you are saying makes no sense, she says, my son is thirteen, why would a thirteen-year-old be detained, there was an airstrike and my son was taken to St James's Hospital by mistake, I have a copy of the transfer papers in my bag. Please, if you just go outside and turn left, you will see the security entrance and you can enquire there about your son. He is looking at the woman standing behind her in the queue, he motions with his hand for Eilish to step away but she cannot move her feet, she is asked again to stand aside and she goes to speak but the words have fled her mouth. She finds herself walking towards the exit, turns and watches the desk without seeing, she is mumbling something, finds herself standing outside watching the sky, this feeling of weight inside her, the weight growing moment by moment so that she is swollen again with child, this sense of mass and burden that is at once her own tissue and blood, the child that is born from the body remains always a part of the body. She walks towards the military wing of the hospital with her ID in hand, she is told non-military personnel are not allowed inside, she is asked to leave but refuses to go, a second military policeman steps outside the guard box and says, I'm sorry but if you stay here you will be arrested, there's no two ways about it. She turns and walks back to the public entrance of the hospital and goes to the desk and cuts across a woman speaking with the clerk. I'm sorry, she says, but there really has been a mistake, perhaps your computer has made some kind of error, you need to check your admissions again, my son was transferred to this hospital at five past twelve last night, it says so here on the transfer document so there is nowhere else he can be but here, please take a look for yourself, this is a copy of the document given to me at St James's. The man twists his mouth in silent apology to the woman standing before him then looks to Eilish, takes the document and reads it. Yes, he says, but I'm afraid this document does not refer to this wing of the hospital specifically, it just says St Bricin's Military Hospital and I can tell you categorically that your son is not a patient in the overspill—— A strange small laugh escapes her mouth and pulls on her terror, she leans with two hands on the desk and stares down at the computer. My son is thirteen, do you understand, how can a thirteen-year-old boy disappear, do you want to tell me that? The damned face before her and she has banged the desk with her fist and everyone is silent and she does not know what she has said, words, words, all of them the wrong words piling up before the cold eyes and small mouth turning to summon the military policeman and she folds her arms and will not move, watching the coming steps of the policeman, watching a middle-aged cleaner in blue overalls as he makes his way backwards across the vestibule as though in some private stupor, the damp mop working in overlapping circles, he bends to adjust a yellow caution sign as the policeman takes her by the elbow and walks her out the door. She stands looking to the sky sensing madness, turns and stares at the high windows and sees them as though she were looking down some barren precipice, standing alone with nowhere to go, she will return now to St James's Hospital, she will return there and root out the error. It is evening when she goes back on foot to St Bricin's Military Hospital, standing motionless before the entrance to the military wing, watching the unmarked cars come and go, a black feeling rising inside her, a small voice that tries to speak but she does not want to hear it, thinking, what is knowing without the facts, it is nothing but speculation, fortune telling and divination, guessing is so often wrong, it is wrong most of the time. She will try for a third time at the admissions wing of the hospital, darkness and light in the sky, she stands watching the hospital building as though staring into the face of the regime, the cleaner in blue overalls has stepped out of the building placing an unlit cigarette in his mouth, their eyes meeting for a moment, he looks away and lights up then steps towards her pulling on the pack, the tremor in her hand as she accepts the offer of a fag, the smell of disinfectant on the tattooed hand that brings the flame to her mouth. I heard you in there earlier on, he says, I hear the same thing in there every day and it's always the same thing. He lowers his head over the cigarette and takes a long pull then lifts his head and exhales the full length of his breath. Your son was most likely detained, he says, they take them to the military wing for interrogation and after that the door is closed and they won't tell you anything, look, there is no other way to tell you this, but you should ask to go to the morgue, you are allowed to ask to go to the morgue, if I were you that's where I'd go, if only to rule it out for today. She stands frowning at the man. Rule what out? she says. The look of agony on the cleaner's face and then he turns and walks away and she is calling after him, why would I want to go there, she says, what business would I have going there?

She is standing before madness without sleep, seeing her son swallowed by the regime, returning day after day to the hospital only to be told the same thing, standing in the courtyard where she approaches Defence Forces personnel, the plainclothes gardaí, pleading with the mouth of some old beggar woman, please, help me find my son, you must help, please, he is only a child, this sense now she is no longer of the body and will come undone into ashes. She watches the others come and go and reads the news on each face, she cannot do what the cleaner told her to do, she cannot do what the others are doing until some obscure power sends her into the hospital building, she is standing before the administration clerk speaking the words she was told to speak, a phone call is made, two military officers converse by the interior door and she is escorted from the vestibule into the main building, following behind a military policeman along a corridor to a door that leads to steps and down a dark stairwell into colding gloom, following the military policeman to another door and a reception area where a man in a white coat slides a clipboard across the counter, her hand shaking as she lifts the pen. She watches the man read the form and she speaks her son's name and the official says, down here, there are no names, just numbers I'm afraid, we do not have names for them when they come in, if your son is here he will be here as a number, you will need to make the identification yourself. She is given a face mask and gloves and looks down at her hands, something has come loose and is rattling inside her, it is not her real self following this man, this keeper of the dead, but some false self, some other self following through a doorway. She says, I don't know what I'm doing here, this is all a mistake. The man does not answer but points for her to go through. It is not a refrigerated room full of stainless steel but a storage space with bodies lying side-by-side along the concrete shrouded in grey zipper bags, the room is not even cold, it stinks of disinfectant. A small prayer escapes her mouth and she has no faith from which to offer a prayer but again the prayer is spoken and she is whispering to Larry, telling herself she must leave this place, watching herself as though disembodied, moving forward, bending to the first body and unzipping to meet a sunken face with no teeth and what looks like the bore of a drill through the cheek and one eye that cannot close, she stands up abject, wringing her hands, she looks to the keeper as though to say she has made a mistake, that she has wandered by error into the land of the dead and must return, but the keeper simply tells her to close the zipper and move onto the next body. She kneels before the next body bag and unzips and whispers this is not my son, moves from body to body, seeing how the regime has left its mark on each face and neck, that murder has a smell of antiseptic, and each time the mouth whispers, this is not my son, the mouth whispering it again and again, this is not my son, this is not my son, this is not my son, this is not my son, and she looks to the keeper who is looking at the time on his wrist and she unzips another body bag saying, this is not my son before she has even taken read of the face, this is not my son, this is not my son, this is not my son, this is not my son, seeing before her the face of Bailey serenely broken, the skin smelling of bleach, and what was bent inside her breaks so that a wretched howl escapes her body and she takes his face into her hands, stares into the face of the dead child seeing only the living child, and she wishes she could die instead, smoothing her hand along the downy face, the hair still wet with blood. She whispers, my beautiful child, what have they done to you? The skin before her clouded with bruising, the missing and broken teeth, she unzips the bag down seeing the nails torn from his hands and feet, seeing the bore of a drill through the front of his knee, the cigarette burns along the torso, and she takes his hand and kisses it, the body washed down so that no blood remains but for the blood clouding darkly under the skin that cannot be washed away. She does not hear what the keeper says as he helps her to zip up the body bag, guides her through the door speaking in a low voice. Number 24, he says, would you care to make a positive identification of your son, Mrs Stack? And he says, once you have filled out the form, your son will be transferred to the city morgue. And he says, just so you know, Mrs Stack, it says here your son died of heart failure. And she turns from the man seeing only darkness, stands lost in darkness, standing in a place where no place can be found.

# 9

She wakes with her head against the window and looks outside without seeing, closing her eyes she travels to a darkness as though moving through water with her heart in pain, squeezing and squeezing her hands. Molly is calling from far away and shakes her mother's arm. Mam, she says, wake up will you, the driver said something just now, I don't know what he said, we haven't moved in over an hour, I'm going to go see what's up. Ben is passed into her arms and Molly follows the passengers towards the front of the coach. The front door makes a hiss and the driver steps down onto the motorway and hitches his jeans, slides a phone into his shirt pocket as people gather around. Ben bouncing on her lap with a malevolent grin, he grabs hold of her nose, beep-beep, he says, beep-beep, beep-beep, and she must honk and honk again, trying to smile as he tweaks her nose, he turns and slaps his hands to the glass. Car, he says, car, car, car, car. She looks outside and points out each word for him, bus, car, van, lorry, woman, child, bird, a meaty rook winging down with foil in its mouth, it empties its beak to poke at a piece of food thrown from the back of a van where too many children are sitting on stacked mattresses inside. People are standing outside their cars reading their phones, the car boots stuffed with outsized items or electrical appliances, the roofs stacked and the belongings sheeted while the motorway winds around a hill pointing north though nothing moves but for those on foot, a silent procession in the lay-by of people walking in winter coats or wrapped in blankets, children strapped to their mothers' chests or pushed in buggies or carried on the shoulders of men who pull on luggage or carry their lives on their backs. A young child stepping ahead of her parents falls onto the road and turns wailing with arms outstretched and Eilish feels nothing watching this child but a deadness inside her and then sudden pain swells inside her chest and she closes her eyes. Ben is jumping up and down on her lap, he grabs hold of her nose again, beep-beep, beep-beep, and she tries to smile but makes instead a broken shape with her mouth, Molly sliding back into the seat, the gaunt cheeks flushed with news. Everything has gone to shit, she says, the driver just said the corridor has closed and they've shut the border just past Dundalk as there's heavy fighting there, he wants to turn around, the traffic has nowhere to go, he says, we'll just sit here like this for days, he says he's going to take the next exit off the motorway soon as the traffic moves forward, the other roads are just as bad apparently and we'd be better off going on foot, the border is about fifty or sixty kilometres away, there's a row now because people are demanding their money back but he says he doesn't have it. Eilish looks across the seat to an elderly man who is showing a map on his phone to his wife or perhaps she is his sister, who is to know, they look so alike, Ben banging his hands on the glass, birdy birdy birdy birdy, he says, and she turns to see a boy going by with a lime bird in a small white cage and she closes her eyes and cannot think what to do, the heart has grown too sick for thinking, the heart now in a cage.

How quickly the day signals for night, the body of the sky filled with bruising and Ben whining for a snack, one step following after another as she carries the child strapped to her chest, her eyes fixed upon some null space, a numb vacancy at the centre of her being. The air is growing cold but Ben refuses to wear a hat, she tries to slide the hat back on his head but he slaps her hand back and shouts no no no. They leave the motorway on an off-ramp and follow the signs for the service station, her left hand cradling Ben's head, her right hand pinched from sharing the weight of a bag with Molly. The forecourt is full of people standing about or sitting on the tarmac with food and drinks while a queue carries out the door. Ben's nappy is full, she changes it on her lap while squatting in line outside the toilets, the pockets of her long coat stuffed with nappies and wipes. She queues for hot food while Molly sits on their baggage by the entrance with Ben in her lap. There is nowhere to sit so they remain on their bags while Eilish watches an electrical socket where a man is charging his phone, she asks Molly to send a message to Áine, a security guard stands over them and asks them to go outside, you are blocking an exit, he says. They place their bags on the tarmac and sit and eat while Eilish watches a rattish young man move like a beggar among the crowd, he steps before them and offers them a place to stay for the night, Molly wants to know what kind of place it is and how much it costs while Eilish studies his eyes, his shabby clothes, the nails mooned with dirt. What did you say no for? Molly says, watching the man move to the next group. Where are we going to sleep tonight? A woman in a yellow raincoat leans across and taps Molly on the arm. Be on your guard from the likes of that, she says, they lure you away and then they rob you, that's what they're doing. The woman slides a packet of biscuits towards Molly and for a time they speak while Eilish does not hear, she is watching Bailey seated on the tarmac across the forecourt with his legs stretched out before him, his hair shaved at the sides, an ear and partial cheek in amber light. He drinks from a can then stands up and stamps it flat with his sneaker and kicks it towards the pumps.

Fire in a darkened field, women wrapped in blankets and children sitting on their laps with their faces lit

by phones while people gather firewood in the trees
and put up tents. Space is made for them by the fire,
a bearded man nipping at sausages wrapped in tinfoil,
he blows on his fingers and insists they have some
while somewhere in the dark a woman calls for a child,
Molly taking a sausage on a twig, she cools it with her
mouth and tears a piece for Ben who holds it with
both hands and nibbles on it. Darkest blue the sky over
the surrounding darkness, the dark blackest around
the fire which unmakes each face then paints it again
so that a young woman asks with ruined eyes where
they are from and where they are going while a man
claws at the shadows on his face as he speaks. It's
best if you cross the border someplace else, he says,
Crossmaglen is probably the best bet from here, that's
where we're going, my cousin got across the border
no bother yesterday, she says the border police are
letting people through so long as you make it sweet
for them. There is talk of people risking arrest by
crossing the border at night, there is talk of violent
gangs that roam the borderlands, of armed patrols
along the border roads and how much you have to
pay to pass. She watches the flames as though in a
trance, watches the firelight dance before their eyes,
the firelight reaching for the eyes that remain in darkness, and who are these people without their eyes and
who are these people with their eyes blinded to the
future, these people trapped between the fire and the
dark? She closes her eyes and sees how much has
been devoured, sees the whole of her love and what

little remains, there is only a body, a body without a heart, a body with swollen feet to carry the children forward—— The woman with ruined eyes is asking if they will sleep in her tent. It's cold tonight and it's going to rain, she says, you can't have an infant sleeping outside and anyhow it's an eight-man tent, we got twelve in there last night.

Ben turns her face with his hand so that they lie breath to breath in the sleeping bag and when he is asleep she lies listening to the long silence of the night, seeing how death follows along the road, it follows into the dreams of those who are too tired to sleep and who must dream with open eyes, the gasps and cries that escape their mouths as though death were parading before them again and again each night so that each death is relived many times, and she lies hearing the sleepers mutter death into the darkness, lies feeling the cold earth to her back, hearing the rain on the tent as though it were a rain that fell millennia ago and outside there lies nothing but uninhabited earth, the world outside a darkness without pain, and to be without pain would be to enter fully into that darkness but there will be no going out, she knows this now, there will be no going out into the darkness after her son though she wishes she could follow, she will stand watching her son but she will not go out to the darkness because she must remain and there is only this for her now, to be a vessel in which to carry the children away from the darkness and there will be no peace and there will be no escape from pain and not even the darkness of closing her eyes is peace. Ben turns, he reaches for her face and begins to cry and calms when she smooths his cheek. She whispers to him though there are no words for a child this age, no explanation for what has been done and yet what the child will never recall from memory will always be known by him and he will carry it as poison in the blood. She looks to Molly and sees the sleeping heart beating the poison throughout the body and yet there is a light coming from within, her skin blue from the dawn brightening the tent but there is a light radiating also from within her body, a light that brings with it an increase of strength, and she does not know where this light inside Molly has come from, this light that shines out of darkness. Footfall on softened ground outside and cigarette smoke drifting towards the tent, a man coughs and children's voices sound the new day while a youth climbs over them to exit. Molly sits up and musses her hair then begins to rub her feet. Mam, she whispers, let me comb your hair. Eilish looks into her daughter's face and sees she has been crying in her sleep. She unzips from the sleeping bag and puts on her runners and steps outside. A low and cold greyness and the fire in ashes, litter strewn about the fallow field. She sits Ben on her rucksack and peels a banana and pours milk into his cup while Molly slaps her arms about her chest to keep warm, Ben toddling about the dirt and then he begins towards the trees. Eilish calls for him to come back but he continues towards the woodland by the edge of the field stamping his feet in the dirt and she follows ignoring the pain in her shoulders and feet. Ben standing in the mossy grass, he waves a stick and beats it off a tree then turns with his eyes agleam and brings up the stick to strike her. No, she says, wagging her finger, no no no, and she takes the stick and waves it before him and says, you do not hit, you do not hit another person, and she throws the stick away and turns him around and sends him back out onto the fallow field, the dead field crowned with weeds and underneath the worms turning the soil and within the soil the remains of the last crop, dead matter decomposing to give nutrient to what grows next, and Ben is running across the field with his fists pointed at the sky and she looks for a moment behind to the trees and sees the grass full of fallen leaves, sees the leaves lying graveless on the grass, yellow their faces among the dying brown.

The minibus comes from behind and clears its throat with a downshifting of gears that sends the walkers onto the verge, the bus slowing and then it pulls up alongside them while the driver with a slapped-red face leans out. I'm going to the border and there's two seats left inside if somebody wants a ride, fifty quid per head. Some of the walkers turn and look at each other and shake their heads while Molly drops the bag onto the grass. Mam, she says, you need a rest and my hand is broken from carrying this thing. Eilish watches the minibus, her eyes adrift as though waiting for some answer to take shape in her mind, there is nothing but silence and darkness, she exhales against the weight of the child as she climbs the steps and the driver does not meet her eyes. She places her sister's money into his palm and then he looks at his hand and shakes his head. The price is fifty per head. Yes, she says, but there's just two of us and an infant. Fifty per person is what I said and I count three. But the child will be sitting on my lap, she says, he won't take up any space. The driver sighs and continues the slow shaking of his head. It's fifty per head or go on foot if you like but you're safer on this bus than being out there on your own, do whatever you like. She is on display for the passengers watching the exchange, a child crying down the back, Molly nudging her from behind when she snaps at her purse and draws another note and throws it into the man's lap, forcing the piglet eyes to look at her, the thin and gobbling mouth. Leave the bags down outside the door, Molly, let this man put them into the hold. Ben wants to walk the narrow aisle, he wants to stand on her lap and bounce and play hide and seek with the people behind, he is hungry and needs to nap, she turns her face towards the glass watching the sun gone from the sky, the country road full of walkers parting to let the bus through, a woman pushing a child in a buggy lifts her eyes towards the window and Eilish sees herself staring back. Molly says something about her father and Eilish turns watching her daughter's face in the compact mirror as she paints her eyes. I didn't hear what you said. I was talking about Dad, she says, it's going to be his birthday soon, what year was he born again? Eilish turns to the window and shuts her eyes. It is not that she has forgotten him, it is that when she thinks of him now so little remains, he has become a shadow, an absence in the place where love used to be, or perhaps some small love remains in a chamber of the heart sealed under so much weight. Ben is asleep in her arms when the bus slows and then it stops and the driver drops his shoulder to yank the handbrake and stands out of his seat to pull open the door. He steps down onto the road and speaks to a soldier wearing a black beret then lights a cigarette while a second soldier steps onto the bus with a handgun buttoned on his hip. They are told to leave the bus, have your security passes ready and take your bags out of the hold for inspection. They step down off the bus and there is no border but open countryside, the border is thirty kilometres away, a man says, almost an hour has passed before they climb onto the bus again. It is evening and then it is night, the bus meeting one checkpoint after another, military Land Rovers or civilian SUVs angled across the road, soldiers from the Defence Forces or militias in surplus army fatigues, shaven heads and hands in fingerless gloves holding automatic rifles at the shoulder pointed towards the ground, different faces each time speaking the same commands, the driver standing away from the bus with a cigarette in his mouth counting the cash he has to pay. IDs must be shown, they must explain where they are going, they are forced to open their bags and place their belongings onto the road and then pack them again and sometimes the bags are a little lighter and each time there is a different price, an exit tax some of them call it, a contribution to the cause you are leaving behind. One road is closed after another, a petrol station looms brightly in the darkness and they stop to use the toilets and buy food and drinks. She can sense the border nearby in the dark, can sense it withdrawing from them as though a tide were leaving the shore behind to barren moonlight. She needs to sleep but cannot, she must wake Molly again and carry Ben asleep in her arms as they step down off the bus for the fifth time, Molly dragging her feet, it is almost 1am, a stone wall and hooding trees, the bus pinned in the headlights of an SUV while flashlights take a read of each face. A bearded militant waves a handgun and shouts them into line, he is dressed in civilian clothing with jeans rolled over the top of his boots. He pulls a middle-aged man from the line and puts a torch in his face. So what do you think you're running from, baldy, why don't you stay and fight for your country you chickenshit cunt? The man remains motionless with his face turned away from the torchlight, his eyes half-closed and then he blinks slowly as though trying to understand what has been said to him. She looks away when the militant kicks the man behind the legs. Get down on your knees and show your ID. She looks again to the militant's face and sees nothing but his malignancy turned inside out so that it is worn openly, she takes hold of Molly's arm and seeks her eyes asking her to look away, watches the driver and sees him rub his eyes from fatigue and understands now his price, better to drive around in circles all night meeting one checkpoint after another than be out here alone in the dark meeting the likes of these, the kneeling man fumbling at the pockets of his coat, his fingers have fled leaving two useless fists, finally he produces an ID. The militant tosses it towards another man who picks it up off the ground and reads the details into a radio, the bearded man nudging at the kneeling man's shoulder with his gun, he brings the muzzle to the man's temple and slides it slowly down his neck then lifts a boot and rests it on his shoulder. So what do you work at you cunt? The man whispers something with his face towards the ground. I didn't hear what you said. The man half-shouts. I'm a technician. A technician of what? The man clears his throat and begins to weep, the militant bringing the torchlight onto the faces of the people standing in line by the bus, static talk on the radio and then the boot comes down and the man's ID is thrown onto the ground before him. The price for you is not the same as for the others, the price for a chickenshit cunt like you is double. She watches the man remain on his knees as the militant steps away, sees him carry his humiliation onto the bus with bowed shoulders, his hands shaking on his lap when he takes his seat. Without thought she has placed a hand on his arm and squeezes and the man looks up and tries to smile but something in his eyes is destroyed.

There should be nothing on the other side but the edge of a cliff that begins the long fall down into nothingness but instead the road continues past the border, the pre-fabs greying in the dawn, the utility wire running with-out interruption across the international line, an artic-ulated truck slowing to a stop as a yawning soldier covers his mouth. They join a queue for those on foot, people trying to sleep or keep warm while propped against their bags or against one another while Molly leans into her mother's arm and falls asleep. She begins to mutter then makes a small cry, sits up rubbing her eyes and Eilish can see in her eyes the terror reaching out from the dream. The queue at last begins to move as the checkpoint finally opens and they drag their bags forward a few paces and sit down again. Watching the last of the night recede, the British checkpoint further along the road growing in definition, the corrugated barriers and the barbed wire and the military watch-tower and the road continuing onwards and she knows that once they walk across this line the weight will begin, that what is left behind will not be left behind at all but will continue to grow in weight and be carried forever on their backs. They stand in a prefab waiting room where all the stackable chairs have been taken by people filling forms on their laps, the floor vibrating as people move in groups towards the glass and she cannot find her pen, she must borrow one from the elderly man standing beside her, he looks into her eyes and smiles but she cannot return the smile and looks to the floor, sees he is wearing two different shoes, one tan and one grey. When she steps to the glass she slides the forms and documents across and stands waiting to be told how much she will have to pay, the going rate changes each time, they look at your clothes and come up with a price, they look and see if they like your smile, it all depends on the time of day, the moon and the tide. She is told she has filled out the wrong form, that she is trying to cross with an undocumented child and must instead fill out another form and await an interview, she must exit the door to her right and go to the next prefab outside. There is nobody in the cold unheated room and nothing to look at but a window of frosted glass and a desk with a PC and an empty mug, she tries to hide the tremor in her hand when they hear quick footsteps outside and a muffled cough, Molly taking hold of her hand and squeezing as the official steps into the room and pulls a chair before them, an angular man with a Roman nose, a pale shirt unbuttoned at the neck, she does not know what he is, a policeman or a military officer or a small-time bureaucrat, he types quickly into the computer and exhales sharply then looks at Eilish as though seeing through her to something else. He asks for their documents and turns to the screen and types, Ben wriggling to be free, she tries to pull him back onto her lap but he screams into kicking and Molly lets down her hair and gives him the elastic hairband to play with, the official turning his head as though to study the child, he is staring at Molly as she combs her fingers through her hair. He asks one question after another and obscurely shakes his head as Eilish gives each answer, scratching the end of his nose with a fingernail, typing quickly into the computer, she believes she is giving the wrong answer each time and begins to bite down on her teeth. She looks into the man's grey-blue eyes and hears his mouth speak but his eyes are saying something different to the questions the mouth is asking, the finger toddling the downward key while the eyes are sizing up how much she is worth, watching a quick slight smile pulling on the corners of his mouth as though he has read her thoughts, it is then that she knows and no longer believes in the substance of the interview. She looks about the empty room seeing it all as a game, she has been fingering the child's birth certificate but leaves it down and sits back in the chair and tries to smile as she leans forward again. We might as well be frank with one other, she says, how much money do you want? The man allows a frowning look of surprise, he regards Molly and seems to tut under his breath as he leans back in the chair. There will be a cost for crossing the border, he says, an exit tax if you will, but there is also an additional cost, you are seeking to leave the state with a child who does not have a travel document, and though this birth certificate proves his citizenship, it affords him no right to leave the state and denies him the protection he would

enjoy as a citizen of this state while travelling in other
jurisdictions, what you must do is buy a temporary
passport for the child, the passport will have no legal
effect after today and later you will have to apply for a
passport in full from your new place of residence, of
course there will be a price, there is always a price for
such things. The man picks up a pen and writes quickly
on a sheet of paper and slides it towards Eilish, she
reads the paper upside down then turns it around and
begins to cry, looking again at the sheet, she shakes her
head and closes her eyes, seeing them forced to run the
gauntlet across the border at night, the military patrols
and the baying dogs, Molly takes a hold of her hand
again but Eilish pulls it free. I don't have this kind of
money, she says, nobody told us it would cost this
much. The man exhales sharply out his nose while doo-
dling with a pen, she looks at the hand that has found
time to divine something from the man's subconscious,
a geometric pattern coming loose into tumbleweed, a
thought begins to pull on his mouth as he lifts his eyes.
It is going to cost you a lot more to pay a smuggler to
take you across at night and half of what you give him
will come back here. She looks at the man and cannot
speak and he sighs again and stands up as though to
leave. Wait, she says, and the official remains standing
before them and when she speaks again he licks at the
corner of his mouth and declines with a slow shake of
the head. That will pay for your son's temporary passport and it will pay for your exit visa, but it will not
cover the cost of your daughter. The voices sounding

outside, the voices and the sound of footfall passing onwards in steady transference across the border and she is biting down on her tongue and there is nothing in his eyes, an agonised smile creeping across her face. But please, she says, surely we can agree a price, I'll give you all that I have. The official studies her a long moment and then he looks at Molly and nods at her. I'd like to interview you alone, he says. Eilish looks towards her daughter and then she looks for the man's eyes but he is clicking at something onscreen, he is searching for the soccer results perhaps, some titbit of useless information, she looks towards the frosted window feeling a sudden nausea. She passes Ben across to Molly and tells her to leave the prefab. I said take the child outside now. Molly stands with a frowning look then carries Ben outside and closes the door while Eilish studies the official. You want to interview her alone, she says, why do you want to interview her alone? Something has caught on the end of her voice as he watches the door, without word he softly shakes his head, then scratches the end of his nose. There have been inconsistencies in the account you have given of your family, it would be best if I speak to her alone. She leans sideways in her seat and looks to the screen, sees that he is playing Solitaire. And for how long do you want to speak to her alone, she says, do you not want to interview me alone, I can paint my lips if that's what you want, I can fix my hair, but I'm not what you want, isn't that right, perhaps the thing you want is something you can only take from a child. The face before her grows very still and then the mouth goes to speak but stumbles, the hand padding blindly for the pen while Eilish begins to unzip a travel wallet strapped to her stomach, she places a sheaf of notes on the table. Look, she says, this is all that I have, surely that is enough when what you are taking from us is everything. The official's face reddens with anger and she sees beneath that anger the coming perhaps of shame, the man exhaling sharply as he puts both hands down on the table. I don't have time for this, he says, do you think I can sit around here all day, this interview is over, leave the money on the table and go back inside to the waiting room.

She tells herself not to look behind as they cross the border, she turns around and a stone forms in her mouth so that she must whisper as she speaks, the stone sliding down her throat so that she must breathe around it as she shows her documents, the soldier on the other side is firm but polite and directs them to a registration centre in a Nissen hut. She is watching for the man they are supposed to meet, there are cars parked along the verge beyond the checkpoint and a handful of people are waiting nearby watching for who comes through, she scans the faces for a quick nod or smile but meets no response, she looks to Molly who is carrying Ben on her chest, she does not know what she is supposed to do, the instructions were so unclear,

another soldier marshals them along and she finds
herself being carried forward. Somebody has come
alongside her and touches her elbow, a resonant smiling voice says, you don't want to go in there. She turns
around and a young man in a fleece pulls her into a hug
and she lets down the bag and stands with her hands
by her sides trying not to recoil until the man lets go,
the intrusion of another body, the smell of sweat and
cologne, the man smiles at Molly and Ben. Eilish, he
says, so good to see yous, come quickly along, this way
to the car. He takes hold of the carry bag and walks with
its weight pulling on his shoulder as they follow him
to a maroon Ford parked tight to the ditch. He is not
the man she has been told they will meet, his name is
Gary and he opens the doors for them, motioning for
Molly to put Ben in the child seat. He puts their bags
in the boot then sits into the car searching the door
pocket and the organiser between the seats, he finds
his glasses and puts them on, turns and smiles at Ben.
Right, he says, sorry about that, I didn't see yous come
through. He turns to fix the seatbelt and his eyes stop
at Eilish who is sitting very pale and still with her hands
on her lap, the stone has grown so that she cannot
breathe, she thinks her heart has stopped. Whatever's
the matter? Gary says, but she cannot speak, the man
looking to Molly for help as she leans forward and
pulls on her mother's shoulder. Mam, she says, what's
wrong? Eilish shakes her head and takes a breath and
releases it slowly while Gary pats her hand. Don't worry,
love, yous are doing the right thing, the wrong thing

would have been going into that registration building back there and signing your life away, they'd have put yous on the bus to limbo land, yous would be stuck in the camps for who knows how long with no right to leave Northern Ireland, yous could be living there for the rest of your lives in one of them tents with the rain pishing down on yous all day, at least when we're done yous'll be free to go wherever you like, yous are doing the right thing, so relax, everything has been arranged.

She sits numbly watching the road, the sky shoreline and foaming wave, Ben bawling for milk but she has nothing to give him, Gary offers to stop along the way. She closes her eyes unable to think or feel, seeking within for some path forward, in the shadows Bailey comes to her and she touches his face and strokes his hair and the numbness in her body swells into a pain that forces her to open her eyes, watching Molly in the rear-view mirror brushing her hair then opening the compact mirror to line her eyes, of a sudden Eilish is reaching between the seats, she grabs the mirror from Molly's hands and snaps it shut, points to a petrol station on the far side of the road. If you don't mind I'd like to stop there. With two fingers she reaches into the lining of her coat and slides out a cigarette of bank notes. She buys fruit and milk, returns to the car with the key to the bathroom, Ben watching her with a livid face as she fills his bottle. She opens the boot and unzips her bag and removes an oval case, knocks on the window and motions for Molly to follow. The pale bathroom reeks of urine and citrus bleach and she catches sight of herself in the mirror seeing the ghost of her future, sees in Molly's face a look of liquid unease as she removes from the case a pair of scissors. Mam, she says, what's going on? Stand still and do not move, Eilish says, I'm going to make sure nobody looks at you again. Molly's face shrinks when she sees the scissors come up, she steps back against the wall and pushes against Eilish who takes a hold of her hair and begins to cut, Molly slapping at her mother, she releases a scream and goes limp, covers her face with her hands. When Eilish is finished she turns to the mirror and begins at her own hair, one savage stroke after another until she sees before her a ruined lopsided crop, Gary knocking on the door. Are yous in there? he says, yer gone an awful long time, we have to get back on the road. He is leaning against the side door of the Ford thumbing at his phone when Molly steps outside with her face in her hands, he looks up and says, what in the fuck, looks to Eilish while shaking his head, watching her as she drops Molly's make-up bag into the bin. He does not turn to look at her when she sits inside and he is silent as he drives, watching Molly occasionally in the mirror, Eilish sitting with her arms folded looking straight ahead. There is no will now, no sovereignty nor strength, just a hollow body reflected in the glass, a body pulled forward along the road through cattle fields and arable land, casual trees and hedgerow, houses

abutting the road with pebble-dashed walls and dogs
inside barking to be let out, the car travelling smoothly
towards the Sperrin Mountains. Gary is checking his
watch, his hand is searching for his phone in the organiser, he fits a headset in his ear and makes a call. Not
long now, horse, he says, just give us fifteen minutes.
The car makes a turn and they drive up into the hills
and soon there is nothing but sky and steepled firs to
one side of the road, the car slowing to take a turn into
forestry and it grows dark inside the Ford, Gary looking
into the mirror where he sees Molly's face in distress.
Don't worry, he says, everything's cool, we'll be there in
a moment. The sunken road gives to a clearing where a
white delivery truck is parked, a goateed face watching
intensely from behind the windscreen. That's us now,
Gary says, let me go have a wee chat with this fella and
then yer on your way. Eilish watches him go to the
truck, he turns around and motions for them to get
out. She tries to wake Ben, brings him into her arms
but he nuzzles into her neck and goes back to sleep,
the goateed man leaping down from the truck with a
mean little face, Eilish watching the way he lopes with
lowered head to the rear of the truck and sends the back
door rolling upward with a clatter. The interior is full
of people and she does not want to climb in, the driver
grabbing hold of their bags, he slides them inside and
motions with his thumb for them to climb up but she is
unable to move, Molly watching while the goateed man
stands before them with an irate look, he wipes his
sleeve across his mouth and shouts, hurry up to fuck.

She is no longer a person but a thing, this is what she thinks, a thing climbing into the truck with a child in her arms, Molly climbing after her, hearing behind them as the shutters go down a strange puling sound from the trees.

From lorry dark they climb out into a factory yard, grey graffitied buildings with broken windows and weeds greening the cement while a lean man in an anorak talks into a phone without turning around, his eyes hidden under a baseball cap. Ben kicks to be free of her arms and he begins to shriek and when she puts him down he is gone at a run and she catches him and must carry him sideways under her arm. The driver climbs into the rear of the truck and kicks a lone duffel bag to the edge then jumps down, points to the man on the phone. That there's the Gaffer, just do what he says and yous'll be alright. They follow the Gaffer through a metal door and along a corridor of peeling paint into a bare industrial room, the smell of damp and squalor, cardboard pallets on a cement floor with brown blankets and three new windowpanes with bars looking out onto a yard. Molly has taken a space beneath a window and she puts her bag down and holds out her arms for Ben while a shapeless woman directs two teenage boys onto the pallets beside them, the woman glancing across at Eilish, she introduces herself as Mona and Eilish sees into her eyes and knows the story of the

woman's life without a word having to be spoken. The
Gaffer by the door thumbing at his phone, he brings up
two fingers and makes a silent headcount and then he
clears his throat. Alright you lot, listen up, this is the lie
of the land, yous will be here just for a few days but so
long as yous are here nobody gets to go outside and this
door will be locked at all times, there's a toilet in that
room with a shower rigged up and there's two bins in
the corner, yous will get three square meals a day until
it's time to go, for those with small children, make a
list of what yous want, nappies and formula, that kind
of thing, I'll come back for it in a while. A man in a
tweed jacket steps forward holding a child while pointing towards the toilet. Are you having a laugh? he says,
this place is unfit for habitation, take a look how many
infants and small children there are and not a single
heater and just one small sink between them, you must
be out of your mind. The Gaffer stands before the man
incalculable, he lifts a hand to his own face and backs it
through stubble without lifting his eyes from the man.
Don't be a stupid cunt, he says, and the man lowers
his eyes and begins to mutter then walks away. Eilish
watching the Gaffer, she feels her chest grow tight as
she searches for the eyes in the shadow of the hat and
imagines there are none as he steps outside and locks
the door. She feels a sudden twist of panic, turns to the
barred windows and puts a hand to the glass, looking
past the yard to the corner of a building and beyond to
maroon shipping containers and further still a bram-
bled field, hills and sky. Twenty-three people in the

room and by evening there are forty-seven, a hard rain pulling down the dark, a pregnant woman has to be helped to sit down on the ground and already people have begun to form small groups. She does not want to talk to anyone, there aren't enough electricity points to charge their phones, Áine will want to know how we are. A young boy with a swatch of grey hair stands at the top of the queue for the bathroom cupping his hands between his legs while his father calls and knocks on the door. Ben is whingeing for his dinner but she has only one cracker left, nobody knows what time the food will come. An elderly man bangs on the main door and shouts for them to hurry up with the dinner, there is no answer, it is a quarter past eight when they hear the door unlock and a doleful young man with his hair in a ponytail steps inside wearing an army surplus coat, his hands ringed with plastic bags full of take-away, a panicked look in his eyes as the people begin to crowd around him. Jesus fuck, he says, would yous ever stand back. He puts the bags on the table and returns with more. It is Mona who brings up her hands and calls for order in the room. Agreement is made to form a queue led by one member from each group. Molly goes and returns with Chinese fried rice and spoons it out onto paper plates. Eilish can eat only a little, she has not seen Molly eat like this for some time, Ben throwing a fistful of rice onto the floor and Eilish sweeps it up with her hand. The dark outside dense against the glass while the room remains in hard light, there is a meeting to decide on the use of the bathroom, it is agreed that it will be used one group a time, nobody can agree on what time to turn off the lights, children are crying and cannot sleep. It is past nine o'clock already, says a man standing up. If you don't turn those lights off now and let my children sleep I'll put those lights off for good.

Days pass by and she watches the rainlight in its rivering drift, the winter taking from each passing day what the days have come to know and yet the heart remains in knowing, this heart that beats like a drum on her grief. There is no word from the Gaffer about when the time will come to go, the people huddling in groups and some of them sleep during the day while she tries to amuse Ben with some toys, he wants to go outside and she cannot explain. She finds herself watching Molly but seeing Bailey, the close-cropped hair and freckled eyes, the gapped teeth in the narrow mouth, only the slender, up-turned nose does not belong and yet beneath the nose lies the philtrum that she painted onto his mouth at birth. She watches him and is present with him and she seeks to remain with him in this null space of looking, Molly giving her a strange look before turning away. When Eilish closes her eyes now she sees only the past, a past that belongs to somebody else and she is emptiness watching from some cold and bottomless dark and is met with the feeling of the world grown intolerable, watching her husband and eldest son taken by a silence that cannot be pierced, it is as though a door opened onto nothingness and each one stepped inside and was gone. Each day she sits with her phone scrolling through the death certificates published daily by the regime, waiting for Larry's name to appear and the relief when it doesn't only adds to her grief. Rain dashed against the windows, sliced white bread and tubs of butter for breakfast with cold cooked sausages. They stand in line for the bathroom while a youth seated against the wall leans into a cigarette and exhales overhead and a woman turns with a child on her breast and shouts for him to put it out while the youth huffs himself to standing and joins a group of men. There is no lock on the bathroom door, the shower is rigged from a wall tap and the cold water dribbles into an open drain, she has only a small piece of soap and a hand towel to dry herself, Molly refusing to wash, she holds Ben flailing in the air while Eilish soaps him with cold water. There is a sick child in the room and it is the same child that has been crying each night, Mona returning from the group gathered around the parents. That woman holding the child now is an intensive care nurse, she says, the child needs to go to hospital but the parents don't know what to do. When the youth comes through the door he is met by the nurse who points to the parents and the child, his hands are full of plastic bags and he has not had time to lower his hood. He makes a face as the nurse follows him to the table. Past three o'clock the Gaffer steps into the room ringing keys in his hand. He squats down beside the couple and pulls back his cap to reveal narrow eyes and a shaven skull, he is older than she has thought, he stands up and looks down askance while shaking his head. I can't bring a doctor in here, he says, soon as the weather turns yous'll be leaving anyhow, yous can have all the doctors in the world then. The nurse steps towards the Gaffer and takes him by the arm but he shakes her off with an angry look. If I take yous to the hospital there's no coming back, do yous hear, there's no getting back what yous paid either, that's completely out of the question, it's not even mine to return, so if yous want to go, yous are deciding to go of your own accord and yous will be on your own, I will arrange for somebody to drop yous up to a hospital, tell me what yous want to do. Music from the keys jangling in the Gaffer's hand and the young parents cannot decide, the mother lowers her head and begins to cry. For Christ's sake, the Gaffer says, I'm giving yous one hour to make up your minds. Eilish watching the child limp in the father's arms and she thinks, it is only a small child, what loss will he be to them, they've hardly had time to live with him yet, and she stares at the small hands and begins to cry and Mona comes forward on her knees and reaches out offering to take Ben, bounces him on her lap. You're a fine boy, aren't you, so big and strong, you'll make a fine athlete I'll bet. Her face goes very still and for a moment she stares into space then shakes her head. So much suffering, she whispers, my husband, he went to the shop and didn't return, I never saw him again, my brother, my first cousin and his wife and their children all missing. For a moment it looks as though the musculature of her face is going to subside and then with effort she rights it again. We were offered visas, you know, to Australia, and we turned them down, my husband said no, plain and simple, he said it was impossible to go at the time and I suppose he was right, and how could he have known anyhow, how could any of us have known what was going to happen, I suppose other people seemed to know, but I never understood how they were so certain, what I mean is, you could never have imagined it, not in a million years, all that was to happen, and I could never understand those that left, how they could just leave like that, leave everything behind, all that life, all that living, it was absolutely impossible for us to do so at the time and the more I look at it the more it seems there was nothing we could do anyhow, what I mean is, there was never any real room for action, that time with the visas, how were we supposed to go when we had so many commitments, so many responsibilities, and when things got worse there was just no room for manoeuvre, I think what I'm trying to say is that I used to believe in free will, if you had asked me before all this I would have told you I was free as a bird, but now I'm not so sure, now, I don't see how free will is possible when you are caught up within such a monstrosity, one thing leads to another thing until the damn thing has its own momentum and there is nothing you can do, I can see now that what I thought of as freedom was really just struggle and that there was no freedom all along, but look, she says, taking Ben by the hand and dancing him, we are here now aren't we and so many other people are gone, we're the lucky ones seeking a better life, there is only looking forward now, isn't that right, perhaps there is a little freedom to be found in that thought because at least you can make the future your own in your thoughts and if we keep looking back we will die in a way and there is still some living to be done, my two boys, look at them, both of them the image of their father, they have their lives to live and I will make sure of that, your children too, they have to live— oh please don't cry, I'm sorry, Eilish, if I said something to upset you, look, let me fix your hair, I'm looking at it now since we got here and it's obvious you did it yourself, it just needs a little fixing, that's all, I used to do a nixer at a hairdresser's during the summers when I was a student a lifetime ago, I can fix your daughter's hair while I'm at it.

Eilish stands at the window watching outside as the mother follows the Gaffer with the child in her arms while the father steps behind with their baggage, the rain striking the concrete, it falls beaded onto the window and she watches her reflection in the glass and sees the shadow of a face grown old, her face that of another. She looks to the sky watching the rain as it falls through space and there is nothing to see in the ruined yard but the world insisting on itself, the cement's sedate crumbling giving way to the rising sap beneath, and when the yard is past there will remain the world's insistence, the world insisting it is not a dream and yet to the looker there is no escaping the dream and the price of life that is suffering, and she sees her children delivered into a world of devotion and love and sees them damned to a world of terror, wishing for such a world to end, wishing for the world its destruction, and she looks at her infant son, this child who remains an innocent and she sees how she has fallen afoul of herself and grows aghast, seeing that out of terror comes pity and out of pity comes love and out of love the world can be redeemed again, and she can see that the world does not end, that it is vanity to think the world will end during your lifetime in some sudden event, that what ends is your life and only your life, that what is sung by the prophets is but the same song sung across time, the coming of the sword, the world devoured by fire, the sun gone down into the earth at noon and the world cast in darkness, the fury of some god incarnate in the mouth of the prophet raging at the wickedness that will be cast out of sight, and the prophet sings not of the end of the world but of what has been done and what will be done and what is being done to some but not others, that the world is always ending over and over again in one place but not another and that the end of the world is always a local event, it comes to your country and visits your town and knocks on the door of your house and becomes to others but some distant warning, a brief report on the news, an echo of events that has passed into folklore, Ben's laughter behind her and she turns and sees Molly tickling him on her lap and she watches her son and sees in his eyes a radiant intensity that speaks of the world before the fall, and she is on her knees crying, taking hold of Molly's hand. I'm so sorry, she says, and Molly looks at her with a frown and she shakes her head then pulls her mother into a hug. But you've nothing to be sorry for, Mam, and Eilish is trying to smile as Molly wipes at her mother's eyes. What time is it now? Eilish says, I need you to send a message to Áine. She takes Ben into her arms and turns and casts an unforgiving look towards a teenager playing loud techno on his phone, says to Molly, do you think he'll ever stop?

The lights are off when the door unlocks and the Gaffer steps into the room shining a torch at the wall. Where's the fucking lights? he says, and a man answers, they're over this side. People sit up rubbing their eyes against the sudden light while the Gaffer wades over the sleeping bodies to the centre of the room. Alright, everybody, listen up, yous are going to be leaving tonight, we're going to come at 2am sharpish, so yous need to be ready to file outside and keep the children quiet, there won't be room for your bags, yous are allowed to take just one small backpack or shopping bag per person and that includes one bag per child, if yous don't do what we ask your bags will be taken away and yous'll go without any, that's all I have to say. He has turned to go when a woman calls out, what do you mean about the bags, nobody told us about the bags, others begin to remonstrate but the Gaffer puts his hands up and stops them. One bag per person, that's all I have to say on the matter. When he is gone out the door people begin at their belongings cursing the man, Eilish laying everything out on the floor while Ben remains asleep, Molly sitting with her arms folded. Mam, I don't know what to take, I don't want to go. Just take two changes of clothes, you can always buy more clothes later on, you must take the things you can't replace. She is holding in her hand a photo frame and she turns it around and prises open the back and slides the photo into her passport, Molly watching and then she lowers her face in tears. Mam, she says, please, why do we have to go, I don't want to go, it's not safe, you know it's not safe, all those people—— Eilish reaches for her hand and squeezes. We've talked about this enough times, haven't we? she says, we could talk about it all night, Áine has arranged everything, there is no other path for us, not now. The door unlocks at 2am and a hand reaches for the lights and it is not the Gaffer but an unshaven man in a beanie hat calling in a Scottish voice for them to remain quiet, Eilish with Ben asleep on her chest and a bag on her back and in her hand a shopping bag with all that she needs for him, she turns to look at their belongings, the room full of abandoned luggage and rubbish and ruined cardboard and the air heavy with sweat and soiled nappies, a freshening cold air outside and the clouds vanished. They follow to the rear of the property where an articulated truck is parked, a man with a torch instructs them to climb into the container and a child is bawling as people begin to mount the step ladder, Molly will not move forward and Eilish nudges her, telling her to follow, she pushes at her back until Molly relents and climbs the step, seeing their way forward by the light of a phone and there are pallets to sit on and everybody is watching as the man in the beanie hat stands at the door and says, this won't take long, remember to keep silent when the truck stops and keep those children quiet. There is a hinged groan as the doors are swung shut and a child screams as they are sealed into the container, somewhere inside a woman begins to pray and Molly grips hold of her mother's hand when the engine starts. Eilish whispering to Larry, telling him that everything is going to be fine and when she opens her eyes the container is filled with white light from phones and people are sending messages and following the truck's route and after some time the truck slows and makes a turn and travels along a road at low speed until it comes to a stop and gasps. The rear door is unbolted and gives to dim light and a man tells them to climb out quietly, Molly gripping her mother's hand as they step through the container. The wish to be at one with the dawn, this feeling of the new day waiting to emerge and a man offers Eilish his hand and she climbs down knowing the shape of the Gaffer standing with his hands in his pockets. An old bungalow leaden in the dark, the night hushed and the world unexpressed but for a breeze that hurries them along. Soon the dawn will come and they walk as a group along a narrow road with children in their arms past a field of silent cattle and not a word is spoken and for a moment the light of the Gaffer's torch powers on and then it is turned off again. It is then the sea is visible, the sound of the ocean woven with the racing breeze as they cross a road and follow a sandy path through dunes onto a beach and she knows the name of this beach, she has been here so many times before, and there is a man standing in a pale anorak with his hood pulled up texting into a phone and she sees two inflatable boats by the water's edge and something inside her is flung when she sees the ocean dark and barren but for the rollers breaking whitely by the headland. The man calls out something but his words are unheard and she follows the others towards the life vests piled on the beach and there aren't enough to go around, she takes one for Molly but Molly refuses to put it on, she is shaking her head and Eilish says, look, I have Ben strapped to my chest, I'd never get it on anyhow, and Molly is crying openly as the man in the anorak appoints one man to pilot each boat, and Eilish can hear what the man is saying as he hands each of them a GPS, direct the motor towards the coordinates and you'll be there in no time. Molly is having trouble with her vest, she flaps her hands and Eilish adjusts the straps and looks into her daughter's face. For an instant it seems the world has been silenced, a silence that belongs only to the mouthing darkness of the horizon beyond it and Molly is pleading with her not to go,

she begins to shout, Mam, please, I don't want to go,
I don't want to do this, and Eilish stands a moment
watching the people climb into the boats and she sees
the wind racing into their mouths as though to wrench
something from out of them and she watches the dim
and sloping headland and she sees in a far field a horse
standing softly blue and she watches the blue horse
and something becomes known to her. She looks for
Molly's eyes and cannot find the right words, there are
no words now for what she wants to say and she looks
towards the sky seeing only darkness knowing she has
been at one with this darkness and that to stay would be
to remain in this dark when she wants for them to live,
and she touches her son's head and she takes Molly's
hands and squeezes them as though saying she will
never let go, and she says, to the sea, we must go to the
sea, the sea is life.

**GROVE PRESS**

**Reading Group Guide**

**by Je Banach**

# PROPHET
# SONG

Paul Lynch

## ABOUT THIS GUIDE

We hope that these discussion questions will enhance your reading group's exploration of Paul Lynch's *Prophet Song*. They are meant to stimulate discussion, offer new viewpoints, and enrich your enjoyment of the book.

More reading group guides and additional information, including summaries, author tours, and author sites for other fine Grove Atlantic titles may be found on our website, groveatlantic.com.

## QUESTIONS FOR DISCUSSION

Consider the opening scene of the novel. How does the author's choice of imagery and language begin to establish the tone of the book? What major themes does the scene foreshadow and how does this set the stage for the characters'—and readers'—introduction to a society rapidly unraveling in the grip of authoritarianism?

———

Who knocks at Eilish Stack's door at the start of the story and how does she respond? Were you surprised by her reaction? Upon the arrival of her visitors, what "universal reflex" (2) does Eilish become conscious of? How does this begin to crack open for readers the feeling of the world she and her family now inhabit?

———

In Chapter 1 Simon tells Eilish that "tradition is nothing more than what everyone can agree on . . . if you change ownership of the institutions then you can change ownership of the facts, you can alter the structure of belief" (20). What does he mean by this and where in the novel do readers find his observation proved true or untrue? What might this reveal about the power of storytelling—including the ways in which narrative can be co-opted as propaganda in order to undermine truth?

———

Why do you think the author chose not to provide an explanation of the events and politics that led to the societal breakdown represented in the novel? What important purpose(s) might this serve? Do you think your relationship to the story would have been different if the author had chosen to include these details? Why or why not?

————————

The author made deliberate choices to eschew quotation marks and paragraph breaks within each section. What impact did these decisions have on you as a reader and why do you think the author made these formal choices? How does the form of the book encourage, for example, a closer understanding of the plight of the characters?

————————

Many critics and reviewers have characterized *Prophet Song* as an example of dystopian literature, but is this accurate? Consider the ways in which the book transcends the boundaries of conventional dystopian novels. Why might it be wrong—or at least imprecise—to categorize the novel as dystopian or speculative?

————————

Explore the imagery of the novel. What recurring images become motifs? How, for instance, does Lynch employ descriptions of light and darkness or the natural world to support the themes of the book and draw us closer to the characters? How does he utilize contrasting imagery? In Chapter 1 Larry watches Eilish breastfeeding Ben and sees the scene as "a sense of life contracted to an image so at odds with malice" (4). How do these juxtapositions allow, for example, the author to underscore the chaos of the time or, alternatively, to illuminate that which endures?

————————

How does *Prophet Song* create a dialogue around memory and the passage of time? Does the book ever answer the question of how our personal histories and our collective history are influenced by both? Is personal or collective memory reliable? How do the various characters in the novel relate to their own distant and not-so-distant but shattered pasts?

———

In Chapter 2 Bailey asks Eilish when his father will be coming back and Eilish responds by lying to her son: "I've told you, love, he had to go away for work" (33). Do you think that she made the right choice? Why does she do this and how does her decision affect their relationship? How does this scene serve as an introduction to a more expansive meditation on the intermingled themes of truth and deception?

———

In Chapter 7 Eilish recognizes that "she has lied to herself about so many things" (235). What are some of the things that she has lied to herself about and what do you think allows her to reach this conclusion? Were you surprised that her realization came so late in the day? Why or why not?

———

How does the novel explore themes of complicity and silence? Who in the book would you say is complicit? Who speaks up and who remains silent? Eilish demands to know "why has nobody shouted stop?" (36) Does the book ultimately answer this question?

———

In Chapter 5 Carole points out that for those in charge "the silence is the source of their power" (165). What does she mean by this? How is silence used by those in power to create an atmosphere of fear that leads to greater control? How do the characters in the book resist or otherwise push back against this?

---

How does *Prophet Song* propose a reorientation of our way of looking at the ordinary and the mundane? What, for instance, does the novel reveal about the banality of evil or that which "hides in the humdrum" (43)?

---

"History is a silent record of people who did not know when to leave" (103), Eilish's sister warns, but at the novel's conclusion how would you respond to this? Why do people like Gerry Brennan and Mrs. Gaffney stay? Why does Eilish hesitate to leave despite the chaos and violence around her?

---

How does the novel paint a complex portrait of grief—its varieties and complexities? Who in the book is grieving and what causes them to do so? How does each character attempt to cope with their grief? Does the book ultimately seem to offer any insight into how we might help ourselves and others in the presence of grief?

---

What does the book reveal to readers about human dignity? How, for instance, does Eilish maintain her own sense of dignity throughout the story? Were you surprised by this? Why might this have been so important to her?

---

Molly observes: "if you want to give war its proper name, call it entertainment, we are now TV for the rest of the world" (160). Where else do readers find the book challenging the way we think about wars and unjust events that occur outside of our own country—our complicity or our complacency?

---

"I used to believe in free will, if you had asked me before all of this I would have told you I was free as a bird, but now I'm not so sure," Mona tells Eilish (302). What does *Prophet Song* have to say about agency and free will? Does such a thing exist? Do the characters of *Prophet Song* have free will or are they simply batted around by chance or fate? How do they attempt to maintain and exert their will? Are any of them successful in this?

---

Revisit the last line of the book. Did you find Eilish's final choice surprising? Why or why not? How does the story ultimately work as an equation that wends its way towards proof of what is contained in the last line—and the inevitability of Eilish's ultimate decision?

---

At the story's conclusion, what is the eponymous phrase *prophet song* meant to signal to us about our assumptions of apocalypse and the world's end? According to the author, of what does the prophet sing? What does Lynch mean when he writes of Eilish looking to the sky and seeing only "the world insisting on itself" (303)?

## SUGGESTED READING

*A Land of Permanent Goodbyes* by Atia Abawi

*All Our Yesterdays* by Natalia Ginzburg

*Azadi: Freedom. Fascism. Fiction.* by Arundhati Roy

*Blindness* by José Saramago

*The Crossing* by Cormac McCarthy

*The Displaced: Refugee Writers on Refugee Lives* edited by Viet Thanh Nguyen

*Exit West* by Mohsin Hamid

*The Girl Who Smiled Beads* by Clemantine Wamariya and Elizabeth Weil

*The Handmaid's Tale* by Margaret Atwood

*Her Side of the Story* by Alba de Céspedes

*History* by Elsa Morante

*I Cheerfully Refuse* by Leif Enger

*In the Country of Men* by Hisham Matar

*In Praise of Hatred* by Khaled Khalifa

*It Can't Happen Here* by Sinclair Lewis

*Milkman* by Anna Burns

*Refuge* by Dina Nayeri

*The Road* by Cormac McCarthy

*Sea Prayer* by Khaled Hosseini

*Steppenwolf* by Herman Hesse

*The Testaments* by Margaret Atwood

*What We Remember Will Be Saved: A Story of Refugees and the Things They Carry* by Stephanie Saldaña

*When the Doves Disappeared* by Sofi Oksanen

**Paul Lynch** is the award-winning author of five novels—*Prophet Song, Beyond the Sea, Grace, The Black Snow,* and *Red Sky in Morning. Prophet Song* won the 2023 Booker Prize. He has previously won the Kerry Group Irish Novel of the Year and France's Prix Libr'à Nous for Best Foreign Novel, among other prizes. He has been shortlisted for many international awards, including the UK's Walter Scott Prize, Italy's Strega European Award, France's Prix du Meilleur Livre Étranger, Prix Littérature-Monde, and the Jean Monnet Prize for European Literature. In 2024 he was appointed Distinguished Writing Fellow at Maynooth University and was elected to Aosdána, the Irish academy for the arts honoring distinguished artists. His novels have been translated into more than thirty languages.